2/97

D0951982

LITTLE
BOY BLUE

Also by Ed Dee

14 Peck Slip
Bronx Angel

ED DEE

LITTLE BOY BLUE

WARNER BOOKS

A Time Warner Company

Warner Books, Inc., 1271 Avenue of the Americas,
New York, NY 10020

ⓦ A Time Warner Company

First Printing: February 1997
10 9 8 7 6 5 4 3 2 1
Library of Congress Cataloging-in-Publication Data

Dee, Ed.
    Little boy blue / Ed Dee.
      p. cm.
    ISBN 0-446-52038-1
      1. Police—New York (State)—New York—Fiction. 2. Homicide investigation—New York (State)—New York—Fiction. 3. Organized crime—New York (State)—New York—Fiction. I. Title.
    PS3554.E32L58 1997
    813'.54—dc20
96-31098
CIP

For my daughters,
Brenda and Patti

Acknowledgments

To Jimmy Franco, Jackie Joiner, Harvey-Jane Kowal, and everybody at Warner for their kindness to an ex-cop; especially Maureen Mahon Egen for her wisdom and Irish soul.

To Sona Vogel, for the third time, making me sound better than I am; and Gail Hochman and Ron Carlson for always being there; Dr. Cook for his artificial eye sketch; Steve and Barbara Crane for their support and classy bookstore.

To all the cops from the old four-eight who are so near to my heart. And to those who shared their street smarts and war stories for this book: especially Don McGuire, my invaluable friend; and John Barna, Bob Bisbee, Bob Browne, Joe Coffey, Al Creighton, Wally Millard, John Murray, Jim Sampel, Harold Schiffer; and the indomitable Frank McDarby.

To my friends and family, especially my wife, Nancy, my first and best reader.

LITTLE
BOY BLUE

1

Every cop I've ever known, no matter how callous, dreaded being the messenger of death. More than any other assignment, it ripped away a piece of your soul. Usually I avoided it by passing the job off to my partner, the Great Joe Gregory. Not this time, he told me in the parking lot at John F. Kennedy International Airport. Absolutely not.

"I got history with this woman," he said.

"No problem," I said. "I'll tell her." But I could hear the echoes of my own history: a woman holding the body of her son in her arms. A woman whose screams followed a young cop from the third floor of a Bronx tenement, through the streets, to the precinct locker room, then everywhere for the last three decades.

"One good thing, pally," Gregory said. "At least Cookie already knows the kid's been shot. It won't be a total surprise."

Eleven hours earlier, young Johnny Boy Counihan, an airport cargo handler, was murdered as he walked into the middle of a huge cash robbery outside a TWA loading dock. The chief of detectives notified his mother, Cookie, but didn't give her the complete details. He omitted the fact that her twenty-eight-year-old son had been butchered in a hail of automatic weapons fire, apparently by a crew of Mafia wanna-bes. He also avoided those three blockbuster letters: DOA.

Gregory said, "I'm going to ask the chief if I can help out on this case."

"Don't bother. He has a standing rule against letting cops work on cases involving partners or family."

"Yeah, but J.C.'s not like a recent partner. We were only rookies when we last worked together."

Cookie's husband, J.C. Counihan, was Joe Gregory's first radio car partner in the Seven Five Precinct in Brooklyn. J.C. retired five years ago and moved to Florida. Last summer he suffered a massive stroke and was confined to a nursing home. We were waiting for the flight carrying his wife, who would hear the worst news of her life alone. From me.

"I just feel like I should be doing something," Gregory said.

"I didn't think you'd even spoken to J.C. in years."

"Yeah, but still, the poor bastard, helpless down there. It's the right thing to do."

The air was cool and crisp. Long shadows darkened the street in front of the terminal as we crossed. Gregory held up his hand with a cop's aplomb, halting a white limo and a Holiday Inn courtesy bus.

"Gate B Sixteen," Gregory said, squinting at the arrivals screen.

"How long have you known Cookie?" I asked.

"Oh shit, how long. Before they were married. I remember a double date. Me and J.C. took Cookie and some bimbette to Jones Beach. Long time ago."

"How about the kid?" I asked. "Ever meet him?"

"Not that I can remember. I didn't see that much of them after they got married."

Cops develop a bond in their first assigned precincts, a bond that extends beyond the job and carries an eternal responsibility. J.C. helped get Joe into the Detective Bureau; Joe always wangled Yankee tickets for J.C. It is this infinite repayment of favors, called honoring your contracts, that greases the very wheels the NYPD runs on.

"Tell me this, Ryan," Gregory said. "What's the deal with the cop coat? Was he a buff, or what?"

To make matters worse, young Johnny Boy had been wearing an obsolete NYPD woolen overcoat that had belonged to his father.

"Old uniforms are trendy," I said. "Kids buy them in thrift shops in SoHo. I've seen kids wearing West Point capes, Russian army coats, and every once in a while one of our old overcoats."

Guards at the security checkpoint decided they needed a supervisor to approve our carrying guns past that point. As we waited, I watched the people; airports have the best crowds. I noticed jogging outfits had replaced business suits as the favored travel attire.

"So this poor kid," Gregory said as we walked toward the gate, "dies because he's wearing a trendy freaking thirty-pound horse blanket of a cop coat."

"So goes the current thinking."

"I don't get the airline food, either. You believe he was actually going out the door just to get airline food?"

The robbery occurred at two minutes after midnight on the Sunday after Thanksgiving, the busiest air travel weekend of the year. Johnny Boy had been working a double shift. His fellow employees surmised he was probably leaving to scoff a hot airline entrée from a steward's cart. That was Johnny Boy's usual practice when stuck on double shifts.

"What I'm saying," Gregory said, "is who the hell goes out of his way for free airline food?"

"Like you never went out of your way for a free meal."

"Yeah, to the Plaza, the Four Seasons . . ."

"Those restaurants make the cops eat in the kitchen," I said.

"The point remains, it was definitely not airline food."

Flight 164 from Fort Lauderdale was on time. A man in tiger-striped pants lugged a crate of oranges on his shoulder. Cookie Counihan was among the last of the tanned travelers appearing in the passenger loading bridge. Gregory pointed her out, then walked away. I waved to her, rehearsed the words one more time, took a last deep breath, and Mrs. Cookie Counihan was in front of me.

"He's dead, isn't he?" she said.

I nodded. Just nodded.

"My husband was a cop a long time," she said. "I know exactly what 'seriously injured' means."

Cookie Counihan was a big woman with a clear pretty face, the type of face that made our GIs go to war. Blue eyes, red lips, and skin so pale that her color flushed when she spoke, as if the words caused red liquid to splash and spread. Like when she saw Joe Gregory and her strong facade crashed. I looked around for a loose chair as Gregory wrapped his arms around her and held her, as her knees buckled and the sobbing came fast and hard.

"Joey," she said. "They sent you."

Joe Gregory's shirt was damp with tears and black with a mascara smudge in the shape of a small half-moon. Gregory had been my partner for most of two decades. He was the toughest cop I'd ever known and, occasionally, the most tender. This time he even managed to look shy when she said, "You still look good."

We walked toward the baggage claim, Cookie between us, talking about Johnny Boy. All of us nodding our heads sadly. Gregory watched Cookie intently, the worry causing his face to glow a shiny crimson. But Cookie was getting strong again. She said that Johnny Boy was a little slow, but a hard worker and well liked at TWA. She said he had the same split nationality as I did.

He looked like her side of the family but loved the Irish roots of his father. Not a day went by when Johnny wasn't wearing the green.

"How's J.C. doing?" Gregory asked.

"Not good, Joey," she said. "And I have to be honest with you, it's all my fault."

"No it's not, Cook," Gregory said. "The Man upstairs runs the show."

Her eyes watered, and I saw it again, in her face, the dance of colors. I felt a sudden appreciation for this woman whose complexion violated the privacy of her thoughts.

"Thanks," she said. "But it was all my idea to move to Florida. J.C. was never happy. He missed New York, he missed being a cop. Me . . . I adjusted. Him . . . you had to see the puss on him. He looked just like his mother, so unhappy. Life was agony. Every day was agony."

Cookie Counihan's hair was a tinsel-silver blond, curled wildly and parted in the center. She walked quickly with short, heel-toe steps. Over her arm she carried a bright red woolen coat with a copy of *People* magazine jammed in the pocket.

"Was J.C. active?" I said. "Did he play much golf?"

"Don't make me laugh with the golf," she said. "J.C. Counihan followed people for fun."

"Followed what people?"

"Bad guys. Everybody was a bad guy. All I heard was 'Look at that guy, he's bad news. Check that creep, he's up to no good. Look at this skell here, that one there.' Skells, creeps, it's all I heard. Twice he left me at the mall in Boca Raton. He drives off on some wild goose chase. I had to get the bus home."

"J.C. Counihan was a bloodhound on wheels, pally," Gregory said, looking over Cookie's head. "He taught me all I know about tailing."

I said, "It's a mistake for cops to retire without something to do."

"He *was* doing," she said. "Following is doing. Outside places taking pictures is doing. At home he had his ear glued to the police scanner for hours and hours. So he was doing, don't say he wasn't doing."

"I didn't mean that," I said. "I meant exercise wise. My father lives down there, plays golf every day. He's in his eighties and he's healthier than I am."

"My husband is sixty-one," she said. "And he's never getting better."

The line at the escalator was held up by a group of frightened third world types who'd never seen one before. Close encounters with crowds of newly arrived foreigners always made me appreciate the bathing habits of Americans.

"You should have seen my guest bedroom," she said. "It was supposed to be for company, it looked like the Fifth Precinct. Charts on the wall, pictures of our neighbors. I took them all down. Can you believe it, our neighbors? J.C. thinks they're in the Witness Protection Program."

"Nothing wrong with that," Gregory said. "Cops are acting normal when they're suspicious."

"Nothing changes; you guys always stick together. But I'll tell you this: My husband used to call the local cops from pay phones to report things, and he'd talk in this phony Spanish accent. That's not normal. He used to write letters about people he suspected, but he used the rental typewriter in Kinko's so no one could trace it. Don't tell me that's normal behavior. That might be cop behavior, but that's not normal behavior."

Late arrivals raced toward the departure gates, faces flushed and sweating. I'd read that heart attack was the leading cause of death at JFK. They averaged one a day. Joe Gregory looked as if he could be today's statistic.

"Now this," Cookie said, sighing. "My son was the one thing that gave my husband joy."

"Does J.C. know about Johnny Boy?" I asked.

"Not yet," she said. "It's going to kill him when he hears. He's going to blame himself for getting Johnny Boy his job with TWA."

"I didn't know that," Gregory said.

"Oh, yeah, yeah, yeah. J.C. knew everybody at the airport."

The three of us stood together at the baggage carousel. I knew that this last contract, a job for his son, would weigh heavily on J.C. Counihan. Joe Gregory was silent, watching a skinny kid in black jeans push his way through the crowd, never seeming to find the right place to stand. I knew what he was thinking: pickpocket. I tried to make conversation but ran out of things to say long before the conveyor belt lurched to a start.

"Where did it happen?" Cookie said.

"Outside the TWA building, near the loading dock," I said.

"I want to go there."

"No, you don't," I said.

She didn't answer me. She looked toward Joe Gregory, who turned away to face the limo con artists and the homeless hustlers scamming for tourist luggage with discarded courtesy carts. I watched Gregory's eyes darting around the room, as designer suitcases and taped cardboard boxes tumbled down the chute. Cop's eyes. Watching everything, every movement. Yet something was wrong. It was as if he were unable to stop, unable to focus on one thing.

All my instincts told me it was wrong to allow a mother to stare down at the fading outlines of her son's blood. But there was so much I didn't know. As a cop for three decades I'd learned that black and white were merely shades of gray. Maybe it would be cathartic, a way of saying good-bye. Standing next to Cookie, I realized how little I understood about grief at its bottom.

"I gave birth to him," she said. "I want to see where he died."

2

Joe Gregory and I lugged Cookie's bags to the curb. He opened the car trunk as a Port Authority cop shouted in the direction of a cabby in a turban.

"My poor father," Cookie Counihan said, shivering and looking around at the push and shove, the horns and grimy cabs. "Still living in this city."

The morning air at John F. Kennedy International Airport smells of salty ocean brine. The airport sits on the edge of Jamaica Bay. Beyond that, only the pencil-thin strip of Rockaway Beach separates miles of runway from the pounding ocean surf. But even the smell of the mighty Atlantic cannot hide the odor of modern Jet-A aviation fuel. Fumes of pure kerosene float up from the underground pipes that carry it throughout the sprawling complex.

"What's the verdict?" I said.

"Let's stop at the scene," Gregory said. "If that's what she wants."

Gregory made a loop around the airport, then turned right

just before the TWA cargo building. He drove down a narrow road bordered by eight-foot chain link fences topped by several strands of barbed wire. The road dead-ended fifty feet past an abandoned guard station at a fence that protected one of the east-west runways. JFK had only four physical runways, but each handled traffic coming from two directions. It gave the tower the flexibility of eight runways. Pilots preferred going into headwinds whether taking off or landing. Never a tailwind. And the wind always blew at Kennedy. Gregory opened the car door and it sucked the warmth from around me.

"I'll wait here," I said.

But I didn't. I walked with them on the path Johnny Boy's killers had followed, through the newly cut hole in the fence, into a storage yard littered with junked forklifts, hydraulic platforms, and metal stairways. The road surface was an uneven combination of blacktop and pebbled-gray macadam, desperately in need of resurfacing. High weeds sprouted from the cracks. We weaved our way toward the cargo building through a canyon of dented aluminum boxes, stacked three high, "Cargo Only" printed in large letters.

"Are you guys investigating this case?" she said.

"No," I said. "The One Thirteen Precinct has it. A guy named Simmons is in charge. Good cop. He'll do a good job."

The case was a brouhaha; I was glad it wasn't ours. The media was all over it, and the feds wanted in. It had all the elements: big money, Mob involvement, three dead bodies. In addition to Johnny Boy, two private guards were ambushed as they wheeled bags of cash toward a safe inside the cargo building. The guards were killed quickly, neatly. Then Johnny Boy stepped through a door and into the hailstorm. A victim of his own spectacular bad luck.

"I wish you two were involved," she said.

A red-and-white pickup truck sat under a sign that said "Domestic Bulk Outbound." A uniformed cop from the Port Authority PD lounged near the door to dock 11, drinking a bottle of Evian water. All three bodies were long gone, cooling in the Queens morgue.

I hoped Cookie wouldn't ask where her son had fallen. Not that I didn't know; I knew exactly where he'd fallen. But for her sake, and mine, I'd play dumb. Cookie walked the perimeter of the crime scene, sliding her fingers along the yellow tape. Gregory grabbed me by the arm and pulled me behind the pickup.

"Did I hear you say Ted Simmons is running the case?"

"For the present he is," I said.

"The guy's an empty suit, pally. He couldn't run a two-car funeral."

"I know, but the Major Case Unit is taking over the whole show, forming a task force. The airline is estimating they lost three million cash."

"They say three, it's probably closer to five," he said. "Tourist money, right?"

The stolen cash was U.S. currency spent by tourists or servicemen in Europe. Periodically it's sent to banks here for credit. Usually when the money arrives it's transferred directly into armored cars, but on weekends it's stored in locked concrete vaults in the terminal and guarded around the clock.

"As a matter of curiosity," Joe said, "is Emil Lutz in or out of prison?"

"Just got out. Three weeks, maybe."

Emil Lutz had been the king of airport crime. Organized Crime Intelligence listed him as an all-star "earner" who'd run JFK scams for the Lucchese crime family in the seventies. Emil had just reappeared on the street after doing major time for the botched Lufthansa job, the largest cash robbery in U.S. history. In Emil's prime, news of a treasure this tempting would have surely been whispered into his ear.

"I hope they're sitting on the prick," Gregory said.

"No doubt in my mind."

Emil Lutz was the undisclosed owner of the Cockpit Lounge, a red-velour cheater's joint on Lefferts Blvd. near the Van Wyck Expressway. Truck drivers, freight handlers, cargo dispatchers, and backfield airport workers hung out at the bar or at the gaming tables in the basement.

Joe Gregory studied the side of the warehouse. He seemed to be counting the bullet holes. Automatic weapons had beaten a tattoo on the corrugated metal wall next to the door.

"You know what's wrong here?" he said softly.

I ignored him and yelled, "Cookie, you must be exhausted. Why don't we get going?"

A silver jumbo jet roared into the brilliant blue sky and made a banked left, following the coastline south. Gregory shielded his eyes against the sun. His lips moved as another jet accelerated toward the end of the runway. I had no idea what he said, but I was sure he'd say it again. He jammed his hands into his suit jacket pockets and stared at the metal wall.

"Your father must be getting worried, Cookie," I said.

Joe Gregory, his face inches from my ear, said, "I don't care what they say. This is way too many bullets to kill a kid wearing an old cop's coat."

"Automatic weapons," I said. "The kid walked through a door, they panicked, started spraying."

"All of them panicked?"

"Panic is contagious."

"They had a freaking epidemic," he said. "Look at the bullet holes, they're all over the place. We're talking fifty or sixty rounds here. Don't you think that's strange?"

In the past I might have agreed with my partner, but in the last few years we'd seen more gun-happy homicides and counted more bullet holes than we had in our entire careers. The thing that did strike me as strange was the fact that young Johnny Boy stepped through the wrong door at the exact worst time. Smart cops don't believe in coincidence.

"It's not our case, Joe," I said, watching a seagull drop a clamshell from above, then swoop down to sit on the tarmac and pick meat from it.

"I'm just playing devil's advocate," he said.

"No, you're not. I know what you're doing. Let Major Case handle it."

We walked back to the car through the narrow path between cargo boxes. Out in the open you could feel the wind whipping across the tarmac, across immense wide-open runways built on five thousand acres of what once was the old Idlewild Golf Course. Away from the main terminal buildings you got the sense of the open flatness of the land. You could only imagine how beautiful it must have been. Above us, two laughing gulls floated in the Queens sky, cackling over some private joke.

On the way to Cookie's father's house in Great Neck, she yelled, "Don't take the Van Wyck." But it was too late; Gregory had already entered the ramp.

"It's Sunday," he said. "We'll take this to the Long Island Expressway. Traffic will move."

"I'll tell you the better way for next time," she said. "Take the Belt west to the Cross Island, then pick up the LIE."

"I know exactly where she gets that from," Gregory said. "Her husband, my old partner, was Mr. Traffic Expert."

"Tell me about it," she said. "I don't know who's worse, my husband or my father. They always argued about the best way here, the best way there."

Distracted, Gregory missed the entrance to the Long Island Expressway. So we crawled past Flushing Meadow Park, sight of the 1964 World's Fair. The Unisphere, newly refurbished and shiny, was visible through the bare trees. In the age of air travel the Unisphere has replaced the Statue of Liberty as the immigrant's first sight of the new world.

Sunlight gleamed off a plane coming in at La Guardia Airport.

La Guardia, the forgotten older sister of JFK with its short runways, built on sandy soil, unable to hold the weight of the jumbo jets. Incoming planes appear to skim the top of the teeming city jail on Riker's Island and touch down inches past the dark waters of the East River.

Cookie told us that her father, Vito Martucci, still ran the family business: a live poultry store on College Point Boulevard. Johnny Boy moved in with Vito after they left for Florida five years ago. Cookie's mother was dead, and her father loved having Johnny Boy around.

"My dad took Johnny Boy everywhere," Cookie said. "Ever since he was a baby. Ball games, the track, everywhere. They were a riot together. Once, at a pool party at the house, my dad gave Johnny Boy one of his old bathing suits to wear. It had a jock strap built in, you know, but attached only at the front. Well, Johnny Boy comes out of the house with the suit on and we all roared laughing, because when he put the suit on, he hooked the jock over his head. He has the straps crossed, and the pouch is sitting in the middle of his chest. He said he thought the pouch was for cigarettes."

Joe Gregory didn't laugh. For all his bluster and street bravado, Joe Gregory came apart when the pain was personal. I wondered if that was why he hid from any woman who started to get too close. The price of love is grief, and perhaps that was more than he wanted to pay.

"You guys break my heart," she said. "You all think you're bulletproof."

I looked at my watch as we crawled past Shea Stadium, slowly enough to catch a full inning, if the Mets had been there. I sat sideways, facing Gregory, but out of the corner of my eye I could still watch Cookie. Both were looking up. Maybe searching for the clear blue skies of the days when they laughed together.

3

"I hope she has family to stay with," my wife, Leigh, said.

We were at the sink, finishing the dishes. The electric clock hummed above our heads.

"Cookie has family all right," I said. "Her father is Vito Martucci, who insisted on telling us he was related to the connected Martuccis."

With the back of her arm, Leigh brushed the hair from her face. For thirty-three years I'd watched that gesture. Her hair, light brown the first time I saw it, was now completely gray.

"Does that mean politically connected," she said, "socially connected, or what I think it means?"

"Mob connected," I said.

"Family is family at a time like this."

I dried the last Tupperware bowl and squatted down to figure out where, in the cabinet, it went. Leigh had a system for these bowls I never seemed to grasp. Bowls on one side, lids on the other. How she matched them again was a mystery to me.

She said, "I guess the important thing is, are they a warm family?"

"They've been a hot family."

"Stop being a jerk, you know what I mean."

"Vito was the only family in the house today. Cookie's mother died several years ago. Johnny Boy lived with Vito ever since Cookie and J.C. moved to Florida."

"Did he seem as though he was going to be supportive?"

"No way in hell. Vito was out of it. Over the top. Cursing at God in Italian. Acting out some emotional wise guy role."

"You sound more like Joe Gregory every day. I suppose you think men shouldn't be susceptible to grief. The man just lost his grandson, what do you expect?"

"It's more than grief, Leigh. The guy was irrational, swearing personal vendettas like in a Mafia movie."

"Sounds like grief to me."

"But it looked like craziness to me. Maybe it's the pinky ring that causes it. All those Mob families have a high percentage of crazies."

"Family makes us all a little crazy," she said.

Our own family craziness was mild compared to what I saw in the world every day. Margaret, our oldest, was living on the Delaware shore with husband number three, a surfboard dealer. Our son, Tony, was in L.A., aspiring to be a rich actor but working as a security guard to the real rich actors. Our house was sadly quieter without them.

"Maybe you're right," I said. "I guess I heard him spouting all the wise guy clichés and it turned me off. Cookie said Vito and Johnny Boy were extremely close. She said he's going to be lost without him; they were like buddies."

Our kids were only babies when we moved into this fading Cape Cod in Yonkers, just a few miles north of the New York City line. The neighborhood was vibrant with small children then. But those kids grew up and moved back to the city we thought we'd escaped or to lives in places their immigrant grand-parents had only heard about. No one sang Beatles songs in our streets anymore. Basketball hoops rusted. The chalk of a thousand hopscotch games washed from the sidewalks.

"Are you going to be involved in this case?" Leigh said.

"Not if I can help it."

"What does the Great Gregory think about all this?"

"He's making noises like he wants a piece of the case. He thinks it's a matter of overkill."

"You agree?"

"I agree they fired an awful lot of rounds into that kid. But we see that more and more all the time. Everybody is gun crazy today."

"You don't find anything hinky about this case," she said. "I can't believe that."

I had to laugh at Leigh using "hinky." Hinky is a word cops use to describe something odd, slightly out of sync. A hinky aspect of a case sits in the back of your head and whispers "bull-shit" over and over again until you deal with it.

"The accidental nature of the shooting qualifies as hinky," I said. "Just as the perps are leaving, Johnny Boy steps through this door wearing a cop coat. That's hinky."

"Accidents do happen, Anthony. No matter what cops believe. Some people have a knack for stepping through the wrong door."

Leigh always reminds me that cops see too much of the worst and focus on the negative, even in their own lives. Things weren't that bad with us. Our neighborhood had held together, a stability owed to a powerful church and the warmth of one venerable bar. Grass actually grew in our backyard now, no longer worn down to bare dirt. Leigh could still walk to her job, as a secretary, at Sacred Heart High School, two blocks away. She loved that job, though the school had changed with the city's population, more Rodriguezes now than Ryans. I see them leaning into the steep hills, coming up from the projects. And I knew exactly how hard that climb could be.

"Let's plan a big Christmas dinner this year," Leigh said. "You know, like the old days. All the bells and whistles. Get everybody, the whole family, here."

"Sounds good to me."

"We should invite Joe."

"Joe who?"

"Joe Gregory. Your partner."

I wasn't being cute; I honestly didn't know who she meant. Although Joe Gregory and I had been partners for most of our careers, we'd drank and caroused our way through too many days and nights, even a few months and years. I couldn't remember the last time Leigh had even spoken more than a few pleasant words to him.

"Don't you think he'd like it?" Leigh said. "Better than going to Brady's Bar."

"Yeah," I said.

I put the knives in their rightful place. I knew Leigh's definition of eating knives as opposed to cooking knives. Knives I remembered.

"Do you mean yeah, it's better than Brady's?" she said. "Or yeah, he'd like it?"

"Both. I'll ask him."

"I'd really like him to come."

One of the underrated benefits of a longtime marriage is that it lulls you into thinking you know someone. And leaves you wide open for surprise. What I did know was that the dumb kid I'd been had made one extraordinarily lucky move in his life. I put my arms around her.

"Do one more thing for me, will you?" she said.

"Sure, what?"

"Tell Cookie she'll be with Johnny Boy again. I know that

sounds corny, but it helps to believe it. I believe it, so don't make fun of it, okay? Just do it for me. Please."

Leigh was a woman whom strangers complimented on her perfume. They'd smile and say, "What are you wearing? It's beautiful." I could never smell it. Maybe I was used to it. Maybe it was beyond me. After all, I'd never gotten past the soft feel of her skin against my lips.

These dreams are always in slow motion. I am always running up stairs, or across a room, or down some nameless, endless street. This one is about a boy, and he's merely opening a door. He turns and smiles at me, looking frail and angelic in that heavy blue overcoat. I struggle to grab him, stop him, but I can't quite reach. He steps out into the light. Then the first incredibly loud barrage jolts me awake, and I lie there cold and sweating. Still seeing his face, the face of my own son.

Leigh took my hand and put it on her leg. It was my need. I needed to feel her skin, her incredible body heat, like a small furnace. Even in sleep, so alive. If only my fingertips brushed her thigh, it was like clinging to life. Normal life, not cop life. That simple touch could hold me still. And if I could be still long enough, I might fall asleep again, before the demons noticed and resumed racing through my head.

We were both sound asleep when the phone rang. It was Frankie Stark, the night desk man in the chief's office.

"I hope I didn't wake you," he said. His famous little joke. I could almost hear his silent cackle. "You need to get your ass out to the One Thirteen. The squad just collared some old man, says he knows you. Guy's name is Vito Martucci. He just emptied his gun into the window of Emil Lutz's place, the Cockpit Lounge."

4

Detectives from the 113th Precinct took their sweet time processing Vito Martucci. But the foot dragging in this case was both a professional courtesy to us and a matter of understanding. The cops well understood the impulse to shatter the grimy windows of the Cockpit Lounge with a barrage of lead. And, after all, no one had been injured, not one solid citizen endangered. Only a few local goons had been in the line of fire, and they were used to ambient gunfire, it was part of goon life in the big city. So even if I hadn't called, the cops might have offered this particular shooter the courtesy of spending the night in one of their wooden chairs. It was far better than waiting for morning arraignment swatting cockroaches and inhaling hot piss in the holding pens at central booking.

I found Joe Gregory in the second-floor squad's coffee room, under the dull green glare of two bare fluorescent tubes. Chest-high metal file cabinets lined the two-tone brown walls. They were alone, facing each other across a scarred wooden table. Vito wasn't handcuffed. Between them, a stack of Italian pastries soaked the bottom of a flat white box.

"I saved something for you, pally," Gregory said, reaching into his pocket. He pulled out a cannoli wrapped in napkins. "Haven't had one of these in a while, right?"

I knew Joe bought the pastries. They came from the Italian bakery around the corner from his house in Bay Ridge. I'd been with him, in the middle of many long nights, when he banged on the back door until they opened. He'd gotten in the habit of "bringing something" wherever we went. Mr. Big Spender had inherited money from his dad, and it smoldered in his pocket.

"Decaf," Gregory said, raising his eyebrows and pointing his chin at the coffeepot. "Since when do cops drink decaf?"

Vito picked at a rum-soaked bun with a plastic fork. I dropped a quarter in a white Styrofoam cup with "25¢" penciled on the side, then sat opposite him.

"So what's the sad story?" I asked, unwrapping the napkin. Orange turkeys squatted in the corners of the stiff white paper.

"Mental anguish," Gregory said. "We're going to throw ourselves on the mercy of the court."

"What's this *we* shit?" Vito said, his voice a bourbon-and-Camels growl. "It's not your battle, amigo."

"We're dealing with a thick bastard," Gregory said.

"This is *my* problem," Vito said. "It's personal, between me and Lutz, that ignorant fucking Polack. It's no cop problem."

"Vito's lawyer says he can plead emotional distress, pally. Say he lost his head, with the grief and all that."

"Sounds reasonable."

"Hey, nobody got hurt," Gregory said, arguing the case. "Vito has no sheet."

"Really?" I said. "No prior record?"

"Just what I needed," Vito snapped. "Another Irish bastard in my life. You think all Italians are criminals, am I right?"

Vito put down the fork and clenched his age-spotted hands on the table. He still wore the same gray suit he'd been wearing when we'd dropped Cookie at his house. In the harsh light I could see a geometric pattern of fine red thread I hadn't noticed before.

"It seems that Vito here is only a distant cousin of the organized crime Martuccis," Gregory said. "Despite what he likes everybody to believe. So, maybe if Vito shows remorse, the judge fines him, gives him a good scare, and we all walk out into the sunshine of Queens Boulevard. Maybe go across the street, bang down a few highballs in Part One."

"Part One is long gone," Vito said. "Where the hell you been?"

"Whatever they call it now," Gregory said. "The place where the deals are made."

"Tell me this, Vito," I said. "What makes you so sure that Emil Lutz is responsible for this?"

"I got the full scoop, amigo. The inside scoop. I got contacts make your head spin. The only mystery you two got to solve is which of those scumbags out at the airport is working for Lutz."

"Vito," Gregory said, "we've got a bulletin for you. You're not a real mobster, you only dress like one."

"Why is this a personal thing?" I said. "Do you think your grandson's murder was an intentional act?"

"You want to know what I think?" he said. "I'll fucking tell you what I think."

I looked down at the arrest sheet for Vito's age and was stunned to read eighty-one. He was thin and wiry, with a full head of slicked-back white hair, pouffed up in a fifties' pompadour. He pointed his finger at me.

"You know that old cop overcoat Johnny Boy was wearing that night? That was my coat. J.C. gave that coat to me when he retired. It was in my closet. I never saw Johnny Boy wear that coat before that night. That strange, or what?"

"It was a cold night."

"It wasn't that fucking cold."

"Okay," I said. "Then what do you make of it?"

"I think he got wind of something going down," Vito said. "Something wrong. Maybe he thought he could stop it by wearing the coat."

I hadn't thought about the hero factor before. Johnny Boy, trying to impress his friends, his cop father, his macho grandfather, dons the police overcoat for a singular act of bravado. It was worth consideration; strange tragedies, even silly ones, happened every day.

"Why wouldn't he just tell security?" I said. "Or the Port Authority cops?"

"I don't know that, amigo. Maybe some buddy of his was involved, he was trying to protect him. He was the type of kid who's loyal to his friends. Who the fuck knows? It just don't make sense to me that he would choose that night to wear that coat. You know what cops say about coincidence?"

"I know what cops say about coincidence."

He opened his hands and stared at the palms. "Those bastards," he said. "Think because they are crazy and ruthless, that everybody backs off. Not me. I'm not letting them walk on this one."

"They're not going to walk," Gregory said.

"It doesn't make sense, Vito, that he'd try to stop men armed with automatic weapons."

"No shit," he said. "My grandson didn't make sense all the time, Ryan. He did a lot of shit you and me know is stupid. But if he did do something this fucking wacky, I blame that Irish broad."

"What Irish broad?"

"He's got this Irish girlfriend, can't understand a fucking thing she's saying. I think her name's Fiona, some shit like that."

"What did she do?"

"She was always playing that diddly-diddly music for Johnny Boy, getting him all excited."

"I don't get what you mean."

"Whenever he was with her," Vito said, "he comes home singing all these stupid songs about fighting and dying and honor and shit. It wasn't good for Johnny Boy to hear that shit. I told him to drop this broad, get a nice, calm Italian girl. Make love, not war. There's thousands of them hanging around the mall. You see them all over. Even a regular American girl would have been better than this piece of donkey fluff."

"She talked him into being a hero?"

"You don't think women can talk men into crazy shit?" he said. "We marry them, don't we?"

"Where can we find this Fiona, Vito?"

"She works in Manhattan, somewhere around Central Park. Baby-sitting for some rich kid."

"Maybe Cookie knows," I said.

"Cookie just left a few minutes ago," Gregory said. "George Raft here sent her home. Tough guys don't need nobody."

"How come you ain't writing this shit down?" Vito said. "You guys here to investigate, or just break my balls?"

"Whatever it takes," Gregory said.

"I've got one thing you can do for me. And only one thing. Bring my daughter to the arraignment. Make sure she gets here safe. That's it."

"My pleasure," Gregory said.

Vito was the poster child for Brooklyn toughness, an inner re-solve street people recognize in each other. Surely he'd never back down from a fight, even at his age, but he lacked the empty-eyed glare of the truly cruel.

"Is Emil Lutz going to press charges?" I asked.

"Emil Lutz can kiss my Sicilian ass," Vito said.

"The squad says that Major Case is sitting on him," Gregory said. "He's holed up in the Cockpit Lounge."

"Let's take a ride," I said. "Give Vito a chance to think about his future."

"Tell that Polack fuck I said he better sleep with his eyes open."

Gregory handcuffed Vito to a pipe, then went to tell the squad we were leaving. In a way I admired Vito. As Joe Gregory's late father said: "The worst thing you can do when you get old is stop being tough." The older I get, the more I think about that line.

"You know what the wise guys say?" Vito said.

"No, I don't. Enlighten me. What *do* the wise guys say?"

Then I figured out what Vito was doing. It was De Niro doing Brando doing Don Corleone.

"It all comes down to the law of nature," Vito said with that squinting smirk. "The big fish eat the little fish, that's all it is. The big fish eat the little fish."

5

The Cockpit Lounge occupied the ground floor of a three-story wood-frame building. Emil Lutz's uncles and cousins lived in the apartments above. Gregory parked at a hydrant, directly in front, but didn't put our official NYPD plate in the window; some good citizen out walking his dog would only assume we were looking for a score. Guilt by association was something we tried to avoid.

"Emil's joint could use some spit and polish," Gregory said.

The shingles were faded, the paint cracked and peeling like a skin disease. The bar's front window was covered with plywood. Tiny fragments of glass, scattered across the sidewalk, reflected purple neon.

"Yeah," I said. "What does it say about our economy when you can't even make a decent living selling stolen merchandise?"

I doubted Emil Lutz would press charges against Vito. Vito did have a familial link to the organized crime Martuccis of Long Island, no matter how thin the connection. Plus, going to court as a complainant would be an act that offended Emil's sense of renegade macho. Too straight. Too nine to five.

But I wanted an excuse to get inside, to get close enough to smell the sour odor of adrenaline, to see if I could sense their perverse exhilaration. I've interviewed Mob guys who talk about murder as if it were the one true holy and apostolic experience. "You ever whack anybody?" one creep asked me. "Then you can't understand the rush. You're fucking God. Guys pull the trigger, come in their pants. One second some poor bastard is eating, bullshitting; the next he's nothing. They all look up at you for a split second, when the bullet hits. They look at you. All of them, I shit you not. Like they don't fucking believe it. Like, hey, I'm Joe Shmoe, I can't fucking die."

Gregory jerked his thumb back toward the garage across the street, toward where a team from the NYPD Major Case Squad was sitting and now watching us.

"What do we do about them?" he said.

"If we talk to them, they'll tell us to stay the hell away. If we don't, we can use the stupidity defense."

"Inspector Decky O'Prey is their boss now," Gregory said. "No matter what we do, he'll be offended, guaranteed. That's his style. I say fuck him, let's just do it."

The Cockpit Lounge was a cross between a cozy ski lodge and a red velour orgy pad. A gas fireplace, framed in fake stone, occupied the corner near the window. The bar itself was bathed in orange light that made your skin appear jaundiced, everyone's clothes rinsed in the same electric Kool-Aid.

"Where's Emil?" Gregory said to the bartender.

"Emil who?" the bartender said.

"The Emil who signs your checks."

In the center of the bar sat two women, both carefully coiffed, overly made up. They talked loudly in honeyed southern accents as a couple of gin mill Romeos circled. Stories of horny stewardesses were legend in some Queens night spots.

"Nobody named Emil signs my checks," said the bartender, who didn't ask who we were.

"Maybe we'll find an Emil downstairs," Gregory said, walking toward a door behind the gas fireplace.

"Hey, nobody's down there," he said, reaching under the bar.

"Then who are you buzzing?"

"That's a private club. You can't fucking go down there."

But we were already on the narrow staircase. I knew it was seven steps down to Vegas in Queens: a private casino, with a roulette wheel and half a dozen card tables, an equal number of blackjack tables, and maybe twenty slot machines. But this night there was no snap of cards or clang of coins in a metal tray, and there hadn't been any action in quite a while. The floor was dirty, the gaming tables in shambles. Gray balls of dust rolled across green felt.

"The great Joe fucking Gregory," Emil Lutz said. "And Professor Ryan. Still on the job. A-fucking-mazing. I thought you'd both be dead by now."

"And your longevity is an even greater surprise," I said.

Emil Lutz and three other men were squeezed into a horseshoe-shaped leather booth. Empty glasses and black plastic ashtrays were scattered about.

"What brings you to Queens?" Lutz said. "Getting shit-faced at some donkey sergeant's retirement party, right? What else is new?"

"Maybe we're here just to visit you," I said.

We pulled bar stools over to the table and sat high above them. But I couldn't see Lutz's eyes, and that made me uncomfortable. Cigarette smoke floated up toward the overhanging lamp.

"What are you up to these days, Emil?" Gregory said as he ran his fingers through the dust on the light's tin shade. "I see you've been too busy to dust."

"Still a comical fuck," Lutz said. "We go way back. Me and these two crazy micks."

Lutz was a fireplug in a sleeveless T-shirt. He had deep-set eyes, bushy brows, and his complexion still had the sickly olive pallor of prison life. His guest list consisted of one pink sport jacket, one suit, one camouflage sweatshirt. I knew only the pink jacket, Larry Russo, scratching his nose with the diceman's stick. Russo was a sleazeball private detective who worked for Mob attorneys. I figured the suit was the attorney. The youngest of the three, the camo sweatshirt, was a squat, dark-haired mirror image of Emil, with a tattoo of something on his right hand.

"Why don't you complete the introductions, Emil," I said. "You *are* the host."

"I don't think so," he said. "I'm a rude prick like that."

"No problem," Gregory said. "We'll check the mug shots later."

I patted Joe on the back, reminding him of what we'd talked about on the way over: This visit was for schmoozing, not for ass kicking. That would come later.

"I see you have a broken window," I said.

"You know what they call our police department?" Lutz said, playing to his audience. "White welfare, white fucking welfare. What gave you sleuths the first clue? The glass on the sidewalk? The bullet holes in my new Moroccan fucking paneling?"

"It must have been a terrible thing," I said. "I wonder why it happened."

"You wonder *why?*" Lutz said. "*Why?*" He snubbed out his cigar in a dice boat. He was shaking his head as he looked up at me. "Who gives a rat's ass why? That senile fucking psycho bastard went too far. That's all you gotta know. End of story."

"It's always more rewarding to contemplate life's deeper aspects," I said. "The mysteries of men's motives."

Lutz touched his lips with his fingertips, his hands in the prayer position, elbows on the table.

"Maybe I haven't had a chance to unravel that mystery," he said. "Maybe I got other mysteries to contemplate."

"Sometimes things remain mysteries," I said.

"Sometimes they don't," Emil said.

"Sometimes it's better they do," I said. "Sometimes the unraveling of an event brings more grief than it's worth."

Lutz looked up at me, his dark eyes ringed and puffy. Prison dandruff dotted his hairline. I could see he'd left a few teeth under his pillow in Attica.

"These events you speak of," Lutz said. "Would this visit be to let me know that this event might be one of those events that could bring me grief?"

"It's certainly possible."

"I mean," Lutz said, "are you saying it might be a good thing if this event didn't bring no grief to nobody?"

"How could that be a bad thing?" I said.

"Good or bad," Lutz said. "The question is, can you guarantee that the angels will look favorably upon my generosity?"

"No good act is forgotten," I said.

"Well," he said, smiling, "I am not one to wish more grief upon a fellow human being. After all, I got all the grief I can handle right now. It's only glass, am I right? What's a little glass between friends?"

"Know your friends," I said. "And your enemies will take care of themselves."

Emil laughed. "You're a piece a work, Ryan," he said. "But all bullshit aside, I want you to remember one thing: You owe me. I want you to remember that. And I expect people to honor their debts."

"Sounds like a threat," I said.

I remembered Emil's laugh from an old FBI tape when he was telling some friends the story of his first contract. He told them how he walked into a Mulberry Street restaurant and put a shotgun into Patsy D'Amato's face. Emil pulled the trigger, nothing happened. He pulled it again, same result. "I bought the wrong fucking shotgun shells," he said over the tape. Emil went on to tell how he ran from the restaurant but returned two weeks later with an Uzi. This time he successfully blew off the head of Patsy D'Amato. "But I fucked up again," Emil said. As his friends howled with laughter, Emil described how he lost control of the Uzi. "My hands are sweating, and the gun slips. It's jumping like a fucking nigger at a Knicks tryout. Blood and glass and shit flying everywhere."

Emil didn't regale his social club friends with the part where a textbook salesman, and father of three, from Upper Saddle River had the misfortune to be celebrating his twentieth, and last, wedding anniversary in the adjacent booth. The fact that this incident was funny to these people spoke volumes to me.

"I'm not threatening anybody, Ryan," Emil said. "All I'm saying is you owe me one. Nothing more. Don't take me wrong."

But there was only one way to take guys like Emil, and that was wrong.

6

It was almost five A.M. when we arrived back at the 113th Precinct. A uniformed lieutenant, half our age, lounged on the front steps, smoking a cigar under the traditional green lamps. Which, in this case, were just bare white bulbs hidden behind warped and peeling plastic covers.

"My gun is older than most of the cops today," Joe Gregory said as we got out of the car. "And they're so little. Like half cops. You notice that, pally? I never saw so many little cops as they got out here in Queens. Two foot three, some of them. I tripped over one in the muster room before."

Gregory parked on Baisley Boulevard, across the street from the precinct and next to two lines of gray wood-frame houses with all the personality of military billeting. Up ahead was the battleship gray overpass for the Long Island Railroad.

"What did you make of Emil Lutz?" I said.

"Prison turned him into a real humanitarian. And they say rehabilitation don't work. What I want to know is, how come he didn't break our balls more?"

"Did he smell guilty to you?"

"He didn't even smell that worried," Gregory said.

The young lieutenant flipped his cigar into the street and went inside the station house. The One Thirteen, a two-story modern tan brick structure, lacked the character of the old station houses. It could just as easily have been a board of ed payroll office or the borough sanitation HQ. A large banner stretched across the front entrance said "Welcome."

I said, "Do you buy Vito's story about Johnny Boy, the night of the robbery was the first time he wore J.C.'s old police uniform overcoat?"

"He's giving us a line of shit. Trying to blame everybody for what happened. We can ask the kid's friends or his co-workers at the airport."

"If it was our case, we could ask them," I said, staring directly at my partner. "But it's not our case, is it?"

"Not that I know of," he said, shrugging.

"I'll write something up for the Major Case Squad. Let them ask. But if Vito's not bullshitting us, it's definitely hinky."

Gregory and I parted ways at the door. He went upstairs to wait with Vito until it was time to pick up Cookie for arraignment. I drove my son's old pea green '75 Volvo to Manhattan. He'd handed it down to me when he left for the West Coast. The only repair I'd made was to scrape off the "Question Authority" bumper sticker.

It was dawn when I emerged from the Midtown Tunnel. I took the FDR Drive south. The sun, just starting to peek over Brooklyn, cast a faint pink glow on the black water of the East River. I thought about Emil Lutz, just out of prison. Why would he immediately take the chance on returning? But three million dollars was a large carrot to dangle in front of a guy like Emil. Guys like Emil love to steal. They lived and breathed elaborate con games and once-in-a-lifetime heists. I've heard them on tape after a big score, giddy like school kids. It was as if they swore at birth never to do anything straight.

At Pearl Street I swung down from the drive, jumped the light, then cut down the side street and easily found a parking spot. In less than an hour that simple act would be impossible. I walked under a dark overpass to the Brooklyn Bridge; the immense and dense stone, over a century old, reeked of history and the homeless.

On the other side was One Police Plaza, a fourteen-story cube that had served as NYPD headquarters since the seventies. In comparison with the bridge it seemed prefab and cookie-cutter cheap. The square, deeply recessed windows made it look like a red brick subway grating.

Only two cops were on security duty, both focusing on two weary uniformed cops from the Bronx. The Bronx cops were following each other toward one of the eight turnstiles. The outside commands had to slide their ID cards through a slot, then wait for it to duplicate on the console. The security cops then compared the picture on the screen with the face before them. Headquarters cops had different cards. I swiped mine through the eye and, at the green light, pushed through the turnstile and stepped into the waiting elevator. I rode alone to the thirteenth floor.

Frankie Stark was hidden behind the radio transmitter in the darkened office. On the wall directly in back of him hung a battery charger with slots for thirty-six portable radios. Tiny redorange warning bulbs glowed like Christmas lights.

"I heard you fucked up," Stark said.

"You spend entirely too many nights here alone, Frankie."

"I heard you stuck your nose where it don't belong." He was polishing a small bronze statue of a Spanish Conquistador. A can of Brasso sat open on the table.

"Who did you hear that from?"

"A little birdie."

"Cut the shit, Frankie. Who said it?"

"My lips are sealed."

"Are they really? You remember all those skin movies missing from the Public Morals evidence inventory?"

"A birdie from Major Case," he said quickly. "Decky O'Prey is pissed 'cause you went into the Cockpit Lounge without clearing it with him first. I'm only telling you because I like you. Your partner's still an asshole."

"He speaks as well of you," I said.

The chief of detectives office consisted of a huge open room ringed by private offices for lieutenants and above. The only windows were located in the offices facing west. If the bosses didn't want to dwell on the setting sun, they could stare at the courthouses of Foley Square. The rest of us sat within cream-colored metal walls in columns of desks that ran the length of the room. My desk was hidden in the far right corner. Gregory had created an L-shaped barrier of file cabinets to cut us off from the masses.

I began typing a memo for the chief. We were reporting directly to him since our boss, Captain Delia Flamer, was attending the FBI Academy in Quantico, Virginia. I was trying to beat Declan O'Prey to the punch; I knew he'd bitch about us going into the Cockpit Lounge. In this job rule number one was Always have a story.

The gist of my story was that we were assisting the 113th Squad in locating and interviewing the complainant in the Vito Martucci case. They'd know it was bullshit, but that wasn't the point. The point was that the boss would hear the story from us first. He'd be prepared when O'Prey came in screaming. He'd be able to say, "I already know all about it." Rule number two: Never let your boss be embarrassed.

As I was sealing the envelope I heard the heavy quick steps I knew belonged to Detective Albie Meyers, the chief's crime analyst. Albie's desk sat just on the other side of the file cabinet from ours. I said good morning and heard something splat on the floor.

"Jesus Christ," he yelled. "You scared the living shit out of me."

I came around the file cabinets and saw him tap dancing around a puddle of coffee. He tossed a stack of folders onto his desk.

"Why so early?" I said. "Long Island Railroad on strike?"

"Naw, I've got all kinds of shit to pull," he said. "O'Prey called a strategy session on the JFK fiasco. Ten hundred hours."

Albie mopped coffee with yesterday's *New York Post* as I flipped through the folders he'd carried in. They contained field reports and arrest sheets going back over forty years. Old booking photos showed groups of guys in fedoras and overcoats standing in front of a wall-length height chart. Surveillance pictures, glued to folder halves, were stacked in the rear; the Cockpit Lounge was depicted from every possible angle.

"Since when do you keep folders at home?" I asked.

"Since fifteen years ago, that goddamn privacy act made us purge the files. Stupidest piece of legislation in history. As if these bastards deserve any privacy."

"So these old files found sanctuary in your basement?"

"Let's make this our little secret."

"You're a regular little J. Edgar Hoover, aren't you, Albie."

"You want to help me, Ryan? Quit busting my chops and run down to OCCB and pull the most recent observations on Emil Lutz and the Cockpit Lounge."

"The most recent observation is on my desk. Joe and I just left the Cockpit Lounge."

Albie stood there, coffee dripping from the wet newspaper. "Tell me you're not shitting me."

"What do you want to know?" I said.

"Was Emil Lutz there?"

"In the flesh."

"What about his kids, Vincent and Rocky?"

"Rocky wasn't there. What does Vincent look like?"

"Like Emil, only crazier. He's about twenty-two, twenty-three. Heavy built, short. Tattoo of a guitar on his hand. Emil named him after his godfather, Vincent 'Chin' Gigante. Like that would help him become a made man. Like for him they'd make a special one Polack exception."

"You have a picture?"

"Of course I got a fucking picture," he said, and gave up wiping to flip through his folders. "This is good, real good. I can say this at the meeting today, right? You'll back me up?"

"What choice do I have? You probably have files on me in your basement."

He pointed to a booking photo. The hair was longer, but it was the same face I'd seen in the Cockpit Lounge. Vincent's resemblance to his father was very evident in early arrest photos of Emil. I thought that we could put together a nice little photo album for the Lutzes. The family that steals together, stays together.

"That's the bozo," I said.

"I thought sure as shit they'd go south. Who else was there?"

"Larry Russo and another guy I didn't recognize."

"Larry Russo, the PI. Sounds like they might be lawyering up."

Albie tossed his coat and sport jacket across the file cabinet. He'd forgotten about the spilled coffee on the floor. Instead he was engrossed in a piece of information that had not yet begun to gather dust. Albie was generally referred to as the "Commanding Officer of Useless Information."

"Has O'Prey considered the possibility someone else besides Emil Lutz did this?" I said.

"No, and he's got to have something under his hat. O'Prey's not the type to go off half-cocked. A regular Mister Conservative."

"What could he have?"

"Beats the shit out of me. I heard they found a gun at the scene, maybe they traced it back to Vincent Lutz."

"Vincent didn't say a word when we were there."

"Vincent's a crazy bastard, Ryan, a real gun freak. He's been running the show at the airport during Daddy's long vacation, and everybody's pissed off. Word is he's causing big problems between the families."

"I hate to see families in turmoil," I said.

During Emil Lutz's heyday the Lucchese crime family happily shared his services with the Colombo family. There was plenty of airport booty to satisfy everybody. Emil's crew stole cash, diamonds, furs, negotiable securities, guns, and credit cards, which led to stolen airline tickets. Sometimes they stole shipments right off the loading docks; other times they hijacked trucks as they left the airport. It was all gravy until Emil went down on the Lufthansa job. The sloppiness of that job embarrassed both families and decimated Emil's crew.

"When's the last time you saw Emil's other kid?" Albie said.

"I haven't spoken to Rocky Lutz in maybe six, eight months. He's a legitimate working man now."

"Yeah, you're breaking my heart, Ryan. Maybe I'll invite him home for dinner some night."

"I'm sure he'd jump at that opportunity."

"Is he still an active stool?"

"He's still registered to me, if that's what you mean. CI number 2662."

"He got Colombo family ties, am I right?"

"Through marriage," I said.

"I got a quid pro quo deal for you," Albie said. "You help me, I help you."

"How do you help me?"

"I know something that will have an immediate effect on your life," he said. "Solid info. But first you got to talk to Rocky Lutz for me. Ask him what he knows about the JFK stickup. I need to verify that the Colombo family is pissed at the Lutz crew."

"It doesn't work that way, Albie. First tell me your end of the bargain."

"Okay. No problem," he said. "What I hear is you're getting the Counihan homicide."

"Says who?"

"Says the chief of detectives. He wants to handle it as a separate homicide. And since Major Case is handling everything else, the chief wants a headquarters team to work it under Inspector O'Prey."

"Joe Gregory called the chief, didn't he?"

"Gregory's your problem," Albie said. "Not mine."

"When were they planning to tell us?"

"At the meeting today," Albie said. "I'm supposed to tell you to be there. O'Prey's going to lay down the guidelines. But if you're uptown looking for your informant, I can't do that, can I? Maybe it gives you time to slip and slide. Get out from under."

"I don't know," I said. "I never worked with O'Prey. Maybe I might enjoy it."

"Yeah, right," he said. "That'll make you his first happy camper. I need to get some paper towels. If you're here when I get back, I'm going to tell you about this meeting."

Declan O'Prey was a rising star in the department and a guy who took the term "superior officer" way too seriously. Joe Gregory says that when he's around O'Prey he wants to kick him in the ass so bad that his leg begins to twitch. I picked up two blank tape cassettes and two new notebooks from our supply stash. Then I grabbed my coat.

7

I drove south, through the Fulton Fish Market, swung around the tip of Manhattan, then north on the West Side. It was faster to make the loop, hugging the edge of the island, than trying to drive crosstown. All cops have their traffic tricks. Gregory taught me this one.

Our informant, Rocky Lutz, was Emil's youngest son, a carpenter at the Javits Convention Center and a wanna-be wise guy. Wanna-bes were good for us because they loved to talk the talk. Rocky also loved to walk the walk, but the only reason the bent noses put up with him was because he'd married well. Rocky Lutz was the son-in-law of the revered Colombo capo Salvatore "Sally the Goat" Corrazzo, who was doing federal time for rigging the concrete bids during the construction of the Javits Center.

Before Sally the Goat left for prison he made sure his dopey son-in-law was given a job with the Carpenter and Joiners Union at Javits. Rocky didn't know a claw hammer from Mike

Hammer. At the corner of Thirty-fourth and Eleventh I called his pager number from a phone that reeked of garlic.

The Javits Convention Center runs north from West Thirty-fourth to the Lincoln Tunnel and west from Eleventh Avenue to the Hudson River. It's a mammoth glass erector set of a building that replaced the Coliseum, up on Columbus Circle, as the venue for major conventions and trade shows such as the auto and boat shows. Unfortunately the Mob also made the trip downtown, clinging to the backs of the trade unions. The Javits Center's employee parking lot now ran a close second to the legendary Ravenite Social Club as the best place in Manhattan to look for wise guys.

Rocky whined, then agreed to be at our usual spot in fifteen minutes. I parked my old Volvo on West Thirty-seventh, behind the River Diner, and tried to think of a way to back out of this case. I hated working in a task force; it was investigation by committee. The real problem in this case was not murder, but money. If all we had were the bodies of three average citizens, we would have worked it out with the detectives who caught the case. Three million missing bucks meant we'd have to climb over the feds, the DAs, and the politicians. My partner has problems trying to be diplomatic with these types—God forbid he steps on their fragile egos.

I took out the new notebooks. On the first one, which would be my official book, I simply put my name and the date. On the other one, for my eyes only, I wrote everything I could remember from the moment I got the phone call to respond to JFK. After that I unwrapped a cassette, wrote "Rocky" on the label, snapped it into the Sony recorder. I read the standard ID heading: my name and shield, the date, and Rocky's name.

It took one more call to his pager before Rocky came shambling across Eleventh Avenue decked out in total Knicks: hat, jacket, T-shirt. Rocky never mixed team logos. I put a piece of adhesive tape over the "on" switch on the tape recorder and shoved it under the seat as Rocky flicked a cigarette at a passing bus. He stopped in the middle of the street to light another. Typical. A rebel without a clue. I was thankful he was one of the few North American males my daughter had not married. I could almost feel sorry for Sally the Goat.

"What's new, Rocky?" I said as he slid into the front seat.

"New York, New Jersey," he said. "New Zealand."

"Good, good," I said. "You added New Zealand. You're getting very international."

We didn't have an exclusive deal with Rocky. He also talked to the FBI, the DEA, and the DA's offices of three counties. The difference was they paid to hear his song and dance. Gregory and I didn't spend a dime on him, nor did we listen to his bullshit. We knew a secret that could get him killed.

"How's the family, Rock? How's Brenda?"

"Fine, thank you for asking."

I looked across the seat and smiled at him. It was a smile meant to let him know that I was back again to squeeze him on the same currency: our little family secret.

"Fuck you," he said.

The secret came from the mouth of Rocky himself. A drunken Rocky, entertaining his bookmaker buddy with a funny story over a tapped phone line. The case never went to court; we heard the story in Brady's Bar one afternoon from two Public Morals Division cops. "It seemed funny at the time," he said when we confronted him.

"Fuck you twice," he said, and took a big, tough-guy drag on his cigarette.

Rocky knew it wouldn't seem so funny to his father-in-law. Sally the Goat believed that his only daughter, Brenda, was severely injured in an accident at home. A pure accident. At the hospital, Rocky told his in-laws that Brenda was vacuuming the rug when the vacuum cleaner shorted, sending an electrical shock through her body, thereby causing her violent fall. She sustained severe cuts to the face and arms. The salesman who sold her the vacuum cleaner disappeared soon afterward.

"Tell me what you know about the JFK stickup," I said.

"I don't know dick," Rocky said. He loved playing tough guy; they all did, at first. "That's the truth."

"You wouldn't know the truth if it came up and zapped you," I said.

The truth of Brenda's electric jolt was all on tape. Rocky telling the bookmaker he'd just gotten home when it happened. Rocky was a party animal, and Brenda was giving him hell about staying out all night. Rocky tells the bookmaker he was sitting in his BarcaLounger with a wicked hangover. Brenda kept breaking his balls, yelling above the noise of the vacuum. Then she bent down in front of him as she vacuumed under the coffee table. Rocky says Brenda had an ass like a Persian mare, and she completely blocked his view of the TV. On impulse, or simple stupidity, Rocky reached into his duffel bag and pulled out a stun gun he'd been using in his collection duties for a Mob loan shark. Fifty thousand volts, right in that big ass. It propelled her, face first, into a newly hijacked thirty-two-inch Sony TV. She never knew what hit her.

I waved the cassette in the air.

"That shit's getting old," Rocky said.

"I bet Sally the Goat won't think so. He gets out this spring, right?"

"I don't know shit about that robbery."

"C'mon," I said. "An 'in' guy like you. You got your ear right to the pipeline. What's Howard Beach saying about it?"

Rocky looked out the window and sighed. "I make one mistake and I got to worry about this shit the rest of my life?"

"Yeah," I said. "That's how it works."

"I'll tell you this much," he said. "Some guys got the wrong idea that some other guys pulled that JFK job."

42

"Would these guys who are wrongly suspected happen to be named Lutz?"

"No names. That's the deal, I don't do names. I'm not a rat."

"The Colombos think your father pulled this off, don't they?"

"I neither confirm nor deny your allegation."

"Or maybe your brother, Vincent?" I said. "Or maybe the whole family. You have cousins, right? Were they cut in?"

Rocky smoked Camels. It was a thing among the young toughs to smoke unfiltered cigarettes, because at one time they didn't allow filters in prison. I noticed he didn't have any carpenter's calluses on his hands.

"This is about respect," he said. "You wouldn't understand."

"Then educate me."

"You know . . . the way you're brought up. You're supposed to show respect to your elders. It's one of the big fucking problems with society today. People got no respect. Hey, by the way, we going to discuss this . . . hypo . . . ?"

"Hypothetically, right. Okay. Say, if someone, this imaginary person, didn't show respect to his elders, then what did he do?"

"More like what he didn't do. Know what I mean?" When Rocky said "Know what I mean?" he ran the words together so quickly that it sounded like "Nomeen?"

"What *do* you mean?" I said slowly.

He looked at me, twisted his mouth sideways, and blew smoke toward the windshield.

"Say you do a job and it turns out well. There are certain gestures you should make to show respect to your elders. See what I'm saying?"

"Emil didn't kick anything back to the boss," I said.

"I'm saying he didn't even fucking do the job. That's my point. If my dad did it, don't you think he'd be the first one in the club with the money? Gift-wrapped. That's the way he was brought up."

There is no written guide to etiquette for the Mob. Emily Post

43

and her peers have ignored this area. But every little half-assed Mob guy knows that when you pull off a big score you duke the dons. It's a must. Within a very short period of time you must arrive at the don's club with a substantial tithe. Not only is it rude to ignore this time-honored practice, it's possibly a fatal error.

"Then why do the Colombos think Emil did it?" I said.

"You gotta ask them that question."

"Maybe your dad was pissed off because they didn't go to bat for him over Lufthansa?"

"You hard of hearing, or what? He didn't do any fucking thing. Now everybody's saying shit, like we're stroking them. Some people want my dad to ante up what he don't have, in significant numbers."

"How significant are we talking?"

"My guess is point five mil. Next week it's a full mil. Hypothetically."

"Of course."

A lunch bell must have rung somewhere. The street was filled with guys in jeans and work boots heading for the River Diner. Most came from Javits, across the street. A few came from behind us, from the run-down auto body shops and sheet metal factories on West Thirty-seventh Street.

"What is this, Macy's fucking window here?" Rocky said. "This the only place you know to park? These guys all know me. We're sitting ducks here. I mean, who else but a cop would own an ugly green fucking car like this?"

"Next time we'll meet on Tenth."

"That's better," he said. "But pick me up here. I ain't walking all the way to Tenth."

I saw the blur of a guy in a black watch cap going through the door of the River Diner. What really caught my eye was the red wool blanket he'd slung over his shoulder like a West Side matador. Although I couldn't make him out in the glare and grease on the diner's windows, I knew he'd stopped in the alcove, in the spot where all diners keep their cigarette machines. All I could see was the red blanket. But I knew he was looking back at us.

"What about your brother, Vincent?" I said. "What kind of business is he into these days?"

"Vincent ain't got the head for business. He's a bit of a dipshit."

"What about the gun business? I heard he's big into selling guns."

"That's more like a hobby with him, Ryan. Vincent's into the NRA, soldier of fortune, all that crap. He can rattle off the specs on any weapon; beyond that, he don't show much interest."

"I want you to keep in touch on this one," I said. "Talk to people for me."

"You know something," Rocky said. "You guys put me in a position where you can get me killed. You ever think about that?"

"Every waking moment."

"Everybody wants my ass, Ryan. The cops, the Colombos, even the Lucchese people are making noises like we screwed them. I been thinking of laying low, taking a short vacation till this blows over. So, if you don't see me around . . ."

"Hey," I said. "Sally the Goat is not going to let anything happen to his favorite son-in-law."

"Not for nothing," he said. "But the guy hates my fucking guts."

"You're wrong, Rocky. He loves you. He got you this job, didn't he?"

"See, that's what's wrong with guys like you. You put too much importance on a simple fucking job. You think he did me a favor? Think again. This job ain't no cakewalk. Alls the Goat had to do is make one phone call. Bingo, I'm in. But no, I'm here all day, breaking my ass like I'm chopped fucking liver. He should have done the right thing by me. You know it's true, Ryan."

"People would kill for your job, Rocky. What do you make, fifty bucks an hour and all you can steal?"

"I'm paying fucking taxes up the ying-yang," he said. "I'm out here Joe Citizen working a shmuck job. I'm family, I deserve better."

"What's better?"

"At the very least," he said, "I should have gotten a no-show job."

The red blanket hadn't moved from the spot near the diner window. Maybe the guy had hung it on a hook, like an overcoat, and all I was seeing was blanket. Maybe he was waiting for a take-out order. If not, what the hell was so interesting about us? As Rocky Lutz walked toward the diner, I put the car in reverse and backed toward Tenth Avenue.

8

Tuesday morning came drizzly and gray, the weather of sad ceremony. Johnny Boy Counihan's funeral mass was to be said at St. Aloyisius, the church he'd attended with his grandfather, Vito Martucci. We were among the last of the mourners to arrive in Great Neck. Gregory parked two blocks from the church and we walked under immense dripping oaks.

"You don't see anybody naming their kid Aloyisius anymore," Gregory said.

"Saints' names are out. Rich-sounding WASP surnames, like Hunter and Courtney, are in."

"And why is that, pally?"

"It breeds success," I said. "It starts a kid out on the way to a seat on the stock exchange."

"So a kid named Joey or Eddie, where's he find his seat?"

"On the benches in criminal court."

"Which side of the cage?"

"Both," I said.

The main drag in Great Neck could have been designed by

Ralph Lauren. Brick sidewalks flanked a wide street dominated by full-growth trees on a center island. The immaculate windows of bricked storefronts were framed in wood painted forest green. Beemers and cabriolets sat at the meters. I imagined the town cops wearing Harris tweed blazers, rep ties, and tassel loafers.

"I was named after St. Joseph," Gregory said. "Patron saint of stand-up guys."

"I thought G. Gordon Liddy was the patron saint of stand-up guys."

He gave me a glance that said "Don't mention that name." Liddy's radio remarks about shooting ATF agents had soured Gregory on his old hero. Liddy's picture went from Gregory's desk to the trash the day after he made the comment.

"Why are we having this conversation about kids' names?" I said. "God forbid you have some poor woman in the family way."

"No, I was just thinking. All these third- and fourth-generation kids today naming their babies Kieran and Maeve. Years ago the Irish tried to get away from the old country names. They wanted to Americanize us, named us Johnny instead of Sean and Jimmy instead of Seamus. Like poor Johnny Boy here, I bet he would've named his kid something like Maeve."

Four slippery marble steps led up through two gothic pillars of white concrete to the front of St. Aloyisius. The church was a modern reddish brown brick, but the cornerstone said "1913." Metallic doors stood tall, dark, and imposing. Gregory reached for the brass handle on the left, the one rubbed smooth and golden from the constant massage of pious hands. Then he stopped in the vestibule.

"What's wrong?" I said. He was frowning and breathing though his mouth.

"Nothing. I'm just a little nervous because I think this church might fall down."

It was his way of saying I hadn't been inside one of these

structures in a long time. He was wrong. I was slowly making my way back to Mother Church. My first few visits had been solo excursions, sitting in the back, listening quietly to the monotone whisper of rote prayers and the click of rosary beads against the pews. Gregory didn't know this yet. It wasn't something I was comfortable explaining. I feel like the returning prodigal, too old to sin and starting to worry about his just punishments.

Gregory blessed himself with holy water, then we sat about five pews from the back. The pews behind us were jammed with Johnny Boy's co-workers from the airport, ready to make a quick exit after mass. Directly in front of us sat two men in oddly formal clothes. One of them was a fat kid wearing a black tailcoat and fussing with the tassel on a beret. The other, a redhead, wore tweed, a heavy tweed meant for outdoors. He held a silky top hat in his lap.

The mass began with carillon bells. We stood and said the prayers together in English. I could hear the strong brogue of someone in front of us, even in grunted responses. It sounded like the fat kid in the tailcoat.

We all said the words together. It's like riding a bike, you don't forget. But I missed the mystery of the old church: the Latin, the incense, the priest with his back to the congregation, murmuring incantations I had no desire to know. We were part of a secret ceremony then. Now it seems too Protestant, all this sing-along and handshaking, like an audience-participation show. Your business with God should be private, between you and Him.

Gregory looked around as if he'd lost something. He checked the bottom of his shoes, as an old nun, reading from a letter from St. Paul, looked over her glasses to remind us solemnly that this was the Word of the Lord.

"Smell something?" Gregory whispered.

"Horseshit," I said. It was horseshit. I'd noticed it on the soles of the engineer boots of the fat Irish kid in front of us. Dried horseshit. I figured they were hansom cab drivers. It would explain the clothes and the smell. The Irish had virtually taken over the horse-drawn buggies parked along the south edge of Central Park. A Sunday afternoon walk from the Plaza Hotel to Columbus Circle had the sounds and smells of old Dublin.

Johnny Boy Counihan's bronze casket sat on rollers in the center aisle. It was draped in the orange, white, and green flag of Ireland. It struck me that Johnny Boy was quite an Irish buff for a half Italian kid from Queens. Perhaps an overwhelming need to identify with his Irish cop father.

Cookie Counihan sat in the front pew between her father and a woman I didn't know. The broad-shouldered Cookie towered over Vito and the unknown woman, who wore a white lace scarf over her dark hair.

"Who is that next to Cookie?" I whispered.

"I think that's Johnny Boy's girlfriend," Gregory said.

"Fiona?"

"Right. Cookie mentioned she'd be here."

The eulogy rang hollow, the priest's words too generic and rehearsed. But when he walked around the casket, swinging the thurible, I heard a soft groan from the front of the church. This was what I loved about religion, the part that could touch your soul: the priest chanting, the clank of the thurible chain as it swung over the bronze casket. Clouds of thick incense rose to the vaulted ceiling as saints peered through the haze. Angled shafts of colored light streamed down through stained-glass eyes.

After mass we filed slowly into the street. People form small groups quickly outside churches, desperate to speak in their own tongue. The hearse and one limo sat in the side street, wheels up on the curb. The ground in the courtyard was covered with ivy.

"Let's pay our respects here," I said. "I don't want to go to the cemetery."

We caught them at the limo, Vito looking across the roof of

the black Caddy, his eyes locked in a thousand-mile stare. The women sat in the back. Gregory squeezed in across from them in the jump seat. I hesitated. I hated this. I knew I should be better with words. Better able to find something healing to say.

I leaned in and made Gregory shove over one seat. I'd resigned myself to cliché but when I felt the warmth of Cookie's hand, I remembered. "My wife wanted me to tell you something, Cookie. She said that she knows you'll see your son again. It's only time, but it will come."

Cookie tried to smile while I watched the light show of her face. We talked a few minutes more, and the smell of perfume made my eyes start to water. I kept glancing at the dark-haired woman looking out the side window, her lace scarf held on with a black comb.

"I'm Fiona Quinn," she finally said. "John and I were close friends." She put a tiny hand in mine and said, "Pleased."

Fiona's small eyes were China blue, like those painted on a doll, her face and frame delicate. She wore no makeup except for a green eyeliner. Her pale complexion contrasted with hair as black as the limo we were in.

"Johnny Boy certainly had a lot of Irish friends," I said.

"And other nationalities as well," Fiona said. "John was a good-hearted man."

Funerals create the most awkward moments. People who barely know each other are thrust together over something no one can understand. I wanted to question Fiona more, but I asked for, and received, her phone number, then stepped out of the limo.

"You talk to those guys out at the airport yet, Ryan?" Vito Martucci said. His white hair was damp in the mist. "The answer is out there, I'm telling you."

"Major Case is handling all the airport interviews, Vito."

Vito had put his hand around my back when I stood up from the limo. He was surprisingly strong for a small, old man.

"I know that," he said. "I saw them out there yesterday. A coupla rookies, going through the motions. Laughing, for chrissakes, like something was funny. You're a smart guy, Ryan, explain that to me. Tell me how a cop can be happy about this."

I reached inside my jacket and pulled my holster away from his fingers, but he only dug them into my ribs. I wanted to be understanding, to try to soothe his grief. But he didn't want an answer.

"I can't explain it, Vito."

"Those guys over there," he said, pointing across the street. "I saw them with Johnny Boy. Maybe they know something. At least talk to them for me."

I peeled Vito's hand from my ribs as I told him I'd talk to them. He'd pointed across the street at the two guys who'd knelt in front of us, the ones with the horseshit on their boots. I walked over and introduced myself. The heavy one with the tailcoat said his name was Dermot Geary, the redhead introduced himself as Mickey O'Brien.

"Are you guys friends of Johnny Boy's?" I said.

"We are that," Dermot said. "We met him through Fiona. He was a fine gentleman."

"'Tis true," Mickey said.

Dermot stood with his hands in his pockets, jingling his change. He was a big, burly guy, almost the size of Joe Gregory. He had green eyes, a protruding forehead, and I could smell the drink on him. Mickey had hair the color of an Irish setter, a snub nose, and his lips were badly chapped.

"You work with horses?" I said.

"Didya smell the shite on me boots?" Dermot said. "I stunk up the church. I know I did."

"No, someone thought you might have been airport workers. I figured, from your outfits, that you drove hansom cabs."

"That's a very fine estimation, sir," Dermot said. "I admire an analytical mind."

"Did you know Johnny Boy well?" I said.

"I'd like to think so, Officer," Dermot said.

"When was the last time you saw him?"

"It was Wednesday night, we were just saying. Last Wednesday night. We were having a few cold brews. Miss Fiona Quinn and the bunch of us from County Cork."

"Did he seem normal?"

"That he did. He was in fine fettle."

"Did he seem worried about anything, like something at his job?"

"If he was troubled, he didn't mention it aloud," Dermot said.

I said, "Where was this bar you were drinking in?"

"The Scratcher, in the Village. Stop by tomorrow night, we'll all be there."

"I'll do that," I said.

"Can I ask you something?" Dermot said. "I don't know if this is the time, but we were wondering if it was required for a person to be a U.S. citizen to become a policeman in this city. We'd like to join up."

"That we would," Mickey said.

"It's better than freezing to death behind the arse of a horse," Dermot said. "And it's a fine profession, as well."

"I don't know," I said. "It's the first time anyone ever asked me. I'll find out."

"We'd surely be interested," Dermot said.

Mickey nodded and licked his lips.

I gave them both my card and turned toward our car, keeping far away from the limo. The old nun waved to me from the top step of the church, as if she knew me. I thought, If the only reason churches exist is to handle this kind of sorrow, then that is reason enough. Plenty of justification for me. Let there be a church on every corner. I kept walking. Away from Vito Martucci, his family, and his pain. Away from the aching grief that only the death of the young can rain down on poor old bastards like us.

9

Wednesday night, after Joe Gregory left for his Emerald Society meeting, I met Fiona Quinn in a bar on Fifth Street in the East Village. The place was called Scratcher, which she explained was the name they called someone on the dole in Dublin.

"The dole is like welfare over here," she said.

I knew that, but I acted as if I didn't. People tend to talk more freely if they think they're more knowledgeable than you.

"But with the price of a pint in here," she said, "I hardly think a person on the dole could afford it."

Fiona was sitting at a table near the bar with two other young women when I walked in. I ordered two Guinnesses, which the barman poured in the deliberate Irish way. Then we sat at a table on the other side of the big open room. The walls were painted earthy shades of brown and orange.

"I met John in here," she said. "About six months ago. He just walks right over and sits down with us. Bold as he can be."

"When did you start going out with him?" I said.

"The following week I did. I told him I'd be here. Who walks in but himself."

Fiona told me she came to Scratcher on Wednesday because people from County Cork met on that night. Cork was her home county, she said.

"What kind of guy was Johnny Boy?" I said.

"Wonderful, wonderful young man," she said. "Truly a nice person."

"Talkative?"

"Oh, Jesus, yes."

"Did he ever talk to you about people from the airport, somebody he might be worried about?"

"How d'ya mean?"

"Somebody that might be in some kind of trouble. Somebody about to do something illegal or wrong."

"Don't ya think that for a second, sir. John was the most honest man I've ever met in m'life."

"I didn't mean that he was involved with bad people, but maybe he had a co-worker or a friend that wasn't completely honest."

"I wouldn't know about that. That whole world out there was strange to me."

"So it's possible he had bad friends?"

"Oh no, not a friend, never in a million years. Not the John I knew. He had no friends like that."

"We all have friends like that, Fiona. It doesn't mean you condone their vices."

Fiona wore a red tam almost covering her short black hair. And her face, which was hidden behind a lace scarf at the funeral, comprised features in miniature. The tiniest nose and mouth I'd ever seen on an adult, and those China blue eyes.

"I'll be honest with ya," she said. "If one thing worried me about John, it was that he was too friendly."

"How can you be too friendly?"

"Oh, you can be, sir. You surely can."

"In what way was he too friendly?"

"Maybe naive is the word I'm searching for. He was naive in the ways of the world. An easy one to be taken advantage of."

If Vito was right, and Johnny Boy had indeed stepped out to stop the robbery, then naive was a gross underestimation. But Johnny Boy's naiveté ran at odds with his ex-cop father, J.C., who supposedly knew everybody at the airport and his grandfather, Vito, so well versed on organized crime.

"Do you know anyone who took advantage of him, Fiona?"

"No, I surely don't, but 'tis a feeling I've had for a while. He was one who tried too valiantly to please."

Fiona nibbled at chips from a bag of something called Ta-tos, which looked like a thick potato chip but smelled strongly of onion. On the opposite side of the room a group of young musicians tuned fiddles and flutes.

I said, "Did you ever see him wear an old dark blue police overcoat? A long knee-length coat, wool, very heavy."

"Oh, many's the time I did. It belonged to his da, who was a policeman. I suppose you know that."

"His grandfather says the night of the robbery was the first time he wore it."

"That crazy old bugger. He used to sneer at me when I was out at the house with John. Physically sneer, screwing up his face to do it. Like this."

She raised the corner of her tiny upper lip in a bad Elvis imitation. I noticed she had a smattering of freckles across her nose, just dots, as if applied by the point of a needle.

"So you saw Johnny Boy wear that coat before?" I said.

"Sure I did. Ask the others; ask the barman, or Dermot or Mickey. Not that I can say I know he wore it to work, I don't know that. But sure, he wore that old coat around sometimes. It embarrassed me a bit, I have to tell you."

I said, "Some people think he might have been trying to stop the robbery when he stepped through the door. Would he have done something that foolhardy, like trying to stop the robbery?"

She looked off thinking hard, then snapped back to face me.

"He was very influenced by bravery, if you know what I mean. He liked his movies with manly heroes."

"Bad guys or good guys?"

"I don't see the difference in some of them. Good, I suppose. But I don't know for certain. Rambo, and his kind. Other than that I couldn't say. Nor would I put it past him trying to act the hero. I could see that very well."

"He was into Irish lore, wasn't he?"

"That he was. He could sing along to all these songs in here, better than some of us born over there."

About a dozen musicians who had gathered in the corner were getting ready to perform. Not a band, they didn't seem that organized. Above them was a sign for Batchelor's Baked Beans.

"He was a good man, John was," Fiona said sadly. "That's what he should be remembered for. Nothing else."

On my way out I stopped by the bar and told the loquacious Dermot Geary and the quiet Mickey O'Brien that I hadn't had a chance to call the recruitment section, but I wouldn't forget them. Dermot wrapped his arms around me as if I were some long-lost brother, begged me to stay for one more drink. But he'd already forgotten me before I walked out the door. He was singing, with a slender woman dressed in black, about youth and death.

10

When I got home that night I could see the look on Leigh's face and I knew something was wrong.

"It's your father," she said. "They said he's not hurt that bad."

My father had carried mugger's money for most of the years he walked the streets of New York City. Forty-two dollars in fives and singles. Enough, he figured, to satisfy your average thief. But he was never mugged. Not once.

"Here's the phone number they gave me," Leigh said.

Ten years ago he retired to Florida and bought his first car. Last night he was carjacked in the parking lot of an all-night golf driving range. The Fort Lauderdale cops had called from the hospital, as a courtesy to me, one of their own.

"How is he?" Leigh said after I hung up. She was sitting on the edge of the bed, sewing a button on the sleeve of one of my shirts. She only sews when she's worried.

"One small cut on his hand," I said. "From a chain link fence. He knew enough to fall down and stay down. They're just keeping him overnight for observation, but he's fine. He's more upset about losing his golf clubs than his car."

"How did he sound?"

"Sharp. Really, with it. The most alert I've heard him sound in a long time."

"Adrenaline," she said. "Should we fly down?"

Whenever I thought about what my father would or would not like, I tried to think what my feeling would be. As I get older I realize how similar we were.

"He likes to think he can take care of himself," I said. "I don't think he'd want us rushing down to Florida. I know I wouldn't."

"He's not as much like you as you think, Anthony."

"You don't think so?"

"I don't mean lookswise. You look alike, maybe you're a little darker."

"You really think we look that much alike?"

"Are you kidding? More every year. Grab a mirror sometime."

"So what's the big difference?"

"He was never a cop," she said.

"He was a bus driver. So?"

"There's a huge difference between cops and every other occupation known to man. I often wonder what you would have been like if you hadn't become a cop."

She went back to her sewing, her hands as steady as ever. The only times I'd ever seen her hands shake were when she'd gone too long without eating something. Leigh was an insulin-dependent diabetic who needed to maintain a delicate balance of food intake and insulin injections. Being a cop's wife wasn't the ideal situation.

"He'll be fine," I said. "He has a lot of friends down there."

My father belonged to a group of ex–New York City transit workers, mostly bus drivers, subway conductors, and motormen. They'd formed a club similar to the 1013 Clubs of retired NYPD cops. They called themselves "the Fun City Survivors."

"You're probably right," Leigh said. "But I don't think he'll come up here for Christmas."

"He's not hurt that bad. They'll release him tomorrow."

"I didn't mean because he was hurt. I just think he's put this part of his life behind him. He's not as in love with this city as you are."

"Maybe he doesn't like Manhattan as much as I do. But he loves this neighborhood. It's his turf. He's a legend down in Morley's."

"I hope you're right," she said. "But just to make it easier, why don't we send him the airline ticket. We'll send a ticket out to Tony, too. As a Christmas present. That way they won't have any excuses."

"Fine, but you'd better start working on that right away, Leigh. Everything gets booked fast this time of year."

"I already have," she said. "I have two choices apiece for them. Now it's your turn. I know how persuasive you cops can be. I'm depending on you to get them here."

"They'll be here," I said. "My old man will be here."

My father loved Christmas in New York. I could remember him and his buddies, walking around the old neighborhood, caroling with silly Santa hats on, searching for the next party. He wouldn't miss it for the world.

"He loves a party," I said.

"In that way he's definitely like you."

"He parties like a cop," I said, smiling.

"Oh, no," she said. "What cops do is a step beyond party. And they don't do it at home with their wives; they leave their party at the precinct."

Leigh always said the most important quality for a cop's wife was trust. She said that was because cops' wives had no idea what was going on in the sordid street world their husbands lived in. In many ways cops' wives existed in the same quarantined bubble as Mafia wives. Leigh said those who couldn't manage blind faith became divorcées.

"We'll have a Christmas party right here," I said. "I promise you that."

11

The following morning at One Police Plaza I read about murder as the sweet smoke of celebration filled the office. Detective Johnny McGuire's sixth Little Mac had arrived, safe and sound. So everybody lit up, the hell with the city ordinance. Although I couldn't help but think about Cookie Counihan's loss, I refused to let it diminish my appreciation of McGuire's joy. Seeing through the thick fog of grief was a trick cops needed to learn in order to survive. It was easy to forget how nice a cigar could smell.

I typed up the DD5 for my interview of Fiona Quinn. Fiona's statement acknowledged the possibility that young Johnny Boy Counihan could have played hero. But she destroyed Vito Martucci's claim that the night of the robbery was the first night he'd worn the old police coat. I crossed it off my hinky list. A simple mistake by a heartbroken grandfather.

From our corner lair, the office was a haze of smoke and chatter. Three feet in front of my face, on the backs of the file cabinets that enclosed us, hung the crime scene photos. The wall of dark green metal provided a background for these pictures, as well as the charts and sketches that complicated cases gave birth to. I did this to remind myself that what I did for a living was not merely a job. All day long I'd catch myself staring. The one thing I absolutely never did anymore was look at their faces. I had enough sad faces visiting my dreams.

Taped to the file cabinet in front of Joe Gregory's desk was a menu from Brady's Bar. The only objects on his desk were a telephone and the chrome bulldog he used as a paperweight. It was a hood ornament from a Mack truck we'd seized in the Fulton Fish Market years ago.

Gregory was downstairs in Major Case, sitting in on the questioning of Nate Auerbach, a degenerate gambler who worked as a Customs shipping broker at JFK. A few hours earlier I'd ridden up on the elevator with Mr. Auerbach and two cops from Major Case. Auerbach was a large middle-aged man with thick black glasses and permed gray hair. He'd already begun to sweat through his sport jacket.

Auerbach, who had ties to Emil Lutz, surfaced when the Major Case Squad inundated the airport complex with detectives digging for the "inside man." It was obvious there had to be an inside man on this job; somebody supplied the shipping schedule. Auerbach was a good bet.

The interview had been going on for three hours when Albie Meyers returned, looking more disheveled than usual. Albie's lone act of bureaucratic defiance was to refuse to button the top button of his shirt. His tie hung permanently at half-mast.

"Auerbach finish spilling his guts?" I said.

"He gave us nada," Albie said. "Zip, zero, zilch."

"You're kidding? He looked like he'd roll over in a heartbeat."

"Oh, the guy's a wreck. He didn't know whether to shit, piss, or go blind."

"I thought for sure he was the inside man."

"O'Prey thinks Emil Lutz put the fear of God into him," Albie said, looking down at my desk. "You still working on those photos?"

I'd spent the morning studying a schematic of lines pointing toward Johnny Boy's body, comparing them to the ME's report. There were so many different entrance and exit wounds, you could only conclude that Johnny Boy had been spun around by the force of the weaponry.

"It's more complicated than it looks," I said.

Apparently the first shots had been fired from middistance. Entrance wounds in the front of his body bore none of the telltale debris of contact or near contact wounds. But some wounds in his side and lower back and one in the back of his head were fired from close range.

It appeared that after he'd fallen, crumpled against the wall in the fetal position, they'd walked up and fired down at him. Powder grains and soot were recovered from his clothes and skin. I was beginning to wonder about Joe Gregory's overkill theory: too many bullets to kill a kid wearing an old cop's coat. Overkill is almost always personal.

"Your partner said to meet him over at Brady's," Albie said. "Bring me back the navy bean soup, if you don't mind. And don't forget the crackers."

"Why don't you come over and eat with us, Albie."

"I got to type the warrants on the Lutz brothers."

"Already?" I said. "Aren't we jumping the gun?"

"Speaking of guns." He handed me a copy of a typed evidence voucher. "Remember that automatic they found at the scene? Rocky Lutz's prints showed up on it."

"Nobody told me that."

"Yeah, well," he said. "Maybe you're out of the loop."

"Are they sure they were Rocky's prints?"

"One is very clear, a thirteen-point print; and one other is a partial. Lesser quality, but enough for the lab to conclude it's also Rocky's."

"I can't believe it. I just talked to him Monday."

"He fooled you, Ryan. It happens."

Brady's Bar sits on Madison Street, directly behind One Police Plaza. I walked three minutes in the sunshine, then down one step into soothing gin mill darkness. Red and green lights twinkled in the mirror. Gregory's voice rang above the buzz of voices and the tinkling of glasses. My pulse quickened, because the simple act of stepping through that door was the most dangerous single thing I did in an average day.

Movies and books focus on the wrong things when dramatizing a cop's world. They make it look like all wild chases and smoking guns. But the true dangers of this life are quieter, more insidious. The rates of divorce, alcoholism, and suicide among cops speak for themselves. This is what frightens me: a darkened barroom filled with the only people who understand my world and that amber laughing liquid only an arm's reach away. It frightens me because I love it.

Gregory stood in his corner, one foot up on the rail. Joe's face, usually bright red, seemed to glow. The stress of interrogation could raise his blood pressure to the red numbers.

I said, "I heard Auerbach stood up."

"The guy's a shmuck, he's not the inside guy on this."

"O'Prey thinks differently."

"O'Prey don't know shit from Shinola."

Brady's Bar was like a private club to old-time Manhattan cops. Johnny Brady, the owner, was an ex-cop, and he'd covered the walls with black-and-white photos of famous cops and criminals. It was the only joint in town where monks chanted Gregorian on the jukebox and where an aging hooker wandered in, every now and then, to do a stunning Billie Holiday for the applause of her cop friends and a few free drinks. Civilians, with the exception of cop groupies, were rarely comfortable among the lethal mixture of alcohol and automatics.

I said, "You hear they found Rocky Lutz's fingerprints on the gun?"

"Just heard it today."

"How many cases do you remember where they found fingerprints on a handgun?"

"Two. Three at most. Except in the movies, where it happens all the time."

"But in real life," I said, "it happens once in a blue moon. There's not that much surface area to accommodate a full print. So I checked the photo of the print. It's under the barrel on the side plate."

"That's possible. Maybe handling the gun, cleaning it, putting it on a shelf, something like that. You could touch it there."

"When's the last time you cleaned your gun?" I said. "When Koch was mayor, right?"

"No, Lindsay, I think."

Gregory and I usually ate at the bar; we didn't need a menu. Patti, the barmaid, put the ketchup in front of us before we said a word. Two Brady cheeseburger specials. The juiciest cheeseburgers in New York are served in Irish bars.

"Rocky give off any guilty vibes when you talked to him?" Gregory said.

"He was a little paranoid," I said. "He told me he was going to lie low for a while. But he seemed more worried about the Mob than us. Otherwise . . ."

Brady's was a cop's joint, that message as bold as purple neon. Occasionally a defense lawyer would mistakenly wander into Brady's during a break in some Foley Square trial. Joe Gregory tells an old Brady's story about Leon, the waiter: One afternoon a pair of nationally prominent attorneys came in for a late lunch. The bar was packed with cops when Leon wheeled by the bar, carrying a tray bound for the dining room. He stopped, lowered the tray, and announced, "This is Mr. Kunstler's soup." Then he spat forcefully into the bowl.

"After lunch let's look for Rocky Lutz," I said.

"How about first we take a ride to Queens," Gregory said. "Cookie called me at home, she wants us to stop out at the poultry store. After that we look for Rocky."

Gregory drained his Coors Light. It was one of the few times I'd seen him drink a light beer. Both of us were drinking lighter. After a decade on the wagon, I'd been having an occasional drink, but not until the sun went down. Usually.

"Did you say Cookie called you at home?"

"You got a problem with that?" he said. "She knows my freaking number. I've had the same phone number since I went to Bishop Lavin High School. She calls all worried about Vito. Thinks maybe we can talk him out of doing something crazy."

Gregory went to the jukebox and played Sinatra while I used Brady's private phone to dial Rocky Lutz's pager number. Although I knew I didn't have my partner's instinct for seeing through a lie, I couldn't believe Rocky had fooled me that badly. I kept the phone on the bar next to me as Gregory stopped to listen to Shanahan from Missing Persons tell a joke. In the rose-colored patch of sun shining though the stained-glass window I could see Joe's face; it was as animated as I could remember.

"He's not going to call, pally," Gregory said, and leaned over to put Brady's phone back under the bar. "And we better get out of here while we can."

I knew what he meant. The noise level around the bar rose to a low roar, like the drone of bionic bees. The place was packed with guys we'd known through decades of scandal and honor. Patti poured two drinks at once and yelled for more ice. Booze and war stories flowed.

"Let me get Albie's soup," I said, but my heart was heavy. My heart would have stayed.

12

"Live poultry is making a big comeback in New York," Gregory said as we parked outside the Martucci family store in Queens. Gold lettering on the front window read "Martucci Poultry, established 1925." Wooden pallets leaned against a side door.

"I thought these places were a thing of the past," I said.

"Cookie says it's all the new immigrants. The South Americans, the Asians, the Africans. They're used to cooking live chickens and stuff like that, where they come from."

The tinkling bell above the door brought on a torrent of squawking and cackling. Feathers flew as hundreds of wings flapped, fluttered, and beat against cramped cages. The noise was bad, the smell worse. Tiny particles of poultry stink floated dustily in the air and up my nostrils, dry and deadly, like mothballs and rotted broccoli.

"Now I know why they call it fowl," I said.

Cookie came through a set of swinging doors, backside first, wiping her hands on a bloodstained apron. Under the apron she wore a red turtleneck sweater, the neck embroidered with Christmas holly. Her cheeks were flushed.

"I see they put you to work already," I said.

"My father hasn't been here all day," she said. "Not that I mind working, but I'm worried. Usually he shows his face for a few minutes."

"When's the last time you saw Vito?" I said.

"Last night. When I got up this morning he was gone."

"Is this about Johnny Boy?" Gregory said, cutting right to the chase.

Cookie looked directly at him and held her gaze, wide-eyed and frightened, as if he'd forced her to remember her Johnny Boy was dead.

"Yeah," she said. "Ever since this happened all he talks about is revenge. He goes to that damn bar, the Cockpit Lounge, and sits outside in his car and watches them."

"Healing takes time," I said.

"You don't know my father. He doesn't heal that easily."

Cookie's beauty seemed childlike and pliant for her age, as if she'd been sealed up somewhere, protected from damage. Her silver-blond hair was shoulder length and too perfect to be natural. I had no doubt she'd kept a weekly hairdresser appointment all her adult life.

"Some nights I'm in bed," she said, "I hear the door slam and his car starts. It's like I'm living with my husband all over again."

"I hope he's not thinking of shooting up the place again," I said.

"I wouldn't put anything past my father."

Dark plastic crates were stacked to the ceiling, mostly filled with big, brown chickens. I saw ducks, turkey, pheasants, and pigeons.

"How does he know all these Mob guys?" I said.

"My dad knew a lot of them personally, from growing up in the neighborhood," she said. "Absolutely hated them. He was always following them around and giving information to the cops. In fact, he taught J.C. everything about how organized crime works in Queens."

"Following Mob guys is his hobby?"

"More like his obsession. He's the one who got my husband hooked on it. J.C. says my father is the best tailman he ever saw."

"That's some compliment," Gregory said.

The store had a handful of customers walking among the crates, making eye contact with dinner. Workers scurried about in white aprons, some with hard hats. Most spoke Spanish to the customers and among themselves.

"I don't know if I should tell you this," Cookie said, "but my father has a police radio in his car."

"So does every half-assed drug dealer in the city," Gregory said.

"What kind of car does Vito drive?" I said. "We'll go look for him."

"A white Lincoln Continental. An old heap, it's like a '78, or something."

"Does he have an address book?" I said. "Or a Rolodex we could see? Maybe get some ideas where to look, if he's not at the Cockpit."

"I haven't got the foggiest. You can check his office, but that sounds too organized for him. He likes to keep everything in his head. Come on, his office is back here through the slaughtering room."

The slaughtering room was past the swinging doors. It was a cold room, half the size of a basketball court and high enough to throw an arcing three-point shot. The walls were cement block, the floor concrete, painted maroon and wet with splattered water, blood, and some gray stuff. I could feel feed or dried bird shit crunching under my shoes.

"This place is a madhouse," I said. "I can't believe all these feathers."

"My father sells about five hundred birds a week now," Cookie said. "Triple his numbers of ten years ago. It's a moving business."

Cookie put her fingers to her lips, then pointed to a bearded man in a tan raincoat bowed over a sink and whispered, "We get a lot of Muslims who must eat poultry killed in accordance with Islamic law. We let some of them come back here and do it themselves. So they can say the prayers just before they slit its throat. It's good customer relations."

I watched as one of Vito's men took the bird from the bearded man and dumped it in a large metal funnel. The blood drained into a sink. Cookie explained that after draining the blood, they bathe the birds in scalding water, then put them into a plucking machine: a large metal spinning cylinder with dozens of rubber fingers. The final process was done by hand and a sharp knife. Entrails plopped into a metal tub.

"Johnny Boy couldn't work here," Cookie said. "He didn't like all the blood."

"Have you looked through Johnny Boy's things?" Gregory said. "I know it's difficult, so we'd be glad to do it for you."

"I'll manage," she said.

"Vito thinks that Johnny Boy might have tried to stop the robbery," Gregory said. "He thinks he was trying to look out for some friend of his in TWA. Some friend that might have been involved in the robbery."

"Dad thinks everything's a conspiracy," she said.

"Did Johnny Boy have many friends?" I said.

"A few at work," she said. "But he never had a lot of social friends. Not even in school. My son was a homebody, mostly. Far as I know, Fiona is the first girlfriend he's ever had."

"Maybe we can find something in his things," Gregory said. "A note or something."

"I'll look carefully," she said. "If I find anything even remotely suspicious, I'll be sure to call you."

"Joe's right, Cookie," I said. "It might be easier for us. We understand your emotional involvement."

"That's thoughtful, but I think I should do it myself."

Vito's office was as cold as the slaughtering room. A small ceramic heater sat unused on the floor. Plants and bouquets of flowers were stacked under a window that allowed Vito to watch his entire operation. The walls were covered with framed movie posters, old gangster flicks: *The Maltese Falcon* with Humphrey Bogart; *Kiss of Death* with Richard Widmark; *Little Caesar* with Edward G. Robinson. Gregory's beeper went off. He asked Cookie if he could use the phone.

"So Vito's still acting strange," I said as Gregory dialed and I went through Vito's desk.

"Strange?" she said. "Let me tell you something: That night, you know, when he shot the window out of that bar . . . we were watching TV, and it comes on the news about the JFK robbery. Well, when that story is over, he just gets up and walks out the door. I looked up at the clock and got this sickness in the pit of my stomach. It was eleven-eleven."

"He didn't tell you where he was going."

"No. But that's not the strange thing. The strange thing is the time."

"Eleven-eleven," I said. "That's strange?"

"Oh, yeah," she said. "Whenever you look at the clock and it's eleven-eleven you know something bad is going to happen."

"Which is more strange?" I said. "Eleven A.M. or P.M.?"

"You don't believe me," Cookie said. "That's okay. Just watch from now on."

A man passed the window carrying a chicken upside-down, by the legs. I watched him tie it onto a scale, then yell out the weight in Spanish. "Voodoo people," Cookie said. "They buy live, for sacrificial ceremonies. My father says don't ask questions."

"We ask too many questions sometimes," I said. "At times like this we can be a bit rough. I hope you understand."

"Forget about it," she said. "I know you gotta do your job. I've been around cops a long time. Ever since high school, when I started working here. Cops were always in here, getting a chicken or a turkey. Dad always told them their money was no good in his store. That's how I met Joey and my husband."

Gregory hung up the phone and continued writing on a piece of brown wrapping paper. I could smell Cookie's perfume over the scent of the stacked flower wreaths. She was so close to me, I could feel her breath on my neck. The effect, even in a room so devoid of the feminine touch, was surprisingly sensual. Then she picked a piece of lint off my suit jacket.

"Guess what, pally?" Gregory said. "They found Rocky Lutz."

"Where?"

"In the trunk of his car."

A pigeon flew through the slaughtering room, hitting the ceiling as he looked for an escape. Finally, he set down on top of a window air conditioner.

"Dead?" I asked.

"What do you think?" he said. "At JFK. I hope you got all your paperwork in order, 'cause O'Prey's waiting for us out there, as we speak."

"No problem," I said.

Cookie Martucci Counihan looked worried enough to cry. I looked up at the clock. It proved to me that bad things can occur at times other than 11:11.

13

They'd covered Rocky Lutz in eyes. Hundreds of artificial eyes. His body lay curled in the trunk of his own Cadillac Seville in the long-term parking lot, legs bent awkwardly under him, his clothes sprinkled with a palette of glass orbs: blacks, browns, blues, shades of hazel, green, and azure. The artificial eyes were hollow and thinly curved, not round like marbles as I'd always assumed. Little hand-painted half-moons. His real eyes were closed, sealed with blood.

"I know exactly what happened here," Gregory said. "This is just a failure to communicate, nothing more. Some Mob guy was instructed to keep an eye on him, right? The boss says badda bing, he hears badda boom, and freaking Rocky is history."

Inspector Declan O'Prey stood on the opposite side of the car, grilling the crime scene boss. He'd been glancing over at us since we arrived, probably worried we'd take off before he got a chance to exercise his need to control.

"Nobody does quality work anymore," Gregory said, looking down at the bizarre scene in the trunk. "Dumb bastard who did this didn't know you're supposed to shoot him first, then put him in."

Rocky had apparently been put in the trunk, then shot. Blood dripping from the bullet holes in the trunk had caused a motorist to call the Port Authority cops. Otherwise Rocky would have stayed planted in the long-term parking lot until ripened by the spring thaw.

"Maybe he wasn't dead enough when they put him in," Gregory said.

"So they made him more dead?"

Declan O'Prey glided over to us as jet engines roared heavily overhead. O'Prey had been one of the youngest inspectors in the history of the NYPD. About ten years younger than us, he was an intense, Irish-born workaholic who ran marathons on the weekends.

"Gentlemen," he said, smiling, rubbing his hand across my back, "at long last I have the honor of working with the legends of homicide."

"Our pleasure, boss," Gregory said.

O'Prey had broad bulldog features that appeared to have been flattened by a brick wall in a cartoon. The small even teeth barely showed when he smiled.

"Detective Ryan," O'Prey said, "I understand you had a relationship with our victim here."

"Rocky Lutz was a registered confidential informant," I said. "And that was the totality of our relationship."

"No need to be defensive," he said. "I'm looking to solve this thing just as you are."

"We're all on the same team here," Gregory said.

"Good point," O'Prey said. "We are a team, are we not? All the players working together?"

"I spoke to Rocky last Monday," I said. "I prepared a DD five regarding the interview and I put it in the system."

"The system has some cracks," O'Prey said. "Why don't you just tell me about your meeting with Mr. Lutz."

"He didn't have much to say. Nothing of substance. He said the Lutzes were being wrongly blamed for the JFK robbery."

"And you believed him."

"Give me a break, Inspector."

He glanced down at his pants, creased sharply enough to draw blood. "Excuse me," he said. "I forgot whom I was talking to. But do this for me, Detective Ryan: Since we are all on the same team, give me one good reason why I shouldn't suspend you from that team right now. Since this is the second time you've spoken to the primary suspects in this case without first notifying your superiors."

"When I met with Rocky, the Lutz involvement was based solely on past behavior. It was just pure speculation."

"Oh, was it?" he said. "And you decided that yourself."

"At that time I was not aware of any evidence against Rocky. I just found out about the prints on the gun today."

I was dying to knock O'Prey on his ass, wipe the smirk off his face, then walk away, put my papers in. The danger of working past the twenty-year mark is that you are constantly tempted to go out in a blaze of glory.

"Perhaps if you'd attend a task force meeting, you would know more about the progress of this investigation."

"We were at a funeral during Tuesday's meeting," I said.

"That's very thoughtful," he said. "But it doesn't help solve our case. It doesn't help the team, does it? Now tell me this, did anyone see you talking to Mr. Lutz?"

"We met in my car on West Thirty-seventh, just behind the River Diner. A few people walked past, mostly workers coming out of the Javits Center for lunch."

"It sounds uncharacteristically sloppy to me, Ryan. Meeting a registered CI in public view?"

"That's the way it works, Inspector. I'm sure the city doesn't want to pay for a hotel room each time a cop meets an informant."

"What's your opinion of those artificial eyes?" he said, pointing to the body in the trunk. "I think that's a message, don't you?"

"Rocky was a professional informant for years, Inspector. It was a well-known fact. But he was a joke among the wise guys, a bottom feeder."

"So this shouldn't have happened, according to you," he said, pointing again to the body in the trunk.

"Rocky was the son-in-law of Sally the Goat Corrazzo, and I would think they'd have to get high-level approval for this."

"Don't romanticize these bastards," he said. "Please."

I imagined young Declan O'Prey growing up in Ireland, never understanding why the other kids relished beating the shit out of him. I imagined him going home after work to a cold, driven woman, nagging him to be as important as her father.

"What I'm going to do," O'Prey said, "is chalk this up to lost opportunity. Right now, my unit will be executing a search warrant at the home of Rocky Lutz. Everyone else, including you, has but one mission, and that is to locate Vincent Lutz. Alive. I want the two of you out there looking for Vincent until further instructions from me. Understood?"

I didn't understand. And I'd had it with O'Prey.

"Why don't we just back out of this case," I said. "I'll tell the chief it was a personality clash, all my fault."

I hoped O'Prey's face wasn't the kind that people referred to as having "the map of Ireland" written all over it. His complexion, now bright red, and his orange hair combined to prove that God was color-blind.

"It's not my intent to break up this task force at this point," he said. "If I do, it will be my decision, not yours. We'll deal with our personality differences when this case is over."

"We'll start looking for Vincent forthwith, boss," Gregory said.

O'Prey got into his Chrysler, and his driver made a hurried U-turn. I counted six antennas sticking from the car.

"What the hell are you looking at?" I said.

"You handled that smoothly."

"He is an irritating bastard."

"I think it's time we lighten the mood here, pally," Gregory said. "Let's start a pool. Two bucks a chance: How many eyes in the trunk? Like jelly beans in a jar. Gimme a guess. Closest wins."

"Counting the two in Rocky's head."

"Why not?"

"Five hundred and twenty-seven," I said as I handed him my money.

"Exactly five twenty-seven," he said. "That's your guess, five twenty-seven, exactly."

"Counting Rocky's two, exactly five twenty-seven."

"Pretty sure of yourself," he said.

"I'm a detective. Hunches are my life."

But it wasn't a hunch. And if Gregory would read the action reports once in a while, he'd know that 525 artificial eyes were stolen from the basement of the Javits Center during the International Vision Exhibition. Mob guys stole everything left unattended in Javits: cars, boats, artificial eyes.

"What do you really make of this, pally?" Gregory said.

"I told O'Prey the truth. I don't know why anyone wasted a bullet on this guy."

"You think the eyes are a message, or what?"

I shrugged and looked across to the other side of the parking lot. Wind carried a hint of the brackish water from the bay.

"What do you see out there?" Gregory said.

I pointed to the international arrivals building. A car had stopped and pulled up onto the grass. The car was a big white American make, shining in the sun. It was a quarter mile away, the windows were tinted, and no one was standing around it, but

I knew it was a Lincoln Continental and I knew who was inside. I looked straight at the Lincoln, then put my hand to my ear in the universal telephone sign. I mouthed the words "Call me," confident he could see me. A tailman like Vito Martucci would surely have the best binoculars money could buy.

14

We spent the following morning watching an empty house in Forest Hills, second-team players in the race for the head of Vincent Lutz. Vincent turned white hot after O'Prey's search warrant team found over a million dollars in the basement of his brother, Rocky. The money was still in the same blue canvas bags as the night it was stolen from JFK. Inspector O'Prey personally assigned us to Vincent's listed residence, the last place he was going to show himself. At noon we pronounced the day a failure and drifted back toward Brady's Bar and our appointment with Vito Martucci.

"Maybe Vincent killed Rocky," I said.

"His own brother?" Gregory said.

"Like it's never happened before?"

"Stop dwelling on this, pally. Whoever killed Rocky Lutz, it had nothing to do with you talking to him. Even if it did, so freaking what?"

As we crossed the Fifty-ninth Street Bridge into Manhattan I realized that I would always be in awe of the city from this angle.

As the car rattles across the metal grating it's like entering a concrete City of Oz. One night my partner, Joe Gregory, hypnotized by this same blockbuster vision of skyscraper, said, "It's all ours, pally." And I knew he was right.

Brady's Bar was cheek to jowl with the phantoms of the Bureau. It was a promotion day, and everybody comes out of the woodwork, sniffing for parties. Gregory strolled to the bar for a quick mingle with the old hairbags from Missing Persons and Safe and Loft. As president of the Emerald Society he was expected to shake hands and slap backs and, more important, buy an occasional drink for his constituents. I hung my raincoat with thirty others, then joined Vito Martucci. He was sitting alone in the last booth, under the picture of Willie Sutton.

"I been in here with J.C. a couple of times," Vito said, sipping from a white coffee mug with a shamrock on the side. "I like this place."

"You like playing cop," I said.

"Listen to me, kid," he said. "One thing Vito Martucci does not do—is play."

Vito's silver hair was slicked straight back. He wore an olive trench coat with the collar turned up. Underneath this was a blue striped shirt with a starched white collar that impinged on the wrinkled flesh of his neck. A diamond stickpin jutted from the center of a red silk tie.

"What were you doing out at the airport yesterday?" I said.

"Last time I looked it was a public place."

"That doesn't answer my question."

"You think I killed that little Polack?"

"I don't know yet."

Vito took a silver cigarette case from his pocket. He tapped one out and put it in his mouth. I wondered if it was all an act, the cigarettes just one more prop. Merit was his brand, and it dangled unlit in the corner of his mouth.

"I was checking the crime scene at TWA," he said.

"Why?"

"It don't smell right to me."

"This is police work, Vito. It isn't selling chickens."

"You don't have to be a cop to know something ain't right."

"Like what?" I said. "I'm listening."

"Somebody inside got to be working for Lutz."

"We've been over that ground, what else?"

I pulled my notebook from my pocket as Vito blew invisible smoke rings at the light. He seemed to live in his own film noir world. I could almost hear the voice-over, see the scene in grainy black and white.

"She used to write him letters all the time," he said. "I can't find them."

"Who used to write?"

"The Irish broad, Fiona."

"How often did she write?"

"Every week or so there'd be one in the mailbox."

"Maybe he threw the letters away."

"Why would he do that? He kept every other fucking thing that was Irish."

Vito's movements were maddeningly slow and deliberate. Every turn of the head, every time he raised his cigarette to his lips. Even his invisible smoke rings seemed to float in slow motion.

"Fiona told me that Johnny Boy wore the police overcoat often, Vito. That night wasn't the first time."

"She's fucking lying," he said.

"Why would she lie?" I said. "What if someone else told me the same thing?"

He turned sideways, showing his profile. It occurred to me I'd never seen emotion in Vito's face—the pole opposite of his daughter. With his hooded eyes he could look bored in a hellstorm.

"Ask around about those letters," he said. "I'm not wrong about that."

"But you're not sure about the coat, are you?"

"Listen," he said. "Maybe I'm not a hundred percent on the coat. But that Irish broad knows more then she's letting on. Trust me on that."

It was becoming obvious I couldn't tell this old man to sit home. No matter what I said to him it wouldn't be enough to keep him off the case. In the reflection off Willie Sutton's picture I saw Gregory pushing buttons on the jukebox; he knew the numbers by heart. Sinatra sang "Stormy Weather."

"I'll talk to her tonight," I said. "Now tell me who killed Rocky Lutz."

"Who gives a shit?" he said.

"I do."

"Rocky Lutz died of a birth defect," Vito said. "He was born with a mouth too big."

"The Colombos or the Luccheses?"

"Oh, the Colombos, absolutely. But they had to get the okay on account of his marriage situation. But, shit, you steal that much money and don't do the right thing, it don't matter who the fuck you're married to."

"Why aren't they after the father?" I said.

"Emil Lutz was having drinks with the right people when the robbery went down. Emil got the benefit of the doubt working for him at the moment. That don't mean he's home free, though."

The death of Rocky Lutz still bothered me. I didn't believe he was killed merely because he was seen talking to me. The theory about holding out on the big bosses seemed more logical.

"I've been hearing some other things," Vito said. "I hear Vincent Lutz is in the wind. After Rocky got whacked Emil sent Vincent packing."

"He'll be back. None of them can stay away for long."

"Yeah, sure," he said. "I also heard you found the money in Rocky's basement. One mil, am I right?"

"Where did you hear that?"

"I got contacts," he said. "You know, I can be very useful to you guys. You don't realize how useful. I know all these Queens mobsters, all the hangouts. I grew up with them, for chrissakes."

"Whatever you hear, call me."

"I think we're talking about a two-way street here, amigo."

"I'll keep you informed."

"I was hoping you'd do better than that. I'm thinking we should be out riding around together looking for that fucking Polack."

"You're from a cop family, Vito. You know we can't do that."

"You won't find Vincent Lutz without me. Nobody knows that crew better than me. I taught J.C. Counihan all he knows about these bastards. Plus, all he knows about tailing."

"You know we can't legally ride around with you in the department car."

"What, you worried about insurance or something?" he said. "I'm not gonna make a fucking claim. All I want is to be there when you pick him up. I want to see his fucking face when he knows it's me that nailed him."

"That's exactly what I'm worried about," I said. "I'm worried about you not being objective. You've already proven that. I can't even think of a good reason why I shouldn't suspect you of killing Rocky."

Vito pushed an empty cup in small arcs around the table. He stared at mottled grain, as if trying to decipher a message from the spirit of the Ouija board.

"You can go your whole life," he said, "and nothing bad ever happens to you. Then it happens and bingo, you know how bad you can hurt. You won't understand that, Ryan, until it happens to you."

"Killing Vincent Lutz won't bring Johnny Boy back."

"But it's going to feel so fucking good."

Vito stood up and I saw the bulge and knew why he'd left his raincoat on. He was carrying a gun again.

"I'm an old man, Ryan," he said. "No one is ever going to love me again like that kid loved me. Think about that, amigo."

15

On the way home that night, I parked my green Volvo among the limos idling in a No Parking zone opposite the Plaza Hotel. I waved to the doorman, Jimmy Kelleher, an ex-cop, flashing the open-handed five minutes sign. The growing network of retired cops working in Manhattan was the only thing making our job easier. Jimmy would make sure my car was safe until I got back from my meeting with Fiona Quinn.

Parking is the one thing all cops hate to pay for. Although the NYPD has come a long way from the days of free meals and Christmas lists, cops will always grab a few feet of illegal curb, on the muscle, as the old-timers say. I knew a detective who kept his license plates on alligator clips, and he'd remove them to run into buildings for short periods of time. Meter maids couldn't ticket the car, because if it didn't have plates it was considered abandoned. They had to notify the Sanitation Department tow truck. He knew he had at least a week before they arrived.

Fiona told me she'd be near the artist's gate on Sixth Avenue. The gates in Central Park have names like scholar's gate, inventor's gate, explorer's gate, women's gate. I ran across Central Park South to Grand Army Plaza and walked west along the park wall.

This part of the park seemed always in a state of festival. A vendor's cart with every New York T-shirt imaginable sat on the sidewalk, the wheels chocked, apparently with someone's permission. Opposite Mickey Mantle's restaurant I spotted a familiar face: Dermot Geary, jingling the change in his pocket, his chubby cheeks raw from the wind.

"It is yourself," he said. I could smell booze.

"Just the man I'm looking for," I said.

"Are ya now? Regular bloodhounds, you NYPD'ers, tracking me down like this."

"Fiona was supposed to meet me here."

"Haven't seen the lovely lass yet," he said, glancing west toward Sixth Avenue. "Not that she'd stop by to see a donkey like myself. Mickey's the one to be helping you."

"He knows her better than you do?"

"That he does," Dermot said, and climbed unsteadily up into his buggy and looked west. "He knows it all."

Dermot's buggy was black and open except for a half roof cover. Victorian sidelight lamps hung outside both sides of the cab. Seats were upholstered in a worn velvety red fabric tufted with brass buttons. A green-and-black Buffalo plaid woolen blanket was tossed across the seat that faced backward.

"There's the lovely couple," Dermot said, and let loose a shrill whistle, his pinkies jammed into the corners of his mouth.

The posted registration of Dermot's buggy said it belonged to Woodrow McTiernan, who'd once been a serious middleweight contender. Bronx-born "Irish Woodsie" became better known to cops for his unscheduled bouts in local bars. After his last undercard debacle he went through a few druggie years, took a number of arrests, but age and family helped straighten him out. He was on the way up again, the owner of several hansom cabs and a bar named the Neutral Corner on Ninety-ninth and First, on the fringes of east Harlem.

Fiona and Mickey came hustling toward us. Mickey wore his top hat and swaggered like one of the Jets from *West Side Story,* ready to rumble. Horses snorted and steamed up the cold night air.

"What happened?" the little redhead said, rolling his shoulders Cagney style. I wondered why the world was so full of tough guys. "We were waiting for you up there."

"I clearly told you Sixth Avenue, sir," Fiona said.

"Sorry," I said. "I parked across from the Plaza and came this way. Is that a problem?"

"There's always a fucking problem," Dermot said. When Dermot said fuck, it sounded like "fook."

"Hush, Dermot," Fiona said.

"With all due respect," Mickey said, "we both try to keep a close eye out for Fiona. She hasn't been over here that long."

I decided that Mickey O'Brien had been in this country long enough to pick up a New York nasal whine.

"I understand," I said. "I just have a couple of questions for Ms. Quinn."

"This fooking city, you can't be too careful," Dermot said, slurring slightly. "Full of snakes, this city. Saint Pat himself couldn't rid them."

"We try to stick together out here," Mickey said.

Dermot snorted as if to say "That's bullshit."

Fiona glanced nervously at Dermot.

"They like to fook you around in New York, New York," Dermot said. "The town so fooking nice they named it fooking twice."

Taxis bobbed and weaved to the whistles of hotel doormen. I could smell roasted chestnuts from a cart. Hooves clopped against the cold pavement between the iridescent high-rise hotels and the black, foreboding park.

"What didya want to ask me?" Fiona said. She was dressed in a long black coat and red tam with matching woolen mittens.

I said, "Fiona, how often did you write letters to Johnny Boy?"

"About two or three times a month. He never wrote back, he wasn't a writer."

"Do you know if he saved your letters?"

"I haven't the slightest idea."

"Maybe he had a bloody roaring bonfire in his backyard," Dermot said.

Mickey O'Brien applied Chap Stick to his lips and glared at Dermot. A watch dealer carrying a telltale black case lurked in the background, whispering, "Rolex, cheap. Check it out," in the sotto voce fashion of drug dealers.

"I apologize for my rude countryman," Fiona said.

"Don't apologize for me, Lady Fiona," Dermot said. "Your royal highness."

"The other night, Fiona," I said, "you told me that people took advantage of Johnny Boy. You have to do better than that. You have to give me some names."

"I didn't say I knew any by name, sir. Just certain types."

"But you think somebody took advantage of Johnny Boy," I said. "Tell me who you think did it."

"I can't say specifically this name or that name."

"People at TWA?"

"I can't say that."

"I'm going to have to subpoena you to the grand jury."

"I can't go to court, sir," she said. "My employer is angry as it is over all these calls from the police."

"Do you have a green card problem?" I said.

"Fooking green card bullshit," Dermot said, spinning a half circle on the heel of one of his engineer boots. "Her legal status makes not a bit of difference in this matter."

"I'll get it off the computer."

"No, I don't have a green card problem," Fiona said.

"What fooking computer?" Dermot said.

"The U.S. Immigration computer," I said, wondering how far I could string this lie, but I knew Dermot's mouth was getting dry, his high wearing off.

"That's purely false," Dermot said as Mickey whispered something to Fiona.

"Go ahead, Fiona," Mickey said aloud. "Tell the detective all the bullshit Johnny Boy was laying on you. Go ahead."

Fiona hesitated as if reluctant to speak, but when she started I got the feeling it wasn't as difficult as she'd anticipated. Behind her, tourists bent to look at pencil sketches of city landmarks leaning against the stone wall that surrounded the 840-acre park.

"John told me things about your low types," she said. "He knew all about your low types."

"Low types?" I said.

"Hoodlums," she said. "Mafia people. Not that he was one himself, but he liked to be around them. John always talked about these people; he liked to brag about it."

"He was trying to impress her," Mickey O'Brien said with a wink. The wink was universal guy language, where "impress" translates into "get into her pants."

"So you think Johnny Boy knew a few Mafia people?" I said.

"More than a few, I'll tell you," Fiona said. "He could rattle off the names."

"Fooking bejesus, he could that," Dermot said.

"Were you with him on any occasion when he met Mafia people, or any low types?"

"No, sir," she said indignantly. "I wouldn't sully my reputation with those types."

"Do you have any direct knowledge that he met with these people?"

"I only know what I was told," she said.

"Do you remember hearing their names?"

"Italian names," she said. "I couldn't pronounce them if I did remember them."

"You ever hear him talk like that, Dermot?" I said.

"I told the bloody fool to shut his mouth. The less you say in this fooking city, the better off you stay."

Dermot wiped his nose on a clean handkerchief, then folded it and put it back into his pocket. A girl in a blue stocking cap wrestled with the leashes of six dogs, probably heading for the deep ruts of frozen hoofprints along the park's bridle path.

I said, "Did Johnny Boy say where he knew these people from?"

"That pub in Queens," Fiona said. "D'ya not remember it, Dermot? The name of it. John spoke of it often."

"He did indeed," Dermot said. "Slips my mind."

"He was always speaking of it," Fiona said. "Where these types congregated."

"Would it be the Cockpit Lounge?" I said.

"I couldn't be positive, sir," she said. "But I know it was near the airport."

"That's the place," Mickey O'Brien said.

"What about Rocky or Vincent Lutz?" I said. "Ever hear him say those names?"

"They have a familiarity," she said.

"I heard him mention them," Mickey O'Brien said.

Yoko Ono walked past us, going toward Fifth Avenue. She was dressed in black leather and looked as if she weighed about eighty pounds, including sunglasses. Two burly bodyguard types walked ahead of and behind her. My three Irish friends exchanged angry glances.

"D'ya have any more questions, sir?" Fiona said. "I have to be getting back to my duties."

"Go ahead," I said. "If I have more questions, I'll call."

Fiona walked hurriedly toward Central Park West. I went the other way, toward my car, thinking that Vito had been right.

Fiona did know more than she'd let on, but it wasn't what Vito expected. It was his grandson, Johnny Boy, whose knowledge seemed a dangerous thing. Joggers, bikers, and in-line skaters zipped and weaved through strolling tourists. Up ahead, Yoko Ono faded into the crowd near the Sherman Monument. I crossed the street at the Plaza, still able to hear Dermot and Mickey arguing. I wondered if I had discovered the elusive inside man.

16

On Monday morning we drove to the Martucci home in Great Neck. Vito's house was like a museum to useless crafts. Every inch of wall space contained a hanging piece of handmade Americana junk. Dozens of embroideries in wooden frames graced the entranceway, all spouting some form of *Bless This House*. Cookie stood in the foyer, watching a woman who was sitting in the center of the living room floor.

"Ariana is smudging the house for me," Cookie said, almost whispering. "To get rid of the negative energy and restore the balance. I can feel evil in this room, ever since the break-in. My chest is tight when I come in here. Can you feel it?"

"What break-in?" Gregory said.

"Shh," Cookie said. "Ariana says silence is imperative for the purification ceremony."

Ariana was a thin woman in a peasant dress, sitting in the lotus position. She was in her late thirties, early forties, with dirty blond hair hanging down to the orange shag carpet.

"What break-in?" Gregory whispered again.

Ariana looked over her shoulder at us, then rose from the floor and walked to an antique oak washstand that held a vase of artificial daisies. We stepped back near the picture window, so as not to disturb the smudging.

"On the day of the funeral," Cookie said. "Someone broke into our house. When we came home we found some mess, I'll tell you that."

"Why weren't we told about this?" he said.

"Daddy said his insurance would go through the roof if we reported it."

"So it wasn't reported at all?"

"Nothing was missing except a few dollars in change, from a cup in the kitchen."

Funeral-day burglaries were common. Bad guys read the obituaries in the paper and assumed the house would be empty during services. This burglary, however, would make my growing hinky list. Cookie crossed her arms under her breasts. She wore only a thin silk blouse, red for the holiday or maybe the purification.

"You're sure nothing else was missing," I said.

"We both checked."

"How did they get in?" Joe Gregory said.

"The spirits?" Cookie asked, wide-eyed.

"No, the burglars."

"Oh, the window in the back was broken. The one near the door."

Ariana cleared off the washstand, then began pulling objects out of a blue canvas bag with the Book-of-the-Month Club logo on the side. First she placed a silver bowl, then candles, incense pots, and statues: the Blessed Virgin, Buddha, St. Anthony, a platoon of angels.

"They broke the window in broad daylight?" Gregory said. "In this neighborhood?"

"Daddy talked to the neighbors. Older people on both sides. They didn't see anything."

Cookie shrugged and held her hands palms upward in a typical New York gesture that says "What can you do?" The houses were close, but the area was heavily wooded. Neighbors probably couldn't have seen anything even if they were spying.

"I wanted to call," Cookie said. "Daddy didn't want to bother the cops. He wanted them out looking for Johnny Boy's killers."

"Crime Scene Unit should dust the place," I said. "Before Ariana heals it completely."

"Daddy says fingerprint stuff makes a mess. The black powder and all. I don't know. What do you think, Joey?"

"Tell her, Joey," I said.

"We should dust for prints," Gregory said.

"Is Vito here?" I said.

"He's in Johnny Boy's room."

We walked through a den, past a white plastic Christmas tree with purple balls. A row of Victorian dolls with crinolines lined the mantel. We found Vito sitting on Johnny Boy's bed. He seemed startled when we opened the door. He stood, suddenly, as if we'd caught him asleep or lost in thought.

"What do you know," he said. "It's the heavy hitters from downtown."

The Americana ended at Johnny Boy's door. The entire wall above the single bed was covered with the Irish flag. Taped above his dresser was a yellowing newspaper photo of Bobby Sands, the IRA soldier who starved himself to death in an English prison. It was a graphic picture of a man in great pain. Gregory stood at the dresser, looking up at a young man's hero.

"Mom bought most of the Irish stuff Johnny Boy had," Cookie said. "Whenever she saw anything Irish at a yard sale, she bought it for him. He was really proud of his Irish side."

"I can see that."

A framed color photograph of Johnny Boy sat on the dresser.

It was taken at a backyard pool. Vito has his arm around him, pointing to the jock strap around his neck. They are both laughing. Cookie picked up the picture, looked closely at her son and father, both so happy, then held it at her side.

"He was saving his money for a trip to Ireland," Cookie said. "TWA gave him so many free flights. So many trips a year, something like that. It was a good deal."

I could hear Ariana muttering some incantation as she walked through the house, placing crystals in all the rooms.

"Is anything missing from this room?" I said.

"He might have had things I didn't know about," she said. "Otherwise everything seems okay to me."

"Like what things wouldn't you know about?"

"I don't know. Boy things. You know boys. We never checked his room, or anything. Even when we lived here. I gave him his privacy. I didn't come in and search his drawers or look under his bed."

A loud *bong* sounded and Joe Gregory, who was still looking at the pictures on the dresser, almost jumped into the air. Then Ariana flew past us, holding a Chinese gong over her head, banging it wildly.

"The gong's vibration chases the evil," Cookie said. "The vibration runs at a higher speed than the negative energy and breaks it up."

"I think she could chase anything away," Gregory said.

Ariana gonged behind doors and leaned into closets and under beds. Cookie watched her intently. Then she left to follow the gong, still carrying the framed picture of Johnny Boy with her.

Gregory picked up an old shillelagh, standing in the corner. It was desperately in need of work. He rubbed his fingers along the grain of the wood. I closed the bedroom door.

"We have a problem, Vito," I said.

I told Vito what Fiona had said about Johnny Boy bragging about knowing the Lutzes and the Cockpit Lounge.

"I'll tell you what I think," he said. "I think Fiona broke in here and stole those letters."

"Stop blaming Fiona for a minute," I said. "The question is, did Johnny Boy know the Lutz brothers?"

"Shit, yeah," he said. "What's the problem with that? He knew all those mutts. Every last goddamn one."

"How did he know them?" I said.

"I told him. We used to ride around together at night. I showed him all the Mob hangouts, told him about how they worked. We sat in the Cockpit Lounge, I showed him the Lutzes. I told him how all the scams went down."

"Why did you do that?" Gregory said.

"He was going to work at the airport, he needed to know who the movers and shakers were. I was afraid he'd get working out there, and you know, he was easy to talk into shit. I was afraid these guys would get him involved in some scam. I could see them sweet-talking him into some shit."

"Sometimes too much knowledge is a dangerous thing," Gregory said.

"That's bullshit," Vito said. "Knowing who the mutts are, and getting involved with them, is two different things. He knew the names, the places, yeah. But I'll swear on my mother's eyes this kid never said word one to any of those people."

The smell of incense began to fill the house. Incense always reminded me of the sixties and all the student demonstrations. During that time I was a cop, but still young enough to roam the campus of Columbia University, wearing bell-bottom jeans embroidered around the cuff. I spent the day talking about love and war. At night I went back to a trailer near Broadway and identified ringleaders for the Intelligence Division. I never felt good about walking into that trailer; in my heart I knew I had more in common with the other side of Broadway. But I was young, and I began to forget which side I was on. Years later I remembered thinking how easy it was to get sucked in.

"You know what you're saying?" Vito said. "You guys are saying that I got him killed. I'm the fucking asshole, because I taught him all this shit."

"Let's take it one step at a time," I said. "We don't know what got him killed. There's no evidence that he ever met the Lutzes."

"I loved that kid," Vito said. "Everything I did, I did to protect him."

Vito leaned heavily against the dresser. I put my arm around him and told him I would have done the same thing. Parenting is about doing what you think is best.

"What you did," I said, "did not get your grandson killed."

The old man put his face in his hands. I looked in the mirror behind him. Jammed around the edge of the mirror's frame were baseball schedules, snapshots, and dry-cleaning receipts. I noticed a number written in pencil across the face of a raffle ticket. It was a 917 number, the area code for pagers. I wouldn't have thought anything of it, but it was a pager number I'd dialed before. I read it three times because I wanted to be sure. It was the pager number that belonged to Rocky Lutz.

17

We spent the rest of the week trolling in the murky wise guy waters, trying to hook a rat who could place Johnny Boy with the Lutzes. But we came up empty. So on Friday night we rejoined the hunt for Vincent Lutz under a full New York moon. Friday night was the best night because it's *goumare* night for Mob guys, the night they take their girlfriends out. Saturday night is wives' night out. It's a system. The essence of the system is simple but important: Friday, *goumare;* Saturday, wife. Never, ever confuse the two.

One time Lenny DePasquale squired his lovely wife, Mary Ann, around to all the hot spots on an unfortunate Friday, a date that coincidentally wound up being their last anniversary together. Mary Ann spotted her brother-in-law, Frankie Fish, swapping spit with the coat check girl from Il Forno. Word quickly got back to Mary Ann's sister, and several ugly scenes ensued. *Goumare* Friday is designed so that wise guys avoid exactly that kind of marital *agida.*

"Not for nothing," Gregory said. "But nobody's going to tell me a kid like Johnny Boy, who was never in trouble a day in his life, was mixed up with a scumbag like Rocky Lutz."

"Then what was he doing with his pager number?"

Gregory and I took the Oldsmobile, which had a citywide radio. We rode through the chain of neighborhoods, from Bay Ridge to Bensonhurst, from Ozone Park to Howard Beach. We covered every known Mob hangout from catering halls with marble fountains and gilded swans to nameless storefront social clubs with steel doors and barred windows—places that looked more like vaults than buildings.

"Are you sure it's his handwriting?" Gregory said.

"The lab says it is."

"The lab's been wrong before."

"When we find Vincent Lutz, we'll ask him. I'll hold on to this raffle ticket until then."

From the very start we knew things in Brooklyn had changed. The Mardi Gras atmosphere of Mob life was not to be found. Gone were the convoys of black Lincolns carrying capos and soldiers from joint to joint as they tossed cash like grass seed into the wind. To the old Mob every decade was the Roaring Twenties.

The Mob we knew had gone underground long before the JFK stickup. It was a series of things: pressure from the law, effective prosecutions, defection within the ranks. Every week a new rat surfaced, and rats begat rats. But not every member was hibernating. The Mob had a generation gap, and the young mafiosa were sorely lacking in discipline. The new generation of wise guys had taken on the values of their Generation X peers. The glue that held the family together was cracking. The long-respected *omerta,* the code of silence, was largely a thing of the past. It seemed ironic that *omerta* literally meant "to act like a man."

Neither of the Lutz cars was present at the Cockpit Lounge. The Cockpit was quiet, but historically it was busier later in the night, well after midnight. A blue Crown Vic from O'Prey's unit sat backed in against the overhead door of a muffler shop. It was a lousy surveillance spot, a poor angle for the front door of the bar.

"It pisses me off that Vincent drives a Lexus," Gregory said. "I never saw an old-time Mob guy that didn't drive an American car. At least you could give them that much."

What's wrong with these kids today? It was a subject discussed daily over short beers by aging cops from Brady's to Elaine's; and over coffee and sambuca in Patsy's and Rao's by eighty-year-old dons. It was obvious the young kids lacked the old world class, the work ethic, and the respect for tradition of their ancestors. But more important, they lacked discretion. Some mobsters privately blamed it on John Gotti; his flamboyance and brutal management methods had triggered the downfall and caused the smart crooks to go underground. At the very least, the fun was gone.

Besides the Lexus, we'd found little information on Vincent Lutz. He had three arrests: two grand larceny autos, one assault. All three were pled down far enough to get him probation. His listed address was a small neat house in Forest Hills that belonged to his mother. I had no confidence in the address, but it was our assigned target.

We picked up a pizza, parked half a block up from the Lutz residence, and I began looking through the file. I found a surveillance picture taken at a block party last summer. Vincent, dressed in tan shorts and white tank top both too tight for him. Expensive-looking two-tone loafers on his feet, no socks. Vincent was wide and burly like his father but seemed more baby fat than muscle. Gregory passed me a slice of pizza. I tuned down the volume on the radio so we didn't have to yell over it.

"Leave it up," he said. "I like this shit. It's the one thing I miss about being out of the bag. I used to love Friday nights, action night. Going like hell all night, next thing you look up and the tour is over."

The radio was hopping; what they say about the full moon is absolutely true. Code 1010, man with a gun at Sutter and Lefferts; 1030, robbery in progress at Jamaica and 189th Street. The dispatcher handled it well, her tone calm, almost bored, as she juggled the precinct sector maps to find available units. Her Queens accent enjoyed a hint of the singsong lilt of the Caribbean.

"We got to find this guy, pally," he said.

"We will. Unless he's already under a ton of new concrete somewhere."

A disorderly man with a machete on Cross Bay Boulevard proved unfounded. A pileup on the Belt Parkway called for two ambulances and Emergency Services.

Gregory said, "I went out to the airport today, with Vito. I feel sorry for the guy."

"Now you're hanging around with Vito."

"The guy's a pisser. Knows Mob stories up the gazoo, and he's more cop than most cops I know. He says his one dream in life was to be a cop. But he was a half inch too short."

"He should have stood on a fifty-dollar bill."

"Seriously, I worked the crime scene over again," Gregory said. "I think Vito's got a point. Something is wrong with the scene. I got some ideas I'd like you to look at."

Reports of a naked woman running through the parking lot of Aqueduct Race Track showed promise of being the night's most interesting call, until the voice of an excited cop with a garbled message. The only clear word was "bomb." The dispatcher told him to slow down, repeat clearly. He repeated the message again: A bomb had exploded. He wanted backup, he wanted Emergency Services, he wanted the fire department, he wanted the sergeant on patrol, he wanted the bomb squad.

"You forgot to ask for the cavalry, kid," Joe Gregory said to the radio. Then the address began to sound familiar. Maybe I'd heard it wrong.

I picked up the transmitter and said, "Ten five that bomb address, Central?"

She said it again. It was familiar. It was the Cockpit Lounge.

"That's the work of your new partner," I said. "Detective Vito Martucci."

"Vito, Vito," Gregory said. "You crazy old bastard."

I slid the pizza box under the seat as Gregory made the sweeping U-turn.

It took us almost fifteen minutes to get there; we got tied up on the Van Wyck. But even from the highway we could see the smoke pouring from the Cockpit Lounge. The entire building was in flames. Asphalt shingles spun in the night air like flaming Frisbees. Gregory drove as far as the police barriers and parked. I couldn't imagine what kind of bomb Vito had used to cause this much destruction.

We stepped over the fire hoses snaked through the wet street. Acrid fumes filled the back of my throat. I gagged and coughed, then tried Gregory's trick of inhaling the damp woolen sleeve of my overcoat. City fires are not romantic, nor do they remind one of the epic power of nature. Rather, the air is filled with the stench of charring cheap paneling, melting plastic furniture, smoldering old mattresses, and nylon carpeting.

Inspector Declan O'Prey stood across the street from the club, talking on a cellular phone. We waited until he'd finished his conversation. Blackened trash flowed in the gutters.

"I want Vito Martucci picked up forthwith," he said as he slid the phone into his pocket.

"Anybody injured?" I asked

"If you consider the dead to be injured, we have at least three."

"Emil or Vincent among the three?" I said.

"Unfortunately, no," he said. "I just hope the money isn't going up in flames."

"Are you sure Vito did this?" I said.

"Just pick him up, Ryan."

Firemen had smashed the window of a car left parked on a hydrant, then they rolled it into the middle of the street so they could clear the hose.

"What the hell did he use?" Gregory said.

I thought we were jumping to conclusions. I hoped we were. Three dead, I thought. Even Houdini couldn't wriggle out of this one.

"We think it was a grenade," O'Prey said. "He drove by and threw it through the window. It landed against the gas fireplace and it all just went up."

"What kind of car was he in?" I asked.

"General Motors product. Two-door. A Mardi Gras or a Grand Prix, something like that. Older model, covered with primer."

"That's not Vito's car," I said. "Did they get a plate number?"

"My men couldn't see it," he said. "But it was probably stolen, anyway."

"What did the thrower look like?" I said.

"White hair . . . Just let me worry about the description, Ryan."

I wondered if O'Prey's men saw anything at all. If they did, why didn't they chase the bomb thrower? I thought about arguing, but I figured it would be better if we just picked Vito up.

"And tell him to bring his lawyer," O'Prey said.

I walked back toward our car, planning the confrontation in my mind. Vito thought he was a cop, and arresting cops was a tricky business. The critical moment is when you ask for the gun. Anything can happen. Gregory stopped to talk to the two guys from Major Case who were staking out the bar. More precinct cops were arriving to deal with traffic and the growing crowd. I walked through the maze of radio cars parked beyond the hoses. Red lights spun around and bounced off buildings.

When I got beyond the sea of flashing red I could see a thin beam of white light coming from the next block. A blinking light, flashing like Morse code. It seemed to be aimed at my eyes. I walked to the light and found Vito Martucci standing next to his Lincoln, wearing a Russian-style fur hat, binoculars hanging from his neck.

"You thought I did this, right?" Vito said.

"Your name came up."

"I was sitting right here," he said. "I saw him pass me."

"Saw who?"

"Fat Paulie."

"Fat Paulie who?" I said. Off the top of my head I could name half a dozen Fat Paulies with the requisite skills.

"Paulie Caruso, that fat bastard. I saw him getting ready. He stopped over here and opened the sun roof. Then he drove to the front of the bar and flipped it out. Grenade, right? Over his head, through the sun roof. Like a hook shot."

"What kind of car was it, Vito?"

"Eighty-two Buick Riviera," he said. "Production model, primer paint."

"O'Prey wants us to pick you up."

"Why? What about the two cops in the muffler shop? What were they doing, snoozing? I don't look nothing like that fat bastard."

"Just tell O'Prey what happened."

"Right. By then Fat Paulie will have his weight in alibis. Come on. I know where we can find him. Get your partner and let's go. They're going to crush that car, mark my words."

I knew sooner or later I'd have a rematch with Decky O'Prey. My retirement speech played in my head as I opened the door to Vito's Lincoln.

18

Gregory was so surprised to see me driving the Lincoln that he ran to the car. He spotted Vito hiding under my overcoat in the backseat but managed to get in and stare straight ahead, waiting for an explanation. I backed down the block and turned toward the highway.

"Vito saw Fat Paulie Caruso throw the grenade," I said. "He says Fat Paulie crushes his car after every job. The Colombo family has an auto junkyard in the South Bronx."

"Take the Whitestone Bridge," Vito said from the depths of the backseat. "Not the Throgs Neck."

I edged through a traffic light, trying to peer around a fire truck.

"So that's where we're going," Gregory said. "The Bronx."

"Fat Paulie is a Colombo guy," I said, working up our "story" for O'Prey. "The Colombos are pissed about getting skunked on the JFK job. Maybe they decided to tell Emil Lutz exactly how pissed, and Fat Paulie was delivering the message."

"Maybe we got a Mob war going here," Vito said.

"That would be nice," I said. "For our sake."

I didn't like driving, especially a car this size; it was like trying to see over the bow of a boat. If it were up to me, I'd live in a place where I'd never have to drive again. I'd begun hinting to Leigh about living in Manhattan. We'd lived on the West Side when we first got married. I could do it again. Get rid of the car and walk everywhere.

"How the hell can those cops think I did it?" Vito said. "The damn car was almost touching the ground on the driver's side."

The only thing Fat Paulie Caruso ever acquired honestly was his nickname. He weighed in excess of five hundred pounds, but he thought his avoirdupois to be golden. Two years ago a team of hitmen from a rival family pumped twelve shots into Paulie, admittedly an easy target. Doctors at Beekman Downtown said Paulie's bulk kept the bullets from reaching a vital organ. Three days later Fat Paulie walked out of the hospital thinking he was a cellulite Superman.

"Where are we now?" Vito said. I told him and he sat up quickly. "What is it with you guys and the Van Wyck?"

"It's three o'clock in the morning," I said.

"But it's Friday night," he said. "Jesus Christ. You can't take the Van Wyck on Friday night."

"It's the best way to the Whitestone Bridge."

"It's the best way nowhere," he said. "Get off here. Next exit. Right there."

Vito directed us to the Grand Central Parkway, which didn't seem any faster to me, then to the Whitestone Expressway and across the bridge to the Bronx.

We came down off the Bruckner Expressway into the no-man's-land of Hunts Point in the Bronx. Hundreds of trucks lined Hunts Point Avenue, diesels idling, blue smoke hanging in the cold night air. They had come from the farms of a half dozen states and were waiting for the wholesale fruit and vegetable market to open. Hookers buzzed around the big rigs like tiny worker bees. A wide-load blonde wearing a tight, hip-length jacket and black stockings jumped down from the step of a tan Mack cab, her huge bare thighs covered only by the crisscross straps of garters.

Four K's Auto Salvage took up an entire block off Viele Avenue, near the sewage treatment plant, in a section dominated by auto junkyards and mysterious factories. I cut the Lincoln's lights and cruised to the front gate.

The third world streets were lightless, signless, and lawless. Skeletons of cannibalized cars were dumped all over broken sidewalks. You couldn't tell where the street ended and the curbs began, pavement more pothole than pave. And everything was black with grease, as if God had swabbed the landscape with a wide, oily brush.

Vito told us that Four K's dealt in every form of automotive business but those considered legitimate. They bought, sold, and even created cars from parts. Twenty-four hours a day a Teletype machine spewed requests for every conceivable auto part throughout a network of local salvage dealers. It was a safe bet that virtually all of those requested parts would be acquired in the hours before dawn.

"Watch your ass out here," Vito said.

A fifteen-foot chain link fence surrounded Four K's. Stacks of car doors, quarter panels, and hoods loomed above the fence forming a metallic hedgerow, insuring privacy for when the telltale acetylene torches of the "choppers" were burning. A pile of Mustang front ends had to be twenty-five feet high, all the little ponies galloping west. I could feel the oily roadway, slippery under my feet.

Gregory found the gate open, the chain lock merely looped through the posts. He began quietly to pull it through. The fence was greasy. I tried to keep my hands in my pocket, my clothes from touching anything but air. The only light came from Four

K's clapboard office and that supplied by the full moon. A car engine was running inside the compound, smoothly and quietly.

"Hear the car running?" Vito rasped. And then a dog slammed into the fence with such force that we all jumped back together, like a Three Stooges routine. The fence shook and bent toward us. Gregory pushed the gate closed. The dog snarled and growled with a deep rumbling rage. The light in the office went out.

"You guys got something to take care of this fucking dog?" Vito said.

"Yeah," Gregory said. "We always carry a couple of drugged porterhouse steaks."

"I don't know," Vito said. "I mean like a tranquilizer gun. Shoots darts, or some shit. I read it in the papers. Maybe it's the feds I'm thinking of."

The dog was a hostile mix of greasy black and skanky brown breeds. I could hear his teeth grating against the metal as he tried to chew his way through.

"Hold this gate, pally," Gregory said. "I'll have to use my tranquilizer gun."

Joe Gregory, who had a checkered history with dogs, waggled his fingers inches from the dog's nose, infuriating the animal. As Gregory moved his fingers, the dog followed, drool spilling from his mouth. He enticed him toward a pyramid of hubcaps where the fence didn't quite touch the ground. Gregory held the fence up until the dog, on his belly, had just enough room to wriggle under. He clawed at the dirt and strained wildly to reach my partner, digging and growling until he'd worked his head completely under, to our side. One quick crack of Gregory's blackjack, the sound of a hollow *thunk,* stopped his progress and brought instant silence. My first thought: He's killed another dog.

"Let's move," Vito said, and swung open the tall gate. It scraped noisily through a gouged rut in the driveway. As soon as we set foot on the oily dirt of Four K's a floodlight swept the gate like an escape scene in a prison movie.

"Let's not give them a legal excuse to blow us away," I said, then yelled, "Police!"

"I don't see no fucking warrant," somebody yelled.

"We're only from Homicide," Gregory said.

I could hear the car, still running, and at least two voices.

"That's close enough," the voice said. It was not Fat Paulie's voice.

Gregory and I meandered, trying to see who we were dealing with, a step here, a half step there. I got close enough to see the car that was running. It was a Cadillac Fleetwood, looked brand new.

"Hey, look, pal," I said. "We don't care what you're doing with this Cadillac. We're working a homicide. Let's cut the shit and talk for a few minutes, or else we'll get Auto Crime over here to turn this place inside out."

We heard one shot and hit the ground so fast that the echo still rang in my ears. But it was like jumping from the fire into the frying pan. I could smell and taste oil. I knew my clothes were ruined.

"Hey, Ryan," Vito Martucci yelled, "I got these pricks for you."

I pushed myself up, feeling the slick grit on my hands. Gregory mumbled something about this being my idea. In the spotlight I could see four hands high in the air. We cuffed the junkyard guy first, a pimply kid wearing a motorcycle jacket and a Springsteen-style American flag head scarf. We didn't bother cuffing Fat Paulie; we'd need hula hoops for that.

"Who the fuck are you guys?" Fat Paulie said.

In a way I could understand Paulie's confusion. Only one of us was wearing an NYPD detective's badge, and that person was Vito Martucci.

Then Fat Paulie said, "Who's this old fuck?" and Vito swung

a glove, a short snapping flip to Paulie's jaw. I heard the crack. Fat Paulie hit the deck and rolled over on his side, soiling the dark suit in several ways. I knew Vito had to have his own blackjack hidden in a finger of the glove, another old cop trick.

"He'll learn to fuck with us," Vito said, landing a soccer-style blow to the ass of the fallen fat man.

"Enough, Vito," I said as Gregory tied Fat Paulie's leg to a forklift with the dog's chain.

Besides my suit and Fat Paulie's jaw, the most serious casualty was the U.S. Constitution. I accepted my suit as a lost cause and didn't give a shit about Paulie, but I hoped we hadn't blown the case by not having legal authority to enter the yard. Then things started looking up.

After a short search Gregory found a sign near the front gate, a hand-lettered sign written in black paint or axle grease, that said "Open 24 Hours." Vito found the primered Buick Riviera under a tarp near the car crusher.

"Don't touch the car, please," I said, and got right on the phone to O'Prey.

When the search warrants arrived we found a traceable hand grenade box in the trunk of the Riviera. In the Cadillac, which was registered to Fat Paulie's pizza joint, we found a Beretta and a half-empty box of Dunkin' Donuts, or half-full, in Fat Paulie's eyes. Crime Scene Unit began dusting both vehicles for prints. O'Prey looked happy.

As dawn peeked over the South Bronx I went out to Vito's Lincoln to write the sequence of events while I could still re-member which details to forget. Hookers were going home, fac-tory workers arriving. The dog Gregory cold-cocked ambled meekly toward the East River.

"Told you, Ryan," Vito said. "Told you he'd be here. Nobody knows these guys better than me."

"You were right, Vito."

Vito had pocketed the detective's badge before O'Prey arrived.

It was a fake badge, an almost exact replica of J.C. Counihan's detective's shield. Replicas were the most common cop retirement gift, legal because they're a millimeter smaller than the actual badge. Nobody can tell the difference. Some working cops use them every day and keep their real shields in a safe-deposit box. The real badges don't come out until they have an appointment at the pension section.

"So what's the good word?" Vito said. "How many less fucking Lutzes we got running around this morning?"

"Neither Emil nor Vincent was in the bar. Disappointed?"

"Absolutely. They'll go way underground now. But we'll find them. I'll get my contacts working on it this morning."

I took a napkin from the glove compartment and tried to rub the grease from my hands. In the daylight I could see my shoes and socks were ruined, too. I tossed the napkin to the ground.

I said, "You sure you're ready to hear what Vincent has to say?"

"I ain't worried in the slightest, amigo. I knew my grandson better than anybody. He had nothing to do with those assholes. No way, Jose."

Next to the curb was a line of half a dozen dead rats. Long-dead rats. I wondered why so many of them had been crushed in that one spot. Did rats travel in families? Were rats pack rodents?

"Vito, how do explain him having Rocky's pager number?"

"That was planted by the scumbag who broke in my house," he snapped.

"It was in your grandson's handwriting."

Vito turned his back to Four K's Auto Salvage and pulled a Smith & Wesson Chief's Special from a shoulder holster. It was a small, snub-nosed .38 on a .32 frame.

"I scared the shit out of those cocksuckers," he said, laughing.

"Not only them."

Vito opened the cylinder, found the spent shell, and pulled it out with his fingernails. He didn't toss it, he slipped it into his pocket.

"Why are you carrying a gun, again?" I said as he replaced the bullet.

Vito held the gun facing the ground and slid the new bullet in from above, using gravity, as we'd been taught in the academy. Vicariously he'd absorbed the lessons better than most cops. He clicked the cylinder closed and gave me a "they can kiss my ass" smile.

"See those rats you were staring at?" he said, pointing down at the gray pelts, dried out and flattened by the wheels of a thousand stolen cars. "You think they're dead, right? You're making that assumption, because they look dead. That's you, Ryan the thinker, thinking it out logically. But not me. I spent too much time around rats. See, I know those rats ain't dead. They're only sleeping."

19

Leigh was up when I got home, sitting at the kitchen table in her red flannel robe, already into her Saturday morning ritual: coffee, bagel, and the *Daily News* crossword puzzle.

"Nice-looking suit," she said. "Detective Dirt has arrived."

"Long story, babe. I'm going to throw these clothes on the laundry room floor and worry about them tomorrow."

I felt pale and exhausted, drained of blood. I wondered how I ever did this for days at a time. Only a few cops work the patrol chart in uniform their entire careers, and it never ceased to amaze me. Eight years was enough for me. Most cops who work revolving tours become old men before their time. The flip-flop of days and nights screws up all your bodily functions and plays hell with your circadian rhythms.

"Call your father before you pass out," Leigh said. "I need to make plane reservations for Christmas. Tell him we'll arrange everything. He doesn't have to worry about a thing."

I'd been leaving messages for my dad all week, hoping he'd call back and make it easy for me. Standing in the kitchen in my underwear, I picked up the portable phone and walked over to Leigh and kissed her.

"I never liked that suit anyway," Leigh said. She poured a cup of coffee and put it on the counter next to my hand. I turned down the kitchen radio so I could hear my father, who spoke softly, like all the Ryans. Leigh couldn't resist snapping the waistband on my shorts.

My father had spent only one night in the hospital. A buddy of his, another retired NYC bus driver, drove him home. I allowed for his hearing problems and let it ring nine times before he finally picked up.

"How are you making out in all that snow?" my dad said. "Looks pretty bad on the TV."

"It's not snowing."

"I saw the news," he said. "Cars sliding all over the highway."

"That storm is in the Midwest. It's a little cold here, low forties. That's all."

Since my father moved to Florida I could count on him calling when he hears the weather is bad. He'd become a typical Sun Belt weather pain in the ass. Joe Gregory's late father couldn't stand living in Florida. Liam said that every night during the winter, TV weathermen show pictures of the same car sliding sideways on an icy highway or someone digging out of a ten-foot blizzard in their driveway. They keep telling everybody how happy they should be, away from all that, living in the land of sun and happiness. In the end it has all the oily reek of a sales pitch.

"Whatever," he said. I knew he didn't believe me. "I thought Hal said New York was socked in."

"We're not socked in. It hasn't snowed yet this year in the city. Maybe they meant upstate New York; they're always getting lake effect snow."

"No, this is a full-fledged storm. Icy roads, snowdrifts, all that good stuff. Maybe you'll get it later this week. That's probably what Hal meant."

I assumed Hal was his local TV weather forecaster. He used shorthand for TV personalities, as if it were someone close to both of us. He's always talking about something Phil said and I think it's some friend of his, but he means Phil Donahue. Weatherman Hal probably did say it was snowing in New York. Eddie Shick, a retired lieutenant who moved back to New York from Arizona, claims that TV weathermen in Phoenix extort payola from the Chamber of Commerce. They talk about snow as if it were a plague.

"Have the police made any arrests in your carjacking?" I said.

"No, and I'll be honest with you, Anthony. I hope they don't. I really don't want to go pick this kid out of a lineup. Truth be told, I don't know if I could, it happened so fast. Damn colored kids, I don't know one from the other."

Until he retired, my father drove a bus for the New York City Transit Authority for thirty years. The M100 route, from Third Avenue and 125th Street, west across the heart of Harlem, then north on Broadway to Inwood. He claims to be the last white man to ride on that bus. Now he can't tell one black kid from another.

I said, "What about your car, they find it yet?"

"Cops don't know what the hell they're doing down here. Not like the good old NYPD."

"How about you, Dad? You feeling any aftereffects, any soreness?"

"I'm fine now that I'm out of the damn hospital. Those are the places that kill you."

"That's right, stay out of those places. But I'm glad you're feeling better, because Leigh and I would like you to come up here for Christmas."

"With that weather! No way you'll get me up there in that weather."

"It's not bad, really."

"But it will be," he said.

"It's an offer you can't refuse. We're going to send you the airline ticket, our gift. The kids will be here, too. Make a big party out of it. Give you a chance to see your old friends. Morley's Pub is decorated to the hilt. All the usual suspects will be there. Just let me know when you can leave and we'll make all the arrangements."

"I don't have the clothes for that weather. I gave everything to St. Vincent de Paul."

I thought, Here I am trying to describe the weather to a man who lived in it for almost seventy years. How do they brainwash them so quickly?

"Come on, Dad. The weather isn't that bad."

"Ah, I don't know, Anthony," he said. "It's a nice offer. But honestly, I can't take the cold anymore. Tell Leigh I appreciate it. But you'll get old someday, you'll understand."

Shortly after I hung up, I fell into a deep sleep. I didn't remember a thing until I heard Leigh tiptoe into the bedroom. In the diffused sunlight filtering through the drapes I watched her reflection in the mirror as she undressed slowly, folding each piece of clothing, laying them across the chair. It was then I remembered the one great perk of shift work: making love while the rest of world toiled. For thirty years I'd watched my wife put her bra on first and take it off last. A ritual that still excited me.

Leigh had a body that fooled you. Athletic yet voluptuous. When dressed she looked tiny, but as the blouse came off you saw the fullness of her breasts straining against the lacy bra and the curve of her hips rounding down from her waist. Naked, she turned into someone else. My gray-haired goddess.

"I knew you were watching," she said as she raised the covers and slid over until she lay on top of me. Her skin was cool, a rare sensation. She arranged her body so one leg lay over mine, her

117

breasts against my ribs, her face buried in my neck as she nuzzled, worked her hips against my thigh.

Outside, wind blew and branches scraped against the side of the house. I turned to face Leigh, both of us on our sides, and she lifted her leg over my hip and I entered her, and we moved slowly in our rhythm. We didn't need to talk, or we could; the beauty of it was we could talk about dinner or fucking. Familiarity is the key, because then you know enough to sense subtle differences, and it's always different. The body temperature, the pebbly texture of a nipple, the degree of need, the words spoken. I reached around and held her as I rolled onto my back and pulled her on top. "Scratch," she said, and I scratched her back as she moved her hips. Then she pushed up on her hands to look down at me, her breasts filling the space between us. Leigh wanted to be touched on every inch of skin I could reach. "Scratch," she said, meaning her arms and her head, and I did until her arms were pink and her hair wild. And I scratched and rubbed as she writhed and ground her hips against me until her skin was so raw that it worried me, then deeper and deeper.

"I love my bed," she said later, as she stretched like a cat, scrunching up the covers and pillow.

Leigh always said she could never be someone's lunchtime quickie. She needed to sleep after sex. Her ability to fall asleep was astonishing; she could turn consciousness off like a switch. On the fingers of one hand, I could count the nights Leigh Ryan has tossed and turned. Somehow I'd chosen the ideal cop's wife.

I put on my jeans and started to go downstairs, suddenly starved. Earlier I'd been too tired to eat breakfast.

"Anthony," Leigh said without opening her eyes, "look out the window for a minute."

I walked to the window and pulled aside the curtain.

"Is that gray car still there, in front of Bracken's house? It's been sitting there for a while. I've never seen it before."

A gray El Dorado sat idling on the corner, blue-black smoke rising into the cold air.

"It's nothing," I said.

Our upstairs was a typical Cape Cod, two rooms with slanted ceiling and a small bathroom in between. The room across from our bedroom, we now used as a den. I walked quickly across the hall, grabbed the binoculars from the shelf, and squatted down next to a side window so I didn't have to move the curtain. I focused on the Cadillac. It was sitting about half a block away, looking into the sun. Any cop would know enough to get the sun behind him. It wasn't a cop.

It was Emil Lutz.

I threw on a sweatshirt, grabbed my gun, and ran down the stairs without saying anything to Leigh. I went out the back door, scaled both sides of McCrudden's fence, cut through Nevin's hedges, and came out on the street behind Emil Lutz's El Dorado. My heart was pounding, and my heart never pounds. All I could think about was the balls of this bastard. Coming to my house. My fucking house. The balls.

I crept along the row of parked cars until I reached the corner. Across the street, a nun carrying altar linens to the sacristy eyed me warily. I could hear myself breathing as I opened the back door and jammed my gun into Lutz's cheek.

"Oh, shit," Emil said, raising his hands from the steering wheel. "Easy, guy. Easy does it, guy."

I slid into the backseat and slammed the door. The heat was turned up full blast; I could feel the cold sweat on my neck and back.

"I'm only here to talk, Ryan," he said.

"Don't say a fucking word to me," I said.

"Talk is all I'm here for. Don't make a big deal outta this."

"You came here?" I said. "Fucking here?"

"So it was stupid," he said.

"Stupid doesn't begin to explain it."

I heard the *thunk, thunk* of a basketball and saw a group of boys walking toward us, coming from the playground. "Drive," I said. "Drive to the end of the block."

I felt fully justified. I was sure he had a gun somewhere in the car.

"I ain't driving nowhere but out of here, Ryan," he said. "You got this all wrong. Let's not make a federal case out of it."

I cocked the gun. How dared this prick violate my life?

"Hey, I'm going, I'm going," he said. "I didn't mean no harm. That's no bullshit."

"How did you find out where I live?"

"It wasn't no big deal, believe me."

With enough phone calls and a half-decent story he might have gotten it from a cop or civilian in our office. Or some scumbag cop might have sold it for Knicks tickets, even for shitty seats. Anything.

"I'll tell you what," he said. "I can see you're upset. I don't want you upset. Let me get out of here for now. You know where Julian's Famous is? The poolroom. Meet me there in a couple of hours. Okay? How about that? Or anywhere you say, Ryan. Just put the gun down. No shit. I didn't mean no harm. They just blew up my bar. I wasn't thinking straight."

I took the gun down, staring at the cocked hammer, realizing how close I'd come. I'd never seen my hands shake like this before, even during my years of bad drinking. I closed the hammer slowly onto my thumbnail, then gently let the hammer down the rest of the way.

"Two hours," I said.

I slid out of the car and waited at the corner until the Cadillac disappeared down the hill. I felt a little dizzy, from hunger and adrenaline. Across the street stood the statue of Jesus. The Sacred Heart, his fingers pointing to the dripping blood.

20

Julian's Famous Poolroom is located on East Fourteenth Street. It was half-empty on a Saturday afternoon. I'd called Joe Gregory, asked him to meet me outside. Gregory spotted Emil in a niche of three tables, situated farthest from the windows and doors. Larry Russo sat on a bar stool behind him, reading *Ring* magazine. We walked slowly, letting them recognize us. Russo slid off the stool and unbuttoned his suit jacket.

"Here come the hustlers," Lutz said.

I hadn't been in Julian's in almost twenty years. I remembered it for its churchlike ambience, with a reverence for concentration, where the click of the balls was the loudest sound. It was still smoky and filled with thirty or forty regulation-size tables, but now they charged a flat admission fee rather than the old method of paying by the hour.

"What the hell is your problem, Lutz?" Gregory said.

"Hey, I apologized already," he said. "I didn't think Ryan would throw a psycho fit just 'cause I parked in his neighborhood."

"You stepped over the line," Gregory said. "That's a mortal sin."

"I said I'm sorry, I'm sorry. *Ming.* Is this all we're gonna talk about, Ryan's problem?"

I said, "You brought my family into this, and now the rules change."

"What happened to your family?" he said. "Nothing happened to your family. That ain't my style. Family should be off limits. That's the way I learned how to play this game. I went there for one reason, to ask you a question."

In the background I heard electronic beeps of video games.

"You couldn't call me at work?" I said.

He shrugged, holding his palms up. "I thought we had a relationship of trust," he said. "I see I was wrong."

"Ask your question."

A giant-screen TV, a jukebox, and a few Ping-Pong tables had also been added to the place.

"Suppose my son Vincent were to suddenly turn up," Emil said. "In your hands. Not that I'm saying this is going to happen. But if it does, can you guarantee he's going to be kept in a safe place?"

"Nobody can guarantee that."

"I need guarantees," he said. "I already lost enough over this bullshit."

"If Vincent surrenders, the DA can request he be isolated from the other prisoners."

Emil chalked the cue and stared at the table. Julian's looked cleaner than I remembered, brighter. Then I noticed the black paint had been scraped from the windows. Sunlight in a poolroom, what's the world coming to.

"What happens then?" he said.

"Then it revolves around what he's willing to say. If he wants to do the right thing, give them somebody with weight, then it's possible he can be placed in witness protection. But I don't speak for the DA's office."

"Okay," Emil said. "But what if he don't want to go that far? All he wants to do is resolve this JFK case."

"Is he going to give us the people who did the job?"

"He don't know who did it, Ryan. That's the point."

"Then why give up?"

"Hey, this is the only son I got left. I'm supposed to wait until they kill everybody in my family? They burned my bar down last night; my poor uncle Stosh, eighty-five years old, an innocent fucking victim."

"What, innocent?" Gregory said.

"See," Emil said, "you think you're the good guys, we're the scum of the earth. We don't deserve justice, right? Let me tell you a story about my uncle Stosh. My mother died when I was sixteen. I'm walking out of Holy Cross Cemetery thinking I got nowhere to go. It's raining like hell, all I could see was black umbrellas. Uncle Stosh comes over and puts his arm around me and says, 'Hey, kid, you know how to steal cars?' Next day I had a job and a place to stay. That may seem weird to you. I don't know how you people take care of each other. But he took care of me. He took care of me the best way he knew how."

"Uncle Stosh was a butcher," Gregory said.

"More bullshit rumors," Emil said. "This city is filled with little punks running around with diarrhea of the mouth."

Stanley "Stosh" Lutz was known as "the Count." During Emil's heyday murders were more common than slot machine jackpots in the Cockpit Lounge basement. The Lutz clan disposed of the bodies by cutting them up, then getting one of the connected garbage trucks to deliver them to the Fountain Avenue dump. Before the butchering started, Uncle Stosh would first hang the body upside-down in the shower, cut the head off, and let the blood run down the drain. That way less blood got on the floor.

"I'll tell you why those old stories are bullshit," Emil said. "My uncle Stosh went blind from sugar diabetes, but still he went to mass every morning. The guy couldn't see ten feet in front of him; he used to feel his way along the cars."

"Must run in the family," Gregory said. "We heard your family came into some money and failed to *see* some important guys."

"What channel you hear that on?" he said. "Channel two, channel four, maybe New York One."

"That's the word, jailbird," Gregory said.

Emil walked around the table, looking for an angle on the nine ball. The floor was a grimy red-and-white checkerboard. A fluorescent light ran the length of the table and buzzed constantly.

"I had nothing to do with the JFK job," he said. "It was a nice job, but I didn't do it."

"They're not saying you're the Lutz who did it."

"Hey," he yelled, and slammed the stick against the table. "I don't care what people say. I did a lot of shit in my life, Ryan. I didn't do JFK, neither did my kids. If they did, I'd sure as shit see to it they did the right thing. Now that's my word, and if that ain't good enough for you and those *gavons* in Howard Beach, then fuck all of youse."

"We have evidence," I said.

"I got your evidence right here," he said.

As he grabbed his crotch, a pair of salesmen four tables away put down the cues and started to leave. They were in shirtsleeves, their sample cases and jackets set on the plastic chairs against the wall.

"Let me ask you something, Emil," I said. "Rocky told me that he wasn't exactly close with his father-in-law. Do you think Sally the Goat may have something to do with a contract being put out on him?"

Emil looked up at me across a mile of green felt. He'd been

bent over, lining up a straight three ball in the corner. I'd forgotten how much longer regulation tables were than the coin-operated ones in bars.

"When did you talk to Rocky?" he said.

"I met him outside the Javits Center, the Monday after the JFK stickup."

"Anybody see you talking to my son?" Emil said.

"Nobody of importance."

Of the thirty or forty tables, only five had players. A girl in a black rubber miniskirt and a guy in sunglasses who'd been playing more with each other than with their pool cues stopped in midwrithe to glance over at Emil.

"You know what I think?" he said. "I think I'm the fuckee here, and I'm getting fucked in both ends."

"What's that supposed to mean?"

"Hey," Emil said. "I forgave that old lunatic Martucci. I apologize to you. Why don't I just put an ad in the paper, 'Everybody welcome to fuck me in the ass'? Why not? What about Fat Paulie, should I apologize to him for having my bar get in the way of his hand grenade?"

"Actually," Gregory said, "we hope Fat Paulie dies a horrible death himself."

"When do you want us to pick up Vincent?" I said.

"I changed my mind," he said. "One of my sons dies after talking to you, now you want me to give you the other one. You think I'm just a thick Polack bastard, don't you?"

"You're the one who called us here," I said.

"That's before I knew certain things," he said.

"Give him up, Emil," I said. "You don't have the resources to protect him from the families. Things changed a lot while you were gone."

"People still die the same," he said. "That don't change. You know how easy it is to cut someone's head off?" He put his finger along the back of Russo's neck. "This bone back here is all there is. It's a little thin bone. It breaks like snapping a pencil. Snap, that's it. The rest is just cutting meat loaf. Throw the fucking head in the dump. Nothing to it."

"Let us talk to Vincent," I said. "We'll meet him in private somewhere. It's better we find him before somebody else does."

"No," he said, seeming to barely control his rage. "He's my kid. I call the shots with my family."

"Then tend to yours and leave mine alone."

"I come to your house for one simple thing," he said. "I come to ask you to help me in this. I don't know what the fuck is going on. I come there to ask for help, and this is the way you treat me, like I'm some fucking nigger, not good enough to be in your presence."

"Don't let me ever catch you near my house again," I said.

Gregory and I walked down the stairs through a greenish black haze of light. At the base of the stairs the marble floor was grooved in one spot, from the heavy footsteps of a million losers. Out on the sidewalk a group of Oriental men in suits took turns posing for pictures, arms around a life-size cardboard cutout of Marilyn Monroe. A dark-skinned man sat atop an eight-foot ladder watching shoppers going through boxes of orange plastic shoes and Ninja Turtle sweatshirts in front of Tito's House of Discount. Nobody seemed to be worried but me.

21

"Maybe we should sell the house," I said. "Move to an apartment in Manhattan."

I said this to my wife as we walked down the hill, through Lennon Park to Lake Avenue. We were going to Sunday brunch at Morley's. Brunch was something we'd started after I began attending mass, again. A feast for the prodigal.

"Anthony," Leigh said. "Is this about this jerk Lutz, who parked in front of our house yesterday?"

"Partly."

"Okay," she said. "I know Lutz is part of a Mob war, that's all over the news. But why, *exactly,* did he come to you?"

"I told you, because one of the other Mob families blew up his bar. They think his sons, Vincent and Rocky, did the JFK robbery and held out on the money. Rocky's been murdered since. I guess the bombing scared Emil enough to where he thought about turning his remaining son over to me. But he changed his mind."

"That's all it had to do with you?"

"Absolutely."

"He wasn't after you personally, or me. Now you suddenly want to move. Isn't going to all the trouble of moving to a new neighborhood a bit radical, or is there something you're not telling me?"

"No, babe, really, nothing else. I've just been thinking about moving for a while. We both liked living in Manhattan when we first got married, right? I've always loved that life. You walk out your door and everything is right there. Any hour of the day or night. You can walk everywhere. You don't owe your soul to a car."

On the outfield grass of the Little League field, a group of young boys was engaged in an impromptu game of six-on-six tackle football. No helmets, no pads, no parental pressure.

"Okay, say we get this little apartment," Leigh said. "And little is all we can afford there. Where do we put the kids when they come to visit?"

"Murphy bed, convertible sofa, roll-away bed. That's not an unsolvable problem."

"What about my job?" she said.

"You can easily find a job in Manhattan. One you can still walk to. One that pays a lot better than working at Sacred Heart."

"But I like *this* job."

We sat in a booth opposite the bar. It was too early for Morley's bar crowd. Not that the middle-aged regulars were a problem. The worst they did was bitch about some politico or the Giants. Nobody bitched about their ex-wives because there was too great a chance she was the sister or cousin of a guy on another stool.

"You think you can handle leaving your old neighborhood behind?" Leigh said.

"I can always visit," I said.

Morley's had mellowed over the years; now it was more of a

restaurant than a gin mill. But once it was a rowdy joint called the Emerald Isle, filled with kids from Sacred Heart High School; every drinker's face was somewhere in the yearbook. Beer was the only drink then, for the sons of cops, bus drivers, and construction workers. I bought my first legal drink at the Emerald Isle bar on my eighteenth birthday and traveled home on my hands and knees.

Leigh said, "What is it you always call the guys who come back for a visit?"

"Returning heroes," I said.

She had me. I'd always made fun of the returning heroes. You see one every now and then, usually on a Saturday afternoon. Balding and fat faced, dressed in Ralph Lauren barn jackets, they come in from Scarsdale or Houston, Texas. They're smiling as they look left for the long, straight slab of a bar where they vividly remember chug-a-lugging from eighteen taps of Schaefer beer. But, surprise, the place has changed. Suddenly unsure, our returning heroes take a seat at the new horseshoe bar in the center of the room and order something clear and expensive, naming the brand: Tanqueray and Schweppes or something with Perrier. They sip and stare into every face. It's as if they actually expect to be recognized because they were once a class president or basketball star three decades ago.

But the neighborhood bar, like life, moves on without you. The returning heroes always leave somber, their drinks unfinished. After a few minutes someone will say, "Who the hell was that, anyway?"

"We couldn't have our big Christmas party," she said, smiling, "in a small apartment in Manhattan."

"That's a point."

"Speaking of the party, I want you to call our son when we get home. Find out when he can leave L.A. I've got to make airline arrangements, or it will be too late."

"He's probably holding off until we're forced into buying first class."

The brunch was "all you can eat," a concept I usually wasn't crazy about, but I didn't mind it in Morley's. I loaded up on scrambled eggs, pancakes, and Irish sausage. On the wall above us were the winners of past football pools and the amounts they'd yet to collect. It was the kind of bar that would hold your winnings for years.

"You can't leave this neighborhood," Leigh said. "Who are you kidding? You love all this tradition and history, especially the Irish tradition. These people know you, they knew your father."

I did like the pace of this place, no one in a hurry. The waitresses always had enough time to chat.

"Tell me about your case," Leigh said. "Do you think Johnny Boy and Fiona fell in love in a place like this?"

"I know you're trying to change the subject, but I think it's more likely they met in one of the hard-core Irish hangouts in Queens or Manhattan. Some of those bars won't serve you unless you have a shamrock between your teeth."

On a wall next to the big-screen TV, a message board had a note in grease pencil: someone trying to organize a bus trip to the Garden for the Knicks-Celtics game.

"I don't know about Fiona and Johnny Boy being in love, either," I said. "I get the impression that Fiona likes the attention of multiple suitors."

"What makes you say that?"

"Fiona's own words for one. She specifically says John was her 'friend.' I think it might have been one of those mutually beneficial relationships. He got to hang around with a real Irish girl, and she got a date, someone to buy her drinks. Then the other night in the park I noticed some tension between two other 'friends' of hers, Dermot and Mickey. It was clearly over her."

"I didn't think Irish girls did that."

"You should have gone to my high school."

I made another trip to the buffet table for the black-and-white pudding. Leigh dipped her spoon and smiled. She wasn't an adventurous eater on her own, but she loved to sample whatever I took a chance on.

"Are these friends of Fiona's the hansom cab drivers you told me about?"

"Sure and begorra," I said.

Barney, the day bartender, came through the door and waved a copy of the *Irish Echo* at us. Barney, a retired Yonkers fireman, graduated from "the Heart" two years before me. A slight foot drag was the only clue to the stroke he'd suffered a few years back.

"Let's do that again sometime," Leigh said. "Remember when we took the kids on one of those buggy rides around Central Park?"

"Margaret's scarf blew off and she never forgave me for not chasing it."

"It was handmade, Anthony. By your mother."

"It blew into the lake."

I paid the bill and went over to say something to Barney. He leaned over the bar and whispered. Barney always whispered, as if any communication over a bar top were a state secret. But this he didn't want Leigh to hear. He told me that a guy we'd played basketball with, and who later made a fortune in the charter bus business, had committed suicide in Palm Beach, Florida.

Outside I said, "Maybe we'll just get a good alarm system, and stay right where we are."

"Now you're talking sensible," she said. "Besides, there's no such thing as a safe place anymore."

22

The front paws of Joe Gregory's chrome bulldog stood on a stack of messages. I flipped through them, trying to find a clue as to where he was. Six messages, all the same: Call Vito. It was almost eleven A.M. and he was late. He swore he'd be in early for Declan O'Prey's task force meeting: eleven, sharp. I quietly asked Albie Meyers if he'd heard from him.

"Maybe he's doing some Emerald Society business," he said.

"They don't have any business that's conducted before Brady's opens."

"Maybe he's over at St. Andrew's," he said. "Isn't this a holy week? Pentecost, some shit like that. Maybe he's praying, what do I know?"

I taped a note to the bulldog's butt and was on my way downstairs when Gregory came hustling through the door. He was motoring, doing his fast walk, what Albie Meyers referred to as "when those afterburners in his ass kick in."

"Nice of you to show up," I said.

"I was out doing what they call detective work," he said,

brushing past me. "I'll explain later. Make my apologies to Iron Balls."

I took the fire stairs down to the tenth floor. It was exactly three minutes to eleven when I entered O'Prey's office. The room was empty, except for the icy Irishman. He didn't look up but sat at his desk, flipping through *The New York Times,* touching the pages only at the edge so as to avoid getting ink on his fingers. A dozen chairs were lined up in front of his desk, in two rows, like third grade at St. Something-or-other. I had my choice, so I chose the back row. Newspaper rustled, a clock ticked.

Not until the final seconds before eleven did the seats begin to fill. They came en masse, as if they'd been waiting in the hall. Then we all sat quietly, as if any tomfoolery would cause Brother Declan to rap our knuckles with his steel ruler. At exactly eleven he put aside the paper and said, "I think we have a quorum."

O'Prey stood up and shut the door. He looked around, nodding his head, taking a mental roll call. The room, which contained more oak than any cop office I'd been in before, smelled of pipe tobacco. O'Prey removed his jacket and hung it on a hanger in a small wooden closet. As usual, he was dressed for success.

"Let's all try to be concise today, ladies and gentlemen," he said. "We have very little time at our disposal."

He was scheduled for a meeting in the eighth-floor war room, where the police commissioner regularly and ruthlessly grilled all commanders. It wasn't a pleasant experience for any of them; the PC had no patience for the old soft-shoe.

"We have another nail for the coffin of Vincent Lutz," O'Prey said as he pulled the cover off a portable blackboard in the center of the room. "ATF has confirmed that the gun found at the scene of the crime was purchased at a gun show, in Richmond, Virginia, by a local in the employ of Mr. Lutz."

On the blackboard was a neatly drawn wheel. In the center of the wheel was a blank circle, but the lines, or spokes, going out from the center all had messages, concise bits of evidence: informant statements, etc. O'Prey added his ATF information in yellow chalk. All of the handwriting bore the look of O'Prey's classic Dublin education.

"They say all roads lead to Rome," he said, pointing to the wheel. "This is the case here as well. All the investigative roads: through informants; through evidence; through modus operandi; through opportunity. All lead here."

He tapped the blackboard with his chalk, then drew a remarkably straight freehand line in the center of the wheel. On the line he wrote, "Vincent Lutz."

"We must find Rome, forthwith," he said, and sat back down at his desk. But I'd heard in his voice the tinny rattle of doubt.

The longest presentation lasted seven minutes, as analyst Kelsey Lucas from Organized Crime Intelligence discussed snippets of wise guy gossip filtering out of the Colombo and Lucchese camps. Colombo family hot heads were convinced that the Lucchese people had conspired with the Lutz crew to deny the JFK score. OC Intelligence believed a major Mob war to be at hand.

O'Prey's face turned deep red when Kelsey said that word on the street was that Rocky Lutz's fingerprints had turned up on the gun found at the scene. The very evidence O'Prey had sworn to keep confidential was common knowledge in the wise guy bars of Brooklyn. O'Prey looked directly at me.

"Does the Central Homicide Unit have anything to add?" he said.

"Not a thing," I said. I had planned to mention that Emil Lutz had parked his arrogant ass in front of my house, but I knew it would fall on unsympathetic ears. O'Prey turned away to stare out the window that faced west across the plaza. City Hall was visible if he looked hard to the left.

Albie Meyers read a debriefing of a top-level federal prison source who claimed that Sally the Goat Corrazzo was livid over the murder of his son-in-law, Rocky Lutz. Sally the Goat's daughter, the widow Brenda Lutz, was making weekly visits to Danbury, dressed in black, breaking the Goat's heart and making him crazy. At Rocky's wake Brenda promised her dead husband "that the streets would run red for him," a line stolen from Crazy Joe Gallo's sister. So Sally the Goat petitioned the heads of the crime families for permission to expunge Fat Paulie Caruso, whom he believed to be the trigger man. O'Prey looked as if he'd like to call a hit on me.

"How about some good news for a change, boss?" said Lieutenant Jesse Keegan from Major Case. "We just received information that looks solid. We know where Vincent Lutz has been staying."

O'Prey stopped as he lifted a cup to his lips. It was a teacup with a delicate pattern of tiny green shamrocks. He set it back down in the saucer.

"Three ten East Eighty-fourth Street," Keegan said. "In Manhattan, apartment six C. It's his mother's address."

O'Prey stared at the lieutenant. "Why aren't we acting on this?"

"I have six men en route, as we speak," Keegan said.

O'Prey wrote the address slowly. Behind him was a framed color picture of one of his New York Marathon finishes. The leaves in Central Park were orange and brown and falling on the cluster of runners and silver-caped volunteers. O'Prey's arms are raised as if breaking an invisible tape. High above, the Manufacturers Hanover digital clock read 3:21:07.

"Detective Ryan came up with it, Inspector," said Keegan, who fully deserved his reputation as a cop's boss.

The National Rifle Association had helped me find the address. But not voluntarily. I knew Vincent was a gun nut, so I had a postal inspector friend of Joe Gregory's search the NRA mailing lists. Vincent's copy of *American Rifleman* was being sent to that Manhattan address.

NYNEX had no listing for Vincent Lutz at that address. Con Ed said the electric bills were paid by an R. Ciccalone. Hudson Property Management, after some melodramatic threats, told us the lessee of apartment 6C was Rose Ciccalone. Rose Ciccalone was Vincent Lutz's mother's maiden name.

"Good work, Ryan," O'Prey said.

Don't put me in for a medal yet, I thought. I had serious doubts that we'd find Vincent there. If he had any brains at all, he would have fled as soon as reverberations of the Cockpit Lounge bombing reached Manhattan. Gregory keeps telling me not to underestimate the stupidity of the kiddie Mafia. But if Vincent had the other half of the TWA cash, he could easily wait out the storm in some safer, sunny clime.

"Let's get going, gentlemen," O'Prey said, lifting his hands like a preacher asking the congregation to rise. "Lieutenant, you'll take care of the warrant and affidavits."

O'Prey, suddenly energized, knew he had a plan to report to the bosses. The room emptied in seconds. None of the investigators hung around to talk. In the old days we would have gone across the street to Brady's and compared notes over a couple of cold ones. These guys intended to get away from the building as fast as they could.

Gregory sat at my desk, still wearing his overcoat.

"What's this all about?" he said, holding up a note from Albie Meyers.

"I asked Albie to look up a couple of names for me."

"These names, what the hell for? You checking to see if they paid their dues to the Ancient Order of Hibernians, or what?"

The note said "No record on Fiona Quinn or Dermot Geary, but three possibles on Mickey O'Brien. I had to wade through about thirty O'Briens; Mickeys, Mikes, Michaels. You owe me big time for this, Ryan." It was signed "Albie M."

"Just being thorough," I said. It was true. I had nothing solid,

136

just a nagging sense that I'd kick myself in the ass if I didn't do it. "I'm going to order the booking photos of the three possible O'Briens."

"You're relentless, Ryan. You can't decided who you want to chase, can you? You thinking maybe Customs nailed Mickey for smuggling bogus shamrocks or shillelaghs?"

Inspector Declan O'Prey still didn't like us well enough to invite us along on the Lutz warrant. In the semi-isolation of our file cabinet foxhole we looked like the kids not picked for the big game. Major Case cops wearing their raid faces dug vests and shotguns from metal lockers. The office filled with the clatter of expensive cop toys and bursts of nervous laughter.

"Where were you this morning?" I said.

"Airport, pally. Scene of the crime. That's where we're going now."

He stood up and held my coat as if I were his prom date.

"You want to tell me why?" I said.

"The great minds do not share their secrets with the masses," he said.

"True, but what exactly is on your alleged mind?"

"Remember, years ago," he said, "that guy who flew the wrong way? He was supposed to go to California, he wound up in Europe."

"Wrong Way Corrigan," I said.

"Well, that's how we've been approaching this case, the wrong way. You remember the first hinky thing you noticed about this case? Johnny Boy coming out the door."

"The coincidence of it," I said. "The perfect timing."

"Well, I figured it out. I can tell you why he came through that door at that exact time."

"Right Way Gregory to the rescue."

"Come with me," he said. "And prepare to have your socks knocked off."

23

Light snow fell as we drove around JFK Airport toward Federal Circle. Only two types of drivers populate airport roadways: those of us reading the color-coded signs and the obnoxious bastards who know where they're going. Inside or out, airports conform to their own odd rules. Even the streetlights are different. On the looping access roads to JFK's terminals the lights are curving metal poles that look like a gauntlet of praying mantis.

"This crime scene has been bugging me from the start," Gregory said. "All those bullet holes in the wall of the TWA building. I knew that was bullshit from the get-go. But I finally got that figured out now, guaranteed."

At TWA cargo we drove right through the gate to loading dock 11. Gregory got out of the car carrying the cheap black attaché case that contained the props and gimmicks he called investigative aides. I was surprised to see brand-new crime scene tape stretched across the alleyway; I thought CSU had shut the scene down.

"I hope you got your thinking cap on," he said.

I knew he was going to walk me through the crime scene. It was standard for the Great Gregory to take a walk in the victim's shoes. We were in a narrow passageway, blocked from the weather, between the corner of the building and stacks of aluminum cargo containers.

"It starts right here," he said, pointing down at the fading blood of a pair of eight-dollar-an-hour uniformed guards. "The perps are hiding here, behind the cargo boxes. The guards come around the corner, wheeling the dolly. The perps shoot the shit out of the guards, no mercy. Maybe thirty seconds, it's over. They grab the dolly, start wheeling it to their car."

The snow was becoming wetter, just a slushy mist. The sky was dark. It was easy to understand why they leave the runway lights on day and night.

"Okay," he said, gesturing for me to follow him. "The perps are moving this way. They're pushing the cash toward the hole in the fence. They get right here and the door opens. Stand right there, pally, where the perps stood. You with me so far?"

Gregory climbed up the three metal steps and banged on the door to dock 11. He looked thoughtfully at the corrugated walls, thinking through the points of his presentation. He opened his attaché case and took out a handful of red-and-white-striped plastic drinking straws. He began sticking the straws through the bullet holes. The straws all pointed down. Strings dangled from some of the straws.

"This is when Johnny Boy opens the door," he said, banging on the door again. He was standing almost on the exact spot where his old partner's son had died.

"Where did you get all the straws?" I said.

"McDonald's. I cleaned them out."

We waited another half a minute until the door swung open. Gregory propped the door back and came down the steps. He picked up the loose strings hanging from the straws in the bullet holes. He pulled them across the blacktop and tied them to the stacks of aluminum boxes.

"I feel like Dr. Watson," I said. "Obviously, I'm watching genius at work."

"Look at the slope of the blacktop," he said. "See how it goes down from here. Now look at the trajectory of the bullets. See what I'm doing? Straws are all pointing down. I'm saying the bullets in that wall were fired from right here on an upward angle. You agree the trajectory is rising from where you're standing?"

"Obviously," I said. "Can we go now?"

A plane dropped out of the clouds, falling quickly. It landed with the screech of brakes on the wet runway.

"Bear with me," he said. He let the strings fall to the ground and climbed the stairs. He stepped up into the doorway of the warehouse. The doorway was at least two feet above the blacktop.

"What they say happened," Gregory said, "is that Johnny Boy opens the door and steps out. The bad guys start firing. Johnny Boy falls down the steps and lands on the blacktop. They keep shooting. He falls right there, rolls over. But not all the bullets were fired from the same distance, were they?"

"Correct," I said. "The medical examiner's report said they probably kept shooting as they walked toward his body. The last few shots were fired at close range."

"So then it's your contention that all the shots were fired from the outside?"

"That's my contention," I said.

"Then how do you explain this?" he said. He reached into his briefcase and took out a different straw, a solid blue. He pushed this one through a bullet hole in the door, then closed the door. The blue straw pointed in the opposite direction as the others, it pointed up. "Where was this shot fired from, the freaking sky?"

"Gadzooks, Holmes," I said. "The blue straw points up."

The bullet hole in the door was the same height as many of the other sixty rounds, about seven or eight feet above the alley pavement, but the trajectory appeared different.

"This can't be, can it?" Gregory said. "The question is: If this shot was fired from the outside, how was it fired at a downward angle?"

"It wasn't," I said, swinging the door fully open, back against the corrugated metal wall. "Because the door was open when that shot was fired."

"Really?" Gregory said. "Then look behind it. Tell me why there's no dent in the wall, no mark where the bullet would have hit when it came through the door. Where did it go?"

It was obvious the entrance hole was on the inside of the door. I took the door and held it at various angles. Perhaps the force of coming through the door weakened the velocity and it fell to the ground before it struck the back wall. I made a mental note to check with Crime Scene to see if a bullet had been found behind the door.

Gregory said, "My money says that shot was fired while the door was still closed. It was fired from inside the warehouse, and aimed at Johnny Boy. It missed and went through the door. Then a second shot didn't miss. That's the one in the back of his head. I say someone fired two shots from inside the building, then pushed him out the door."

"So who fired that shot?"

"That's the question, pally. That is the sixty-four-dollar question."

I heard a sound off in the distance. A definite gunshot, it sounded like a kid banging a kitchen pan. I looked toward the end of the runway; it came from the grassy marsh beyond the tarmac.

"You see one of those Texas jackrabbits out there?" Gregory said. "They say there's hundreds of them living out there now. A crate of them broke open out on a runway couple years ago.

141

They ran away into the marsh. You know, those giant Texas rabbits with the big ears?"

"No, I heard a shot."

"Oh, that's just French Willie," Gregory said. "He shoots birds. That's his full-time job for the airport. They hired him after that starling incident at Logan Airport in 1960. He rides around the runways in that orange truck and shoots birds. They got geese, ducks, all kinds of birds that could get sucked into a jet engine. French Willie is licensed to shoot them all. Even some protected species."

"How do you know all this?" I said.

"Vito told me. He knows all about this place."

I'd read where environmental groups were incensed that airport officials were pouring oil over bird eggs in the sanctuary in Joco Marsh, trying to keep down the population.

Gregory said, "You see my point here, right, pally?"

I stepped up into the doorway with my partner. He did have a point, the kind detectives hate to hear, because it raised too many new questions.

"I see your point," I said. "But if a shooter was inside the building, we have to consider how he got in. Somebody let him in, didn't they?"

"It appears to be so. But now watch this."

Gregory opened his old attaché case, which was a cross between a cop's tool kit and a vaudeville trunk. In it was a baseball hat with a fake ponytail hanging out the back, dark glasses, horn-rimmed glasses with no lenses, a set of lock picks, a telephone repairman's headset, a stack of fake IDs wrapped in a rubber band, and a box of aluminum foil to insert in the hats of the city's paranoids in order to protect them from demon rays from outer space. He brought out his tape measure.

"Johnny Boy was my height, six foot two," he said. "We know that from the ME's report."

Gregory put a small mark on the door, like a father measuring his growing son against the bedroom wall. Then he made a second mark five and three-quarter inches below that. The bullet that entered Johnny Boy's head, just below the base of the skull, entered through his neck, five and three-quarter inches below the top of his head.

"Check this out," he said, pointing.

The lower pencil mark was almost directly even with the bullet hole in the door, just to the left.

"The shooter was a short bastard," he said, bending his knees and pointing his finger like a gun. "About five five, no more than that. Five five is the exact height of that scumbag Vincent Lutz."

"A lot of people are around that height," I said.

"Not in this case."

"I'll tell you what," I said. "Let's talk to the medical examiner before we go to O'Prey with this."

Gregory reached for his beeper and squinted at the number. "Vito again," he said. "There's a phone in the manager's office. I'll give him a quick buzz." He walked down the corridor toward the inside of the warehouse.

I could see how it might have happened, how someone with a gun stood behind Johnny Boy and jammed it into his neck. The hole in the door could have been the first shot, a hurried miss, although there was no way to tell which bullet had been fired first. It could have been the second, an accidental discharge as the killer pushed Johnny Boy through the door into the waiting barrage.

I reminded myself it was only one possible scenario among many. But all the scenarios I could think of raised the same questions, questions that Joe Gregory didn't seem willing to address: Who let the killer into the building, and why would the slow-witted son of a cop be executed in this fashion?

I looked across the asphalt toward the reedy wetland. In the distance I could see a gang of garbage-eating gulls hovering over the hills of a city landfill.

Gregory returned, his face pale.

"What happened?" I said.

"J.C. Counihan died."

"I'm sorry to hear that, Joe."

"Yeah, shit. I don't know. The guy had to be miserable living like he was. I know I would be."

He began packing up his straws and string. The Sherlock act was over, a deep frown spread across my partner's face.

"Maybe you should take a ride out to Great Neck," I said. "See how Cookie's doing?"

"I'm thinking that."

The tang of marine salt was in the air as we walked back to the car. Then the wind picked up, the metal building rattled, the ground started to shake. For a brief second I thought it was rolling thunder. I turned to see a spindly white object hurtling down the runway, its nose pointed down. Gregory and I stopped to watch the Concorde, and I could feel its deafening bass boom in my chest, white flames shooting from the exhaust, its power like a freight train barreling inches away from your face, moving your body, rocking it. We stood there with our hands over our ears. I wondered if we had just opened a door on something we couldn't control.

24

I asked Gregory to drop me off at the medical examiner's office while he went to comfort Cookie. We drove through Springfield Gardens and St. Albans, areas of working-class blacks living in brick two-story houses, windows framed in white. Wrought-iron rails were painted white. Tin awnings covered the front steps.

"I'll give you two hours, pally," he said. "By the time I get out there, and all."

"Two hours is plenty for me in this place."

The Queens Hospital Center Complex is located at 164th Street and Goethals Avenue near Grand Central Parkway. The complex consists of five or six austere public hospital buildings that ring three sides of a city block; the fourth side is closed in by an eight-foot iron fence.

Before I went up to the window in the ME's office, I sat in a molded plastic chair and took the Counihan file from my black canvas briefcase, a briefcase that suddenly seemed dull compared with Joe Gregory's magic bag. I pulled all the photos. I wanted to go over them one more time before I spoke to the doctor. If Gregory was right, the bullet found in Johnny Boy's head was fired while he was standing. I wanted to know if the ME could verify that.

It was a matter of basic ballistics. When a bullet leaves a gun it's preceded by fire, then smoke, then the bullet emerges. More smoke, and grains of both burned and unburned powder follow the bullet. If the weapon was held close enough to the body, this debris forms a pattern on the skin or clothing.

I felt secure about the front torso. The frontal wounds to Johnny Boy Counihan didn't have any tattooing or powder marks. The bullets came from too great a distance. But seven wounds marked Johnny Boy's back. Several of them had burned and stained his thick wool NYPD coat. Minimal smudging marked the skin. We'd assumed they'd come after he'd fallen, while they stood directly over him. The head wound appeared to be the coup de grâce.

The head wound was the question: first or last? Gregory said we had it backward. Johnny Boy Counihan's lone head wound was an angled contact wound, one in which the gun is held directly against the body, but on an angle. Only part of the barrel actually touches the skin. What happens is that escaping soot, powder, and vaporized metal mark the skin to the side of the barrel that isn't touching skin. In this case the mark was a fairly large, pear-shaped smudge directly over a smooth round entrance hole. The blacked skin blended into the bottom of his hairline.

"You need help, sweetie?" said a woman half my age, wearing a skintight black turtleneck. She had an earring in her nose, another in her lower lip, her orange hair in dreadlocks.

"I need to see Dr. Rachman."

Dr. Sy Rachman wasn't in the morgue or the medical examiner's office. Orange Dreadlocks said he was on his break. She pointed out the window and told me where to find him.

In the center of the complex is a private area, consisting

mostly of a gravel parking lot. Adjacent to the parking lot, but hidden by a small forest of full-growth trees, is a lone park bench. Rachman, she said, would be there.

Many years ago I happened to be on the rooftop of the Airport Holiday Inn and I remembered being surprised by all the trees, by how green the borough of Queens appeared from above. It's something you don't appreciate from the sidewalk. I've noticed it in the other boroughs as well. Manhattan is particularly surprising, the upper half densely verdant. I've always thought that if we New Yorkers survive the ravages of city life, the stress, the air pollution, we have our trees to thank.

Rachman was on the bench, as predicted.

"Every day I come out here," the doctor said. "It gets me away from that cadaver factory. It's quiet. You can relax and talk to yourself without people staring."

From the green wooden slat bench you could barely see the buildings. It was an oasis.

"It must be nice out here in summer," I said.

"Oh, the children play here all the time. Kids from the hospital. I come out to hear them laugh. Like a breath of fresh air, if you know what I mean. Makes it easier to go back to the table."

I wondered if hearing the laughter of children would make it easier or harder for me to go back to work. Small manicured bushes outlined the children's playground: a slide, an old set of rusting monkey bars, and three swings. The concrete turtle sat alone. I asked the doctor if he remembered the Counihan autopsy.

"If it would make you think better of me," he said, "I would say yes, but the truth is I don't remember the names. Do you have a copy of the protocol?"

Rachman wore a long nylon parka, the hood pulled past his face. He was eating a sandwich, liverwurst and onions on white bread. The sandwich disappeared into the fur frame of the hood. I handed him the protocol and the photos.

"Detective Joe Gregory is your partner," he said, chewing. "One of my favorites. The Great Gregory. Big, deep laugh. I love his laugh. Too few people laugh out loud anymore. And you're the one with the bad stomach."

Bad stomach is how Gregory explains my absence during autopsies.

I said, "I don't laugh out loud enough."

The doctor's glasses had two lens, one on top of the other. The outer lens, hooked at the top, flipped up like an outfielder's sunglasses. But, oddly, he flipped up the outside lens for reading, then back down for distance. It seemed illogical.

"Ah, suddenly this is important," he said. "They send a detective with a serious face. Those other two, the first two from the precinct. I don't remember their names. They had more pressing matters than observing my work."

The cops he was talking about were from the One Thirteen Squad, the team who initially caught the case. At that time they were locked on the trail of the Lutz family. The autopsy seemed as if it would be a rubber stamp for the first hot hunch. I pointed to a photo of Johnny Boy.

"This head wound," I said, "is an angled contact wound."

"Go to the head of the class. Of course it is. You see the stippling here?" He pointed his finger, like a gun, at the dark smudge just above the bullet hole.

"What about the other wounds to his back?"

"Midrange wounds. See the tattooing present? This is tattooing, not powder burns, as some of your colleagues insist on calling them. These marks here are abrasions."

A gray squirrel stopped and looked up at us.

"How far away would you consider midrange to be?"

"Maybe ten, twenty centimeters." He held his hand about a foot apart.

"Was he alive when these midrange wounds occurred?" I said.

"Difficult to say," he said. "See, the tattooing doesn't have quite

148

the normal red-orange color that would occur in antemortem wounds. But he was wearing thick clothing, so that may have something to do with it."

"So is it possible he was already dead from the head wound when they walked up and shot him in the back?"

"Officer Ryan, is it? So many Irish names to remember. I cannot be sure merely by looking at these photos. These things are not always that clear-cut. Let me review my notes and I'll call you back."

"What I'm getting at," I said, "is the head wound. Is it possible he was alive and standing when that shot was fired?"

"These bullets were fired within a very short space of time," he said. "It's quite possible he was alive for all the wounds."

"But was he standing for the head wound?"

"I don't know whether or not I can give you an unqualified opinion."

"Then consider the angle for me."

"You mean the track of the bullet," he said. "Let me see . . . the bullet penetrated the head, here at the hairline. It traveled up, perforating the brain, then the top of the skull. It came to rest under his scalp."

"Is that consistent with a victim who was upright?"

"It's possible. It could have happened either way. Considering the angle at which the weapon was held."

"This is important, Doctor," I said. "Would you please review the case for me?"

Rachman stared down at the photos while he ripped small pieces of bread from his sandwich and threw it toward the squirrel.

"Interesting," he said. "This is a very interesting problem you've given me, Officer Ryan."

25

"He's never going to call you back," Gregory said, maneuvering the Olds aggressively between lanes of traffic on the Belt Parkway. "Sy Rachman never commits."

He'd picked me up at the ME's office and filled me in on Cookie's funeral plans. We were on our way back to Manhattan, and snow was still falling off to our left, into the dark waters of the Atlantic. My partner seemed to be in a hurry to get somewhere.

"You never know," I said. "Give him a couple of days."

"What coupla days? We're running around with our balls taped to our leg, pally. What this case needs is a major goose. Where the hell is this kid Vincent, anyway? Freaking kid is harder to find than Hoffa."

Gregory surprised me with this sudden intensity. What was the rush all of a sudden?

"Maybe we really don't want to find him," I said.

"Why, because you think Johnny Boy was involved with the Lutz crew?"

"Isn't it obvious?" I said. "He had Rocky's pager number, now it appears his murder was intentional. Johnny Boy gave them the money shipment schedule, then they decided they couldn't trust him, so they killed him. He's right in the middle of it, Joe."

"Middle of nothing," he said. "What happened to Mickey O'Brien? I thought you were chasing Irish guys now."

"You can't even acknowledge the possibility that Johnny Boy was involved?"

"I acknowledge that Vito is probably right," he said. "I think, at most, it's possible the kid found out about it and tried to stop it. Vincent Lutz came up from behind and blew him away."

"So we find Vincent Lutz, we find the truth."

"I'm thinking that, too."

Gregory's theory didn't make any sense and he knew it. I could have taken it apart, but why bother. He was only creating his own justifications, so he could operate in peace. We all go through life telling ourselves lies to protect our self-image. In this case, everything came down to squeezing some form of the truth out of Vincent Lutz. And that truth might break the hearts of people Gregory cared for. Of course, first we had to *find* Vincent Lutz.

"My point is," Gregory said, "what possible reason could Johnny Boy have for working with Lutz? He had a good family, he didn't need the money, he wasn't on drugs, he wasn't a gambler. The kid was never in trouble in his life, so suddenly he starts hanging out with creeps like the Lutz brothers. What's the motive?"

"I think it's about belonging," I said. "This was a kid who desperately wanted to belong to something."

"So he joins up with these bastards?"

"You never had kids. Some kids are like that."

I saw the big gray Chrysler slide out from the exit ramp off

Sheepshead Bay. He had to be after us, the way my partner was driving. In less than a mile he pulled abreast of us. A cop from one of the motorcycle units: The crumpled hat was a dead giveaway. Bad weather forces them off their beloved bikes. I took the official department parking plate down from the visor, showed it to him, and shrugged apologetically. Gregory slowed and pulled over to the inside lane.

"Where do you figure this mook Vincent is?" Gregory said. "Say he left the country, what's your guess?"

"Rome," I said.

"What, the freaking pope is hiding him, or what?"

"Just kidding. It's an O'Prey thing, you weren't there. He used this visual, a wheel chart, all roads lead to Rome."

"Whatever," he said. "It's not a bad thought."

"The pope?"

"No, but somebody just as big. Not for nothing, but I can't believe how well this kid is hidden. All the pressure we been putting on, and nobody is ratting. That ain't the way it should be."

"So, eliminating the pope, that leaves us with the president, or who?" I said.

He stuck his chin out toward the windshield, and it took me a few seconds to figure it out. Gregory usually doesn't resort to pantomime.

"Chin?" I said. "Chin Gigante?"

"Who else?" he said. He proceeded to tick off the reasons on his fingers. "First, he's the kid's godfather. He cradled little Vinny in his arms at the baptismal font. That creates a sacred bond. Second, the kid is even named after him. Vincenzo, am I right? Third, Emil Lutz and Chin were either altar boys together or did time in the same joint; one or the other, I can't remember which."

"Chin is nuts, Joe. He's a lunatic."

"That's a matter of opinion," he said.

The new boss of bosses, the head of the Genovese crime family, a man known as "Chin" because of his name Vincenzo, can be found every day scuffing through the streets of the West Village, muttering to himself, unshaven and wearing his bathrobe and slippers. He carries a laminated plastic card with his mother's address. Several psychiatrists have judged him to be mentally incompetent. Despite that, the street diagnosis of Chin's psychosis pegs it as pure fresh bullshit.

"It's all an act," Gregory said.

"It's a great act," I said. "I'm sold."

"Albie Meyers says all the big informants including Sammy the Bull say it's all a scam to avoid the courts. Hey, if not Chin, then somebody over there is running the show. That's for shit sure. If not Chin, somebody close to him."

If it was an act, it was the most untypical role ever taken in the macho-conscious culture of the Mafia. It would make him the first godfather to portray himself as a babbling idiot. A far cry from his dapper, made-for-TV predecessor.

"Let's talk to Chin, pally."

"You're crazier than he is. What makes you think he's going to talk to us?"

"You got a better idea?" he said.

Whatever was going on, it was working for the Genovese family. They were the only New York crime family that hadn't been decimated by the successful prosecutions of the past few years. They'd survived by going underground. Members of the family never talk on the phone and are rarely seen together anymore. When they are spotted, they are poorly dressed, riding in old junk heaps, if any car at all. They learned from the excesses of Gotti. Even the famous Mafia kiss was now forbidden.

"We can't just go there hat in hand," I said. "The Mafia is a quid pro quo organization. The first thing they're going to say is, What did you bring me?"

"So we bring something."

"Like what, Italian pastries from your friend in Bay Ridge? What could we possibly offer that would make them give up Vincent Lutz?"

"It's not going to be that tough, pally. I'm telling you, Chin don't like all the hassle this is causing him. Inspector O'Prey is all over the families. He's locking up little old men playing euchre in the social clubs, for chrissakes. He's hassling the numbers guys, the bookmakers. The sooner we get Lutz, the sooner O'Prey stops breaking their balls. Chin's whole game is a low-key game, and the Lutz crew has become too high profile."

We passed under the Verranzano Bridge, the Sixty-sixth bridge in New York City history and the one that Joe Gregory hated. Joe Gregory joined the navy in 1956. Construction of the bridge began in 1959 and displaced eight thousand of Gregory's Bay Ridge friends and neighbors. This occurred only two years after the Dodgers left Brooklyn for the West Coast. When Gregory came home from the service his whole world had changed. He blamed it all on the bridge west.

"The Rocky tape," I said, reaching into my canvas briefcase. "We give Chin the tape of Rocky Lutz."

I dug around, pulling out old reports and crime scene photos, until I found the tape—the one where the late Rocky Lutz describes how he zapped his wife, the former Brenda Corrazzo, in the ass with fifty thousand volts.

"Why is that a primo offering?" Gregory said.

"Because it shows that Rocky Lutz was an asshole, and it takes Sally the Goat off the Chin's back. Sally the Goat has been screaming for vengeance. He's not going to want to avenge the guy who assaulted his daughter."

"Sounds like an idea, pally."

Gregory reached into his inside suit jacket pocket and handed me his address book. The leather cover looked as though it had been made from the sandals of wandering Ti-

betan monks. Cocktail napkins, business cards, pages ripped
from telephone books, and bar coasters with barely legible
phone numbers were jammed between the curling pages. It
was all held together by a thick rubber band.

"You ever meet Chin?" Gregory said.

"No."

"Me neither. You know anybody in his operation?"

"Nobody that's currently breathing."

"Who owes us?" Gregory said.

"Everybody owes us."

"Start looking through my book for somebody who can
make the connection we speak of. We need an entrée, an ice-
breaker, somebody to handle the intros."

"Let's go to Brady's and work on this."

"Absolutely," he said.

The Gowanus Expressway approaching the Brooklyn Battery Tunnel rides above decrepit old factories and tenements.
Although Queens is considered the borough F. Scott Fitzger-
ald actually had in mind, this area always reminded me of "the
valley of ashes" in *The Great Gatsby*. I began putting everything back into my briefcase: stray pieces of paper and ME
photos.

"You still don't look at the pictures of the victims' faces, do
you?" Gregory said.

"Not really."

"I didn't think so."

"Why do you ask?"

"I was just trying to figure out what I did to deserve such
a weird guy for a partner."

At Red Hook the road swings northwest and brings into
view the carnival of skyscrapers jammed onto the tip of that
little island of glass, glitter, and promise. At that moment I felt
as I did thirty years earlier, when I was a young cop in mid-
town Manhattan with a brand-new badge in my pocket. Here

I was, at middle age, with the best friend I ever had in my life, and we were going for a drink in a bar I loved, in the greatest city in the world. And we were planning a caper. Who had it better than us?

26

It was late when I got home; the outside light was on. Leigh was in the living room, reading. I hung my coat in the closet, trying to do everything slowly and deliberately. The drinker's slow-motion shuffle.

"What happened?" she said, padding down the hallway, her eyes searching my face to see how drunk I was. "God, you smell like smoke."

"J.C. Counihan died."

"Oh, Anthony," she said, placing her hand on her chest. "Is there anything I can do?"

"Give Cookie a call, maybe. I don't know. A mass card, write her a note. I think she'd appreciate that."

I knew I used J.C.'s death to avoid any hassle over my drinking. It wasn't a lie, exactly. Although I hadn't really seen Cookie, I did know what had occurred at Vito's house. And all I did was direct Leigh's eyes to the day's headline: J.C.'S DEAD. My drinking was only small print on the back page. Cops become good at this; we are the spin doctors of the night. Our coded messages scrawled between the lines, our punctuation a wink and a nod. And we wonder why our marriages wind up in the toilet.

"Cookie's handling it pretty well," I said. "Everybody seems to think it's for the best. She's flying to Florida tomorrow."

"Is he being buried down there?"

"They're going to have a small service in Fort Lauderdale, then fly the body back to New York. J.C. wanted to have his funeral mass said in St. Camillus in his old neighborhood in Rockaway."

"What about flowers?"

"Cookie said no flowers. St. Camillus is a poor parish now, and the family is suggesting contributions to the church in J.C.'s name to help a needy family through the holidays."

"That's a beautiful idea."

"They're nice people," I said.

Leigh was giving me the benefit of the doubt because of J.C.'s death. This night was not in my past just yet. The subject of my drinking would resurface later. Leigh says my friends and I make a distinction between alcoholics and drinkers and every one of us considered ourselves the latter.

"Did Gregory seem upset?" Leigh said.

"Yeah, actually he did."

"You sound surprised."

"Well, he hadn't heard from J.C. in a long time."

I went upstairs and put my gun onto the top shelf and changed into jeans, an old sweatshirt, and a twenty-year-old pair of Topsiders, ripping at the seam. I wore the old deck shoes around the house; I'd never worn slippers in my life. Or pajamas. Leigh says it's because those clothes are too relaxed for me. She says that even my house clothes are the kind I could wear to chase a burglar into the street.

I ate nuked fried chicken, standing at the sink. My voice was rough and gravelly from booze and inhaling bar smoke.

"Margaret called tonight," Leigh said.

"When are they coming?"

"They're not," she said. "They've decided to go to Florida for the holidays. She said they're going to stop in and see how your father's doing."

"Really?" I said. "They're driving all the way to Florida just to see my father?"

"Well, that, and Cliff is going to a surf board manufacturers' convention in Miami."

"I knew it. I knew it would be some self-serving shit like that."

"Anthony," she said, "Margaret was really upset. She said she hoped we understood. Cliff needed to go for his business."

"Yeah, his business is playing with surf bunnies."

"You can be so hard sometimes," she said. She stomped away from me, barefoot, across the hardwood floor.

I wasn't surprised they'd canceled; it wasn't the first time. Cliff was uncomfortable around me, mostly because I didn't fall for his laid-back surfer dude act. But what really hurt was that Leigh's Christmas party plans were falling apart by the minute. I followed her upstairs.

"I'm sorry, Leigh," I said. "I know you were counting on this Christmas party."

"Don't use me as an excuse to vent your anger at Cliff."

"The guy pisses me off, I admit that."

"Get over it," she said. "It's your family. At least give them the same consideration you'd give your cop drinking buddies."

I fell asleep the way I always fall asleep when I'm drinking—instantly. My eyes feel as though they're spinning, then they slam shut as if a curtain dropped. I snore for about fifteen minutes; I only snore when I'm drunk. Then I wake up and lie there for the rest of the night, trying to put the pieces together, sew the time frames in some order, replay my own drunken dialogue. Hoping I wasn't too much of an asshole.

Leigh was right: I could be too hard, especially on the people

I loved most. I try not to blame the job, but I see so many cops, their hearts poisoned by the constant diet of anger and deception. Happiness seems like wishful thinking. But that's another excuse.

I'd left Joe Gregory in Brady's without a solution. He was still mulling things over between rounds of Old Bushmills. I thought about how the death of J.C. Counihan had deeply affected him. How he seemed determined to avenge the death of J.C.'s only son. He wanted Vincent Lutz desperately. But we couldn't just walk up to Chin Gigante on Sullivan Street. No way he'd act like anything but a lunatic.

As soon as the phone rang, I knew it was my partner. I snatched it up halfway through the first ring. I could hear Sinatra in the background, "Nancy with the Laughing Face."

"One word," the Great Gregory said. "Pauline."

27

Pauline was a hostler. She loved horses but not men. I made a phone call to verify she was working the day tour, locked my desk, and met Gregory in the headquarters lobby. The morning crowd of clerks and desk cops streamed through the turnstiles. Eight cops scanned the IDs on the screens. Gregory was reading the plaques in memory of slain cops, of which there were far too many.

"Let's collect, pally," he said. "Miss Pauline is overdue."

One of the advantages of a long active career in police work is that you accumulated many debtors. No favor is a small favor to the wise detective; each good deed is an investment. Gregory and I were the First National Bank of the IOU. Everybody owed us at one time or another. Some investments paid off when we least expected it.

Pauline was a civilian employee of the NYPD, working in a two-hundred-year-old stable, Mounted Troop A, 19 Varick Street. Pauline also lived on Sullivan Street, over the Soho Trucking Company, one floor below the mother of Vincenzo "Chin" Gigante. More important, she owed us.

The day was bright and sunny as we parked behind an NYPD horse trailer on the west side of Varick. Mounted Troop A was directly behind the First Precinct. Drivers making the loop out of the Holland Tunnel drove downtown, blinking in the sudden brightness, as Gregory pushed open the big green wooden door. It was like entering a movie theater in the daytime. A pigeon waddled past us, apparently knowing where he was going. We hesitated at the door, to let our old eyes adjust.

We'd come across Pauline twenty years ago when her name surfaced in a lesbian love triangle murder in the East Village. She asked us to keep it quiet; she said she came from an old Italian family of cops, priests, and hoods. They wouldn't understand. And mostly, she didn't want to lose her job working with the horses.

"Pauline, you in here?" Gregory yelled, his voice echoing.

"Who wants to know?" a voice came from the back of the long, narrow warehouse of a room. As my eyes adjusted I could see a line of stalls on the right, barely wide enough to hold a good-size dog. Yellow metal poles stood at each side of the front of the stalls. The sides consisted of a variety of wooden boards, painted NYPD blue. Above the wood was a somewhat fancy touch, an arc of yellow metal grating, pencil-thin vertical bars. The smell was horseshit and wet hay.

"Pauline," Gregory yelled, squinting toward the rear of the high-ceilinged room. A heavy equine flank thumped against the old boards. The concrete floor was as cracked and uneven as a sidewalk in a Mexican back alley.

"Nobody here but us horses," the voice replied.

We walked toward the voice, stepping over a black hose dripping into a floor drain. I counted eighteen stalls, at least half of them filled with big brown horses, rumps higher than our heads.

The stalls didn't have gates. Only one low-slung chain, covered with rubber hosing, separated us from their hooves.

"Gregory and Ryan," the voice said. "This must be my lucky day." A woman stepped from a stall on the opposite side of the room. It was Pauline, heavier than I remembered and her hair almost white.

Gregory walked on until he was face-to-face with the horse Pauline had been working on. He looked surprised at what they looked like without jockeys. Above the horse was the name Finbar, after a cop Gregory knew well. Finbar was famous for his days in the Emerald Society pipe band.

"What are you guys doing here?" she said, her breath congealing in the cold room.

"Gregory wants to ride one of these horses around the block," I said.

"In his next life," she said.

"How come Finbar is over here?" Gregory said.

I wondered if Gregory, the president of the NYPD Emerald Society, felt some need to be an advocate for a horse named after one of his most famous constituents. Bedding hay clung to Finbar's hooves.

"That's our medical stall," she said.

"What's Finbar's problem?" Gregory said.

"What's your problem?" she said.

"Hoof and mouth disease," he said.

"His is sleep deprivation. Some of them, especially the ones we get from racetracks, won't lie down in the narrow stalls. They try to sleep standing up, and they can only get away with it for so long. Then, like this big lug, they start nodding, until they just collapse. They get all scratched up."

"I've done that many times," Gregory said.

"But they're sober," she said.

Above us, a curled brown roll of flypaper hung from a fluorescent light. Balls of dust and pieces of straw clung to the light.

The flypaper was fully occupied. Gregory blew on his hands to keep them warm.

"C'mon, I've never been on a horse before," Gregory said.

"We can strap him on," I said.

"No kidding around," she said. "What are you doing here?"

"We came to visit you," Gregory said.

"Come on, assholes, cut it out. I'm around enough horseshit all day as it is."

"Why don't you turn the heat up in here?" Gregory said. "Looks to me like some of these horses froze their balls off already."

"No heat, no air-conditioning," she said. "The horses must stay in the natural environment, or they get sick."

Finbar's tail rose suddenly and Pauline pushed us back, under a loft of damp-looking hay bales. We followed Pauline past other horses named Radio City and Daily News, after the corporations who donated them. McDonald was named after a cop killed in the line of duty.

"Step into my office," she said as she led us into a tiny room lit slightly better than the stable. A cracked leather harness lay across the arm of a greasy club chair, padding peeking from rips in the fabric. Saddles hung from the walls.

"Let's get down to business," she said. "Tell me what you want."

I could see a web of small lines around her eyes, but the white hair softened her look. Her complexion was red and fresh from working outside and in the cool, airy stable.

"You still live in the same building?" I said.

"I knew it," she said. "I know what this shit is all about. And the answer is no."

"We need a big favor," I said.

"Listen, I owe you guys big. But not that big. You think you're the first cops to come around asking me to do something? You're not, by a long shot. I have a rule: I don't get involved with those people for nobody. Period. End of story."

"You are involved," I said. "Your mother is always with his mother. You talk to them all the time."

"Yeah. Hello, how are ya. Nice day, blah, blah, blah. I don't talk about their business. Besides, the guy is a walking vegetable."

"It's an act," Gregory said.

"Well, if it is, he deserves the Academy Award."

"All you have to do is deliver a package from us. Nothing more."

"Oh, just a package. That's all. Just a package. People go to jail for the rest of their lives for just delivering packages."

The package contained the tape of Rocky Lutz telling his bookmaker how he zapped Sally the Goat's daughter, Brenda, with a stun gun. With it was a polite note addressed "To Whom It May Concern," stating that we'd appreciate being put in contact with Mr. Vincent Lutz. We left a phone number: the chief of detective's red emergency phone.

"They're not going to do anything to hurt you," I said.

"I'm not worried about them. I'm worried about you."

"What's the big deal, it's a package."

Behind Pauline was one more small room, about five feet deep. An anvil sat in the center of the room. Spot-welded to it was a horseshoe with four steel lumps, like cleats.

Pauline said, "How do you know they won't just tell me to fuck off and throw your package in the garbage?"

"Because you'll tell them what great guys we are," I said.

"In a pig's ass I will."

"You owe us, Pauline," Gregory said.

"Fucking extortion artists."

"Here, take the package," Gregory said.

She put her hands up in the air, refusing even to touch the paper. "Go ahead, tell everybody I'm a lesbian. Go ahead. Hey, everybody knows about me now anyway, so what's the difference. They accepted me years ago."

"You weren't so tough twenty years ago," Gregory said. "Crying like a baby. 'Don't tell my mother.' And we were there when you needed us, weren't we?"

We heard the echo of footsteps and stopped talking. In the dim light I could see the yellow cavalry stripe down the side of a mounted cop's blue uniform pants. They were the only cops allowed to wear that historically significant stripe. I watched the stripe rise and turn as the cop climbed the black metal circular stairs to the locker rooms above.

"Come on, Pauline," I said. "It's the first favor we've asked for in twenty years."

Gregory and I stood there looking down at her. We knew it was a matter of time. That's the way it is with nice people: in their hearts they want to help you. So you wait until your persistence tramples their common sense.

"Give me the damn package," she said, snatching it out of Gregory's hands. "I'm tired of your whining."

28

We left Pauline and went back to the office to wait for Chin's people to call our people. Albie Meyers tap-tapped on his calculator, scrutinizing his paycheck. Albie was a guy who knew exactly how and when the city screwed him out of three cents. I ran the chief's red phone line out to my desk and hooked a suction cup to the earpiece. The smell of French onion soup wafted from Albie's desk as I signed out a brand-new tape recorder, new batteries, and a new package of tapes. I asked him to call me from another phone to test the red line. It had to be right. The Mob doesn't do retakes.

We had time to kill. According to OC Intelligence, every wise guy within a mile of Mulberry Street was out looking for the baby Jesus. The infant was a valuable antique stolen from the crèche in Our Lady of Most Precious Blood. Old ladies in black were wailing in protest in front of Little Italy's social clubs. Jesus was top priority. No other business was likely to be handled until he was recovered—and the thief crucified.

Three booking photos of various Mickey O'Briens were

spread out on my desk. None of them were even close to Mickey the hansom cab driver. I'd told Gregory I was just being thorough, but in truth Mickey's brogue sounded more phony every time I heard it. I know that sounds paranoid, but he just seemed too oily for me, although my wife says I put entirely too many people into the oily category.

Gregory had his feet up on my desk, reading *SPring 3100*, the NYPD magazine. The cop bimonthly is named after an old headquarters telephone exchange, from the days when phone exchanges had personality, like MUrray Hill two, or BUtterfield eight. SPring 3100 was an ancestor of 911. Gregory turned right to the back inside cover of the magazine, the obituary page, or, as Gregory calls it, "the Irish social page."

"Guess J.C.'s name will be in here next time," he said. We knew more names on the back page than in all the weddings and new babies reported from the uniform commands.

"How do they find out those guys are dead, anyway?"

"From the pension section, pally. They find out right away, so they can stop the checks. J.C.'s pension stopped the moment he croaked. Cookie won't get another dime from the city."

"That's our kind and liberal city," I said. "Too bad he wasn't on welfare instead."

The obit page listed active members first, usually five or six names, then three columns, well over a hundred recently deceased retirees. Their last listed commands were long forgotten or housed in buildings that had since met the wrecking ball.

"Say we do grab Vincent Lutz," Gregory said. "What's our leverage?"

"The gun found at the scene is traceable to him. His brother Rocky's prints are on it."

"Say he denies everything and lawyers up?"

"This kid has been in hiding since the bar blew up. He knows the Colombo family is looking for him. Plus, he never did time.

I don't foresee a problem. But if that doesn't work, we'll dig out your old rubber hoses."

"What about the monkey?" he said.

"What monkey?"

"I never told you that story?"

Taped to the file cabinet, behind Gregory's head, was a large handwritten note outlined in black Magic Marker. We'd been ignoring it for weeks. The heading said "Personnel who have failed to attend the indoor shooting cycle." Five names were listed, and Gregory and I were among them.

"This is a great J.C. Counihan story," Gregory said. "He's working in the Two Eight this one night. And this black guy comes in and he's drunk and got a monkey on his shoulder."

"A real monkey?" I said.

"Of course a real monkey. Well, the black guy starts bitching about something, gets rowdy, and push comes to shove. A fight breaks out. They throw the black guy out into the street. But the monkey is lost in the scuffle, no one knows where.

"A couple of days later, some cop is at his desk eating a hero sandwich. The freaking monkey comes flying out of nowhere, snatches the sandwich out of the cop's hands, swings up to the pipes, and sits there nibbling, holding the sandwich in his little monkey hands. This goes on and on, night after night. The monkey keeps grabbing food and disappearing into the bowels of the house.

"But then J.C. figures out a use for him. They start feeding the monkey. They get a bell and ring it whenever they have food. But they put the food inside the prisoner's cage so he won't make a mess. Ring the bell, monkey comes flying, goes right into the cage.

"Pavlovian confession, J.C. calls it. Whenever they get a prisoner who's a real hard-on, they'd hide some food in the cage, throw the prisoner in, and lock the door. Then they'd ring the bell. The monkey comes screeching like a maniac, spitting and clinging to the cage, screaming and clawing to get in. Bingo, instant confession."

It was almost three P.M. when the red phone finally rang. A gruff voice spoke quickly. The instructions were specific. I could hear street traffic behind him and what sounded like Jimmy Roselli singing "Little Pal," the wise guy national anthem. We had to play the tape back several times to make sure we had it right.

When we told O'Prey we'd found Vincent Lutz his face lit up like the tree at Rockefeller Center. Green eyes danced, cheeks blushed crimson. He invited us into his office, closed the door, arranged our chairs around his desk, and listened.

"Kudos, gentlemen," O'Prey said when the tape ended. "Kudos."

He went right to work, a carrot-topped whirling dervish. I had to admit he was a great organizer. He even invited us along this time. The gruff voice had told us to be outside the Travelodge hotel at JFK Airport tomorrow, at nine A.M. O'Prey set our meet for dawn.

When I got home Leigh was making lasagna from my mother's old recipe. Under her apron she wore the black silk blouse that I'd bought on her last birthday. She always seemed to look her best when she was mad at me.

"I'm sorry about last night," I said.

"It's okay."

"No, I mean it. I shouldn't be drinking like that. You'd think I'd learn."

"You would think that, wouldn't you," she said.

Leigh says she doesn't believe that most cops' wives worry about them while they're doing their job. She used to say that as soon as I backed out of the driveway she forgot about my profession. The problem, she believes, is "the job" itself—the fraternity, the closed circle of guys with drinks in their hands telling war stories until the sun comes up. Cops who get off at midnight are too jazzed to go home to a quiet house and a sleepy wife. At two A.M. cop bars are packed with armed men telling weird stories that are lost on those outside the brotherhood. Leigh says that if the phone rang in the middle of the night during my younger, dumber years, her first thought would have been that I'd been killed in a car accident.

"I'll try to do better," I said.

"I know you will, Anthony. I know that. I just hope we all stay lucky."

That night Leigh fell asleep as we watched TV in our bedroom. She was curled up in her nightgown on my side of the bed. I put on my jeans and sweatshirt, then went back down to the kitchen and put a bottle of beer in the freezer to cool it down quickly. It was a Brooklyn lager from a case Gregory wanted me to try. He bought anything that had "Brooklyn" written on it.

At the kitchen table I began making a list of questions to ask Vincent Lutz, the most dramatic of which was to ask him his relationship with Johnny Boy Counihan and how he got Rocky's pager number. I knew the answers would devastate Joe Gregory.

I wrote for about twenty minutes, then took the beer out of the freezer. My father would have been horrified to see me put beer in the freezer. Forty-five degrees is perfect; you ruin it otherwise, he would say. He kept his beer in the vegetable bin in his refrigerator, so it wouldn't get too cold. I wondered if the hot Florida weather had changed his drinking habits.

The beer had already gotten a little slushy on top. The slush felt cool and soothing on my dry throat. It had been a day in which I'd talked too much.

When I finally went to bed Leigh was naked. I squeezed in behind her and put my knees in the crook of hers. As Leigh got older she'd become more adventurous, more spontaneous. New scents, hairstyles. She'd added another hole to her earlobes, wearing three earrings now.

"You figure it out?" she said sleepily.

"Figure what out?"

"Whoever your man is. You always get your man, Ryan."

"And my woman, too," I said.

"Not when she's sleepy, you don't," she said. "You took too long downstairs. Just lie close to me, Anthony. Hold me."

I squeezed closer and put my hand under her breasts, between that plushness and the solidity of her rib cage. It was a touch that never seemed the same twice. One I couldn't bear to lose.

29

The morning sun over Brooklyn reflected pink in the charcoal gray clouds, like the colors I wore to my high school prom. Gregory and I were heading for JFK Airport, on the Belt Parkway approaching the "goddamn" Verrazano-Narrows Bridge. Just past Owl's Head Park an oil tanker rode high in the waters of lower New York Bay. A handful of early joggers and bikers leaned into the wind as a wave crashed against the seawall and splashed onto the footpath.

"What a piece of crap this car is," Gregory said. "The front end goes into convulsions soon as you hit forty. I can guess who handled the auto requisitions."

O'Prey had arranged a small fleet of undercover vehicles from the Motor Transport Division on a one-day loaner basis. He'd assigned us a yellow cab from Street Crime. But Street Crime's cars always took a merciless beating. The seats were patched with duct tape, and the car clearly had an exhaust problem. I kept my face turned to the cold air blowing through the half-open window, trying to breathe in as little carbon monoxide as possible.

"We taking Vincent Lutz to the One Thirteen Precinct?" Gregory asked.

"No, the bat cave. O'Prey's idea."

"At least that's good thinking."

The "bat cave" was an underground garage in Queens where the NYPD stored its surveillance vehicles and electronic eavesdropping equipment. Few cops know about it. And only on extremely rare occasions is anyone brought there, usually to escape the Mob or press scrutiny. In Vincent's case both reasons were good. What we do is blindfold them until safe in the subterranean office.

"You think you're going to get enough time to ask all those questions?" Gregory said. I was still writing them down, as they came to me.

"I'm optimistic."

"My money says this kid got strict orders to clam up. That's the only reason they're giving him up. He got the word, and it ain't Thunderbird."

He was right. After I'd thought about it, I didn't quite understand why the Mob had given Vincent up, either. Although he was just a fringe player, sometimes they're the ones who fool you. There was no way for them to be sure how much he really knew.

"Maybe he really doesn't know anything," I said. "Everyone says he's in desperate need of an IQ enhancement."

"If J.C. Counihan was here, Vinny Lutz would be singing the blues before lunchtime. He used to have this one act that was a classic."

I wasn't sure I could take another J.C. story. Gregory had been inundating me with J.C. Counihan stories all morning, as if J.C. had been a hundred cops rolled into one.

"When J.C. worked in the Four Eight Precinct," Gregory said, "that was a crazy freaking squad. They did this thing; you know when you come across a skell you know is guilty, but he just won't admit it? Well, J.C. would go in and put on this judge's robe he kept in his locker. Then they'd have about a five-minute trial. J.C. would slam down the gavel, 'guilty as charged.' Then they'd throw a rope over the water pipes, and get ready to hang the prick. That's when the truth spilled out."

"And people don't trust cops," I said. "Can you believe it?"

"Hey, you know what I mean, pally. You work in those busy houses . . . if you can't have a couple of giggles, you go nuts. Wind up hanging yourself. What, we got nine cop suicides so far this year? This is the only job I know of where a guy has a minor traffic accident and steps out of the car and blows his brains out. Not me, no way, baby. I'm going to laugh at a lot of politically incorrect shit before I eat my gun."

For a guy who tended to put himself in unnecessary danger, Joe Gregory had a spooky attitude toward death. When Joe's father died he told me that now he had stepped up to the front lines. It was like soldiers going to war, he said, our grandparents' line, then our parents', then us. When you're in front, you've got to fall.

I said, "When I die are you going to tell all these great war stories about me?"

"You wish you had some war stories," he said.

The floor of the cab was sticky, as if something were spilled, a Coke or beer, maybe blood. I wondered how much contraband had been shoved down behind the backseat. Usually the little things that are missed in the quick pat-down on the street disappear on the way to the station house. How many razor blades spit out from under a tongue? How many drug-filled condoms yanked from an orifice? It's amazing what some people can do while handcuffed behind their back. No sane cop reaches behind the seats anymore. In our minds we can see a filthy hypodermic needle, wedged out of sight, a death sentence on its tip.

"I don't get this taxi bit," Gregory said. "Two white guys, look like us, sitting in the front seat of a taxi. Who are we supposed to be fooling?"

"They should just issue us monkeys, robes, and ropes," I said.

"Gimme a freaking break," he said.

The instruction we'd received from Mulberry Street predicted that Vincent Lutz would come walking out of the airport Travelodge at exactly nine A.M. That's what they said: exactly. They said he'd be walking to a car, which was not his usual car. And he was heavily armed.

We knew we couldn't take Vincent in a crowded hotel lobby, but the outside area was ideal. Just a wide-open service road, no pedestrians, no other buildings. O'Prey's plan was to block off the service road the instant he started his car. We'd let him drive away from the hotel parking lot, then we'd take him on the deserted service road. The radio code word was "Rambo." That word alone was indicative of the average age and personality of the cops we were working with.

Gregory and I were not assigned to the parking lot, because Vincent might recognize us. We were assigned to help block off the service road and stationed in the bushes across the street. Just before Federal Circle we turned off and drove past the rental car return. Gregory jumped the curb as the old car shook and rattled. It sounded as though the bumper fell off.

We drove across the frozen lawn and pulled the car behind two huge fir trees. We were at least a quarter mile from the hotel. In front of us was a pyramid of Christmas lights strung to a point on three leaning poles. I pulled the binoculars from the seat between us.

The Travelodge hotel appeared to be under renovation. An unmanned scaffolding stretched across the upper floors. Workmen had been either painting or resealing around the window frames. The front entrance was covered by a concrete canopy. A Carey Transportation bus was parked under the canopy. We couldn't even see the entrance, but he certainly couldn't see us, either, as we were swallowed up between the two overgrown pines. The trees were damp and fragrant and smelled richly of clear mountain air.

"Nice place for a picnic," I said.

"Now that you mention it," he said, reaching into his brief-case. "On the way in I stopped at Sarge's on Third Avenue. Picked us up a little Jewish feast."

"Pastrami," I said. "For breakfast?"

"Breakfast of champions."

I'd thought I could smell pastrami earlier, but I'd assumed it was left over from the previous occupants.

"Thick as your fist, these sandwiches, pally. That great mustard. I love that mustard. I scoffed some extra pickles, those great sour pickles. A couple of bottles of Dr. Brown's Cel-Ray sodas. It's like the old days. J.C. Counihan loved these sandwiches."

"The tailman's picnic."

"And they pay us for this job," he said. "Can you believe it? What a job, right?"

"Speaking of picnics," I said. "Do they still hold the steakout at the outdoor range?"

"It's become a big event, pally. They moved it to the Marina del Rey. I'll get us tickets this year."

The steakout started as a little cookout, a get-together of investigators, an informal bonding picnic for NYPD and the feds. The joke was that you could tell your wife you were going on a "stakeout." Certainly no cop's wife ever bought it. Gregory said the steakout had become a big affair; they sold tickets, drew five or six hundred. Rarely in New York did a week go by without a big cop party somewhere. Some old-timers hit every one, because except for a few thieves and rats, we were all lifetime members of the club.

"A lot of women attend now," he said. "Feds and cops, it's a nice affair. J.C. would have loved it, he was a true ladies' man. Broads used to fall all over that bastard. God rest his soul."

"I didn't know that."

Here we go again, I thought. I stepped right into this story. It seemed as if he'd just realized his first partner was dead.

"I heard this one story," he said. "About when J.C. was picked up off a foot post to guard this DOA. No biggie, just this well-to-do male junkie that croaked sitting right at his kitchen table. Like he nodded off with the needle still in his arm. Somebody had to wait for the ME to arrive; you know how long that can take. So the boss comes and gets him, but J.C. has lunch plans with this policewoman he's looking to boff. The story goes that the boss comes back to check on J.C. He smells something cooking. He walks in and finds J.C. and the policewoman broiling a couple of steaks. J.C. says no sense letting all that food go to waste. The three of them are sitting there at the table, the wine is open, candles lit, the whole nine yards. J.C., the policewoman, and the DOA."

I put down the pastrami sandwich; I could hardly get my mouth around it. I'd been leery of these big sandwiches since our old boss, Lieutenant Eddie Shick, had his jaw lock up trying to get his mouth around a Sarge's Deli sandwich. Albie Meyers had to walk him over to Beekman Hospital with his mouth gapped wide open.

Gregory picked up the binoculars and reported that the Carey bus had moved from the front of the hotel. A group of Oriental men and women were clustered under the canopy, sticking close to their luggage.

"Was J.C. still a ladies' man," I said, "after he married Cookie?"

"No way, pally. Cookie wouldn't stand for that shit. I can tell you that much."

"How did he meet Cookie?"

"I introduced them. I knew her long before J.C. did. They only went out about a month or so, then flew to Reno. Shocked the shit out of me. He didn't even tell me he was going."

The radio started to crackle, I could hear the voice of Declan

O'Prey. The transmission was mostly static, but I could make out the brogue. It sounded like Radio Free Dublin.

"You forgot napkins," I said.

"Cops don't use napkins. On your toes. Here comes Vincent."

Gregory handed me the binoculars. I shoved the remains of the pastrami under the seat. I could see Vincent Lutz, a shoulder-wagging strut, moving across the parking lot. He was moving fast, as if someone told him he was hot, red hot. Maybe that was how the Mob got him out, a well-timed phone call. Vincent started to jog. Then he cut between two parked cars, and I lost him. The door of a dark car opened and closed quickly. I focused the binoculars on that car and buckled my seat belt with one hand, listening for the word "Rambo" to come over the air.

"Naw," Gregory said. "J.C. Counihan was a different guy when he got married. Stopped being fun. I tried to get him out bouncing with me, but he wouldn't. Straight home. Then Cookie got pregnant. J.C. transferred out, looking for a straight day assignment."

It sounded like a pop at first, then a deeper, more rumbling boom. A ball of red-orange flame rose silently into the sky above Vincent's car, and glass and metal flew through the air.

Gregory floored the accelerator, and the back wheels spun and smoked. We slid sideways on wet pine needles, then drove straight ahead, blasting through the trees, branches scraping across the windshield like the brushes in an automatic car wash. We fishtailed across the frozen field, barely missing the pyramid of lights.

The black smoke began to clear. A dozen cops ran around the car as if their legs were stuck in quicksand, the scene still playing in slow motion. O'Prey yelled into the radio. Someone else screamed, "Watch the gas tank!" I could smell burning rubber.

The driver's door had been blown off. Vincent's blackened

body hung half in, half out. The hood of the car stood upright, hanging on an angle, waving in the air like a flag of surrender. I wondered how long it would take Emil Lutz to blame me for the death of a second son.

30

Two hours later it was still midmorning, and Brady's Bar retained a peaceful homeyness. The Christmas tree was lit. Pots and pans clattered in the kitchen. Brady himself, pale from his annual vacation at the dry-out farm, nailed pictures to the wall. A busboy swept under the antique church pews. Chalk screeched across the blackboard as the new waitress filled in the lunch specials. But I wasn't hungry. I could still taste the pastrami I had for breakfast and smell the flesh of Vincent Lutz.

"No baked Lutz on the menu," Gregory said. "I figured the special would be baked Lutz, or Cajun-blackened Lutz, maybe barbecued Lutz."

"Enough already," I said.

Brady gets his waitresses from NYU or the arts community around SoHo. Slender young women, with long straight hair and baggy clothes. Nice young women, who surely hid what they thought of Brady's principal clientele. I wonder what she thought about us, New York's Finest, having a drink before noon. One quick pop, Gregory had said. We were on our second in the back booth, still in our overcoats, a dull light coming through the window.

"O'Prey is going to arrest Vincent Lutz posthumously," I said.

"Hey, it won't be the first time somebody snapped the cuffs around a dead wrist," Gregory said. "Just as long as I don't have to print the crispy critter."

"He's going to close the case pending further information."

"No way, pally. The powers that be aren't going to let him do that until *all* the money's found."

"They don't need a homicide team for that."

The clock seemed to be moving too quickly; I needed to do something before Leigh left work. I didn't want her going home alone. Emil Lutz was a loose cannon, and I didn't want to take a chance. I glared at a retired sergeant who was tying up the phone, getting the spread on tonight's entire college basketball schedule. I tapped my phone card on the table.

"Leigh got anyone she can stay with for a couple of days?" Gregory said.

"Yeah, but she'd never do that."

"I'm telling you," Gregory said. "Say something to O'Prey. He'll do the right thing. He's got the personnel to sit on your house."

Gregory seemed to be lighter since the death of Vincent Lutz. Perhaps he figured the story of Johnny Boy's criminal involvement died with the Lutz boys.

"Tell me honestly, Joe. Am I overreacting? Am I going to frighten Leigh more than protect her?"

"It's your call, pally. If it worries you, it worries you. Err on the side of caution. What's the worst can happen if you ask someone to sit on your house . . . you look a little silly, that's all. Nothing wrong with that."

It wasn't the first time in my career I worried about some psycho taking it out on my family. But Emil Lutz was different. Murder meant nothing to Emil, and now he had nothing to lose.

The underworld clique he'd courted for so long had sent him the strongest of rejections. Maybe he'd decided to go out guns blazing, show those guinea bastards what tough was all about.

"I'm going to ask my son to come home now," I said. "He's coming home for Christmas. Maybe I can get him in a few days earlier."

"Suit yourself," Gregory said. "But maybe until he gets here, you gotta learn to let other people help you."

"O'Prey is just going to assign some empty suit to my house. Or request somebody from the Yonkers PD, some guy who doesn't even know me."

"Why don't you take off a couple of days? You got the time coming to you."

"Would you do that?" I asked. "Would you sit at home?"

"No, but I'm a solo act."

The jukebox was silent. Three or four day-trippers were at the bar, their voices clear and loud in the empty gin mill. The day-trippers were elderly neighborhood guys who manned their stools as soon as the doors opened and nursed short beers until the lunch crowd arrived. Then they stumbled home for a nap but were back at three to do it again, at least until the dinner crowd came through the door. Same guys every day, all unshaven, wearing moth-eaten cardigan sweaters and arguing their tired cases over and over while smoke floated in a beam of sunlight above them.

"We're not closing the homicide," I said.

"Absolutely not, pally. No way do we close this."

When the phone finally became free I took out my address book and dialed my son's number. Three hours' difference. It would be seven forty-five A.M. out there. My son picked it up on the second ring but was out of breath.

"I was out running, Dad," he said. I was always surprised by his voice, how much he sounded like me. "I did five miles."

I wondered if that were true. I always felt lost with our kids, not sure if I was being fed the story they thought I wanted to hear. I asked him when he was coming home. There was a long pause.

"I can't make it," he said.

"When were you going to tell us?"

"Tonight, but I should have called earlier, I know."

I felt the fist inside me begin to tighten. "Your mom is going to be disappointed."

"That's not the half of it," he said.

"What *is* the half of it?" I said, and the little fist squeezed. A cop hears volumes of bad news in his life. You learn to suck up your feelings, but there's a price to pay.

"Mom's not going to like it," he said. "I don't think she appreciates the irony."

"Just tell me, Anthony. I'm sure whatever it is, we can deal with it."

"I'm going on the Phoenix Police Department," he said.

"Phoenix, Arizona?" I said.

"I figured you'd find out through the grapevine. They did an extensive background check."

"I didn't hear a thing. When do you start?"

"Monday," he said. "It happened quick. I was supposed to be in the next class, the June class. But an opening came up, some guy turned it down at the last minute. Maybe I should have done the same thing."

"No, you did the right thing. If that's what you want to do."

"Weird, isn't it?" he said. "I never thought, in a million years."

I wished him good luck, asked him to call on Christmas Day, then hung up. Johnny Brady resumed working with a small hammer. He'd stopped banging when I was on the phone and idly picked his fingernails with a picture hook. His hands, though still scaly and blotchy red, weren't shaking quite as bad as last Christmas.

"I got the solution to your problem," Brady said. "Pick Emil

Lutz up as a material witness. We used to hold guys for weeks like that."

New York black-and-white photographs filled Brady's walls. In the corner near the fireplace hung a new one, a photo of Pope John Paul II riding down Broadway in the rain. The pontiff, standing with his upper body above the sunroof of a stretch Lincoln, waved to the crowd. An aide, behind him, held an umbrella over his head. The other picture was also in the rain. Young Phil Rizzuto, alone on the wet grass of Yankee Stadium. World Series banners hung limp along the rails as the Scooter peeked skyward from under an umbrella, as if imploring the rain to stop.

"This your umbrella collection?" I said.

"I didn't even notice," he said. "Everything is connected, ain't it, Ryan? That's why you're the best, you see all the connections. Just think about what I said, though, okay? Material witness. It's a legit move."

Brady once told me that he wouldn't have a drinking problem if it wasn't for guys like me and Gregory. Brady says that when you own a bar your friends are always offering to buy you a drink. You can't refuse your friends; they're too easily offended. But they forget you're in there seven days a week, night and day. In the world according to Brady, it's your friends who kill you in the end.

"Maybe we should contact Chin again," Gregory said as I sat back down. "He's got a way of making troubles disappear."

When I told Gregory that my son was going on the Phoenix PD he buried his face in his hands to keep from laughing out loud.

"It's not that funny," I said.

"Yes, it is," he said. "Leigh is gonna love this news. Her baby becoming a cop."

"You want to come home with me tonight?"

"Not me," he said, pointing out the window. "Take him."

On the corner of Pearl and Madison Streets, a huge white Lincoln backed into a parking spot behind a Sabrett hot dog wagon, a spot reserved for Central Booking. Vito Martucci got out under the blue-and-white hot dog umbrella and started coming toward Brady's.

"How does he find out about these things?" I said. "Is there a CNN for Mob guys?"

I finished my drink and waved the waitress over. She wore thick wool socks, Birkenstock sandals.

"I'll have another," I said.

"Make it two," Gregory said.

"And a coffee with sambuca," Vito said as he slid into the booth. "You guys stink like you were burning fucking garbage."

"That's exactly what we were doing," Gregory said.

"I knew that was going to happen," Vito said. "The wise guys couldn't take a chance on Vinny turning rat on them."

Vito handed me a white envelope.

"What's this?" I said.

"One of those goddamn letters I told you about."

"Where did you find it?"

"The One Thirteen Precinct called me to pick up Johnny Boy's car. This letter was in the glove compartment. It's from that Irish broad."

"You read it?"

"You shitting me? That fucking backwards writing, I never saw writing like that."

"What backwards writing?" I said, and opened the envelope.

The waitress returned with our drinks. She smelled of patchouli oil, a fragrance I remembered from the sixties, the days I hung around the Columbia University demonstrations. Hippies used the strong-smelling oil in lieu of bathing. It smelled like lumber, wet cedar.

"Hey, Vito," Gregory said, "how did you find out about Vincent blowing up?"

"How many times I got to tell you?" he said. "Contacts make the world go round. I got contacts up the yin-yang."

"Maybe your contacts know Chin Gigante?" Gregory said.

"Is Chin dead?" Vito said. "I ain't talking about *him* until he's dead."

The early lunch crowd, the crew from Missing Persons, came through the door. Shanahan went right to the jukebox and played Sinatra in Joe Gregory's honor.

"You thinking about a meet with Chin?" Vito said. "I'll give you this advice: Never turn your back on a seventy-year-old man with a nickname."

I started reading the letter, then I thought about something Gregory had said. I was sure he'd said it to be funny, but the more I thought about it, the more sense it made.

"I need your help, Vito," I said.

"Anything, amigo," he said. "Whatever I can do, I'll be honored to do."

"I need you to come home with me," I said.

31

My wife is a pushover for a sob story, especially one involving family. I called her from Brady's and laid it on thick about this nice old man who'd lost so much, alone in his big house. It was just for a few days, I said, until Cookie got back. Leigh said Vito could stay as long as he wanted.

And it was a good thing I did call, because Vito's Lincoln was in my driveway when I got home. He must have flown out to Great Neck to pick up his things. As I hung up my coat I could hear them talking in the kitchen. Dean Martin sang "That's Amore" in the background.

"Vito's teaching me how to make his special spaghetti sauce," Leigh said.

"Gravy," Vito said. "It's gravy. Your wife is so American, but so beautiful. I don't know what she sees in an ugly mug like you."

Vito wore one of Leigh's silly Christmas aprons over a red V-neck sweater. Around his neck, a tiny gold revolver hung on a tight chain. As he spoke, he waved a wooden spoon like a symphony conductor. Leigh's eyes followed the spoon and the red sauce dripping from it. I knew exactly what clash number one would be.

"Vito brought wine," Leigh said. "It's wonderful. Where is that wine, Vito?"

Leigh had the spoon in the sink before Vito knew it was gone. Vito draped a little white towel over his arm and began to pour. A stack of tapes filled the top of the refrigerator: Dino, Jerry Vale, Jimmy Roselli, and of course Sinatra. Vito, his back to Leigh as he poured wine, looked up at me and winked. Leigh winked at me from behind him. It was a cop's dream: living in two separate conspiracies.

"What kind of mushrooms are these?" Leigh said.

"These mushrooms," he said, recorking the bottle, "are special mushrooms."

I'd begun to wonder if I was out of my mind to set up a thing like this. Bringing an eighty-one-year-old man into my house to protect the woman I loved. Especially a guy who probably slept with a picture of Carlo Gambino under his pillow. Although I had to admit the wine was excellent.

"These mushrooms can only be picked two weeks a year," he said. "In June. You have to get them during those two weeks in June, or forget about it."

"Do the supermarkets carry them?"

"What supermarkets? I dig these myself, then I can store them for the rest of the year. Don't worry, *cara mia*, I'll get you some."

"Where do you get them?" she said.

"Flushing Meadow Park in Queens."

"The park?" I said.

"In June, the perfect climate," he said. "Let me tell you a story about these mushrooms."

"These are mushrooms with a story," I said.

"Everything worthwhile has a story, amigo. I always picked these mushrooms with my grandson, Johnny Boy. At night, so no one sees us and asks questions."

"Sounds a little dangerous," I said. "Flushing Meadow Park at night."

"Exactly what my son-in-law said. J.C. insisted on picking us up in the patrol car. He drove us right into the park and the three of us dug mushrooms like crazy. Two-and-a-half bushel baskets."

Vito stopped to refill Leigh's wineglass. The house smelled of garlic and oregano. My wife grew up in North Carolina and had no idea what nationality she was. She watched Vito with fascination.

"We loaded the mushrooms into the front seat," Vito said. "Because me and Johnny Boy are crouching down in the backseat. Remember, we're in a marked car. It's a warm night and J.C. is worried about somebody seeing us. So he decides to drive without headlights. We're going slow, everything is fine. Then a signal ten thirteen comes over the radio, cop in trouble, front of Shea Stadium. Two blocks away. J.C. hits the gas . . . ten seconds later . . . wham, bam. He hits another police car, TPF."

I saw Leigh's face, this look of horror.

"Nobody was hurt, thank God," Vito said. "But mushrooms were all over the car, all over J.C., my grandson, myself. J.C. had to do some fast talking that night."

Vito put on a Pavarotti tape and told a story about how he once saw Pavarotti sing for free on the steps of St. Patrick's Cathedral. He rolled the name beautifully off his tongue . . . Pava-rrr-Oh-tee.

I slipped away from the table, not that they'd notice. Vito was dictating ingredients as Leigh wrote on a recipe card. Leigh and I hadn't had a chance to discuss our son and the Phoenix PD. But she and Vito were working so hard to entertain each other, it seemed a shame to interrupt. Besides, things tended to look less serious the longer you let them cool.

In the living room, I took out the letter from Fiona. It was a letter I'd read several times already, and it bothered me more each time. Vito was right about the penmanship; it was remarkable.

The paper was clearly writing paper, but it was lined horizontally and vertically, creating small boxes, like graph paper. The writing followed the lines perfectly, so incredibly precise that it looked as though it had been done by machine. Her letters were printed, but with a style that appeared to be painstaking. In contrast, her name was signed with a swooping flourish in big, fancy script, merely "Fiona."

What surprised me was the content. Fiona's letter was a love letter. So emotional, I was uncomfortable reading it; it was like hiding in their bedroom closet. I had no idea she and Johnny Boy were this intimate. The letter spoke of marriage and children and a life for them alone. I wondered if Fiona was trying to convince him to run away with her.

I called Joe Gregory. I wanted to get his opinion on the letter, because Fiona had certainly fooled me.

"Women always fool guys like us," he said. "We're easy."

"Yeah, but a woman who wears a hat to mass?"

I read the letter to him quietly, and when I finished he asked me to read it again. The second time, hearing it aloud, I noticed the repetition of the same phrase: "ourselves alone . . . we must do this for ourselves and ourselves alone. . . .

"Sinn Fein," Gregory said without hesitation. "The IRA political wing. That's what Sinn Fein means. 'Ourselves alone.'"

32

The NYPD Intelligence Division moved from Hudson Street in Manhattan to Poplar Street in Brooklyn. They'd swapped locations with the Internal Affairs Division, which had become a bureau. Intelligence got the worst of the deal, being forced from the West Village to the gloomy building in the shadow of the Brooklyn Bridge. It had been my job to visit Intel, but now it was in Brooklyn, so I asked Gregory to stop by on his way in Thursday morning. He said he truly hated that place. He claimed that Internal Affairs had left the building haunted, and he could hear the voices of old cops trapped behind the walls. He refused to go. He said he'd meet me at the river.

"What is your problem with this?" I said as I put my coffee on the dashboard. "I asked you to check a couple of names. That's all."

We were having breakfast in the car, just north of the Fulton Fish Market, a spot we'd used for decades when we didn't want the whole office listening in. Fiona's letter sat on the seat between us.

"I thought you already checked these names out with Albie," he said.

"I did. But that was for criminal records. Now I want to see if they have any IRA connections."

"I suppose you want all three names checked?"

"Right. Fiona, Mickey, and Dermot. And get a list of IRA hangouts in New York while you're there."

"Don't tell me you're thinking this crew pulled off the JFK robbery."

"It's not rocket science," I said.

"How do we connect these people with the Lutz brothers?"

"I don't know, yet," I said. "But we still have to take a look."

We were parked under the FDR Drive, facing the sun rising over Brooklyn. The nose of the car was against the pilings, the bumper looked down into the river. The fish market was quiet, the action finished before dawn. Tugs bobbed in the water as the world's fattest seagulls feasted on the scraps in the gutters behind us.

"I'm not comfortable with this," Gregory said.

"Then don't do it. I'll take care of it myself."

"You don't see the problem, do you?"

"I guess not."

"You don't see that here I am, the president of the Emerald Society, and I'm going off on this fishing expedition hoping to find some criminal connection to my own people?"

"Is that what really bothers you?"

"I got a public image to consider."

I didn't believe him. The Great Gregory never spent a second of his life considering his public image. The problem was that he thought the specter of Johnny Boy's criminality died with Vincent Lutz. What bothered him was that I might be resurrecting the issue.

"I don't agree with you," I said. "But if you think that's some sort of conflict, I'll check the names myself."

The windshield was damp with the steam from the hot cups. Gregory had a fried egg sandwich on a hard roll, extra ketchup. I had poppy-seed bagel with butter. With the exception of family meals at home, I'd eaten more meals in cars with Joe Gregory than anywhere else.

"Not for nothing," Gregory said. "But aren't you projecting a little here? You're taking the contents of one letter and projecting a whole scenario."

"That's what they pay us for."

"But within reason, pally. You have to have just cause."

I'd gone over the possibilities in my mind, and the choices were few. All we had was a love letter that possibly mentioned the IRA. We had no other proof linking the three Irish friends to the robbery and murder, only the fact that they knew Johnny Boy Counihan. And Johnny Boy wasn't around to help us.

"I didn't ask you to renounce your people," I said. "Just to check three names for me."

"All right already, I'll check the damn names. But if we come up empty, we let it go. Agreed?"

I didn't answer him, but he knew I wouldn't agree. This was a sore subject between us. He'd criticized me in the past for being too eager to dig into anything that hinted of IRA. And maybe he was right.

"I'll meet you in the office in an hour," he said.

"I'll be there."

"I can't help it," he said. "I just can't picture little Fiona with an Uzi."

"Neither can I," I said. "Welcome to the nineties."

I stopped by our office only long enough to check our messages. Then, without even putting my coat back on, I took the elevator to the lobby and jogged the fifty yards across the plaza to the City Building. The rounded arch of the City Building faces Chambers Street and forms a tunnel where the wind whistles eternal. I ducked in quickly and took the stairs to the second floor. The Marriage License Bureau was in room 252. The line was already about twenty deep, all happy couples. Way too happy.

The fee to get married in New York City is thirty dollars, the fine for bounced checks is two hundred. I caught the attention of a tall black woman in a denim skirt and told her I needed help. She stared at me and my identification.

"Just get in line," she said reassuringly. "The line moves fast."

"I don't want a marriage license," I said. "I just want to check on these two names as part of an investigation."

"What kind of an investigation?" she said.

"A love gone wrong," I said.

"I'll get my supervisor."

The supervisor introduced herself as Milagros Flores and said her son was a uniformed cop in the One Two Two Precinct in Staten Island. Good start, I thought.

"My son wants to be a detective very badly," she said. "Is there anything you can do for him?"

She handed me a piece of paper with her son's name and shield number. I advised her he'd be better off in a busier area.

"Tell him to get himself transferred to Harlem or Bed Stuy," I said. "A couple of years in uniform there and he'd have a better shot."

She snatched her son's name out of my hand and asked me what I wanted. I gave her the names Fiona Quinn and John Patrick Counihan Jr.

"No problem," she said. "What's the date?"

"I don't know the date. All I have is the names."

"Then it's a problem."

Milagros Flores, who suddenly decided her son didn't need to be a detective, disappeared behind a glass partition and dusty stacks of paper. Four clerks behind computers interviewed four couples to the clack of keyboard keys. A guy in a leather jacket with the logo of the Broadway show *Guys and Dolls* gave me the evil eye, as if I had line jumped. No one else seemed to care; the mood was holiday giddy. The clerk nearest me spun the computer screen around and asked a couple to verify the information. Then she warned them sternly that they must wait twenty-four hours. More giggly couples joined the line: entirely too much merriment for a city office. I tried to find a corner out of the way.

Across the hall in waiting room 257, the crowd was even noisier, overflowing into the hallway. A sign on the wall said "Rice Throwing Prohibited: Slippery Floors." The people in room 257 had waited the twenty-four hours and were now bursting with whatever it was they felt: joy, terror, some mass rock-and-roll coochie-coo. Whatever happened to the city that bred negativity?

I figured I could match most couples by age or wardrobe, but some exotic types defied any pigeonhole. I wouldn't begin to guess. Each time the chapel door opened, the crowd cheered and applauded. A groom in a blue Midas muffler jacket, with the name "Leon" in a white oval patch, raised both hands to the cheers, as if he'd scored a touchdown by snaring a tiny, barefoot contessa in pink taffeta.

The small chapel was bare except for a lectern, a single cardboard wedding bell, and crepe-paper streamers crisscrossing the ceiling. A sign said "Request Foreign Language in Advance." The bridal parties didn't dally long in the chapel—faster than a New Yorker at an ATM machine. I timed them: in and out in ninety seconds.

When I got back to One Police Plaza Gregory was on the phone, his coat tossed across my desk. He gave me the thumbs-down sign.

"No record on any of them," he said after he hung up.

He handed me a list of suspected hangouts of known members and associates of the Irish Republican Army. It read like the social life of most cops I knew. Irish bars, mostly in Manhattan and Queens. I'd been to most of them myself, a few quite frequently.

I showed him the marriage application. Fiona and Johnny Boy had not only paid the thirty-dollar marriage license fee, but they'd also shelled out twenty-five for their ninety seconds in the wedding chapel. In advance. The date they'd set was November 27. The Monday after the JFK robbery.

"Fifty-five bucks just to get married?" Gregory said. "How much did you pay?"

"Who remembers?" I said. "Whatever it was, it was a bargain."

"So what does this prove?" he said. "It doesn't prove anything."

"It proves she lied when she said they were only friends."

"She's shy; she didn't want to make a big deal about it. Come on, pally. First we're hot to trot on the Lutzes. Now we do a one eighty and go after these freaking losers. We're spinning so fast we're making ourselves dizzy."

On the bulletin board was a new crime stoppers poster with six photos of wanted criminals, three of the photos taken from bank surveillance cameras. Reward amounts and the 800 phone number were outlined in green. Someone had pasted a photocopied snapshot of Inspector Declan O'Prey over a picture of a transvestite hooker wanted for murder.

"Here's my take on Fiona Quinn," Gregory said. "This is a girl desperate to tear up her green card. She sees Johnny Boy as a way out. So she goes all out to charm this nice kid, and tried to seduce him to marry her. Pulls out all the stops. Even invokes the romance of the IRA, for which he has this strong emotional thing. But all she really wanted was to become a wife and quit that bullshit job. It's story as old as time itself."

"What about the immaculate burglary at Vito's house?" I said.

"Nothing missing at all. I'm thinking the burglary was to recover the other letters that Fiona wrote to Johnny Boy. But they missed one of them, this last one that he stuck in the glove compartment of his car."

"Jesus, are you reaching," he said. "Answer me this: If they did this, why are they still hanging around?"

"Because they think they got away with it. And maybe they did."

Gregory slammed his hand down on the desk. "Let's get it over with now," he said. "I say we go up there and roust them, scare the shit out of them. See who cracks first."

"Don't underestimate these people, Joe. Especially if they're IRA trained."

"Dermot Geary will cave in a heartbeat. I'll lay odds he'll cave."

"Get his address," I said.

"Who licenses those guys, Taxi and Limousine, the ASPCA, or who?"

"Try Consumer Affairs."

So we drove up the West Side, then crossed Central Park South. I didn't see either Dermot or Mickey out there, but it was early for tourists. Hansom cab drivers make more money at night, when passengers have a few drinks in them. In fact, drivers have been known to suggest they stop by a liquor store and pick up a bottle for the ride.

"Cookie gets in tomorrow," Gregory said.

"When is the funeral service?"

"Monday. Ten A.M. in Rockaway. I'm going to go straight from home."

We drove past buildings with intricately carved gargoyles and cherubs. New York is filled with old buildings, landmarks to craftsmanship. I'd read where architectural tours were becoming commonplace. But cops' landmarks are not about arches and cornices, they're about tragedy. And all the lights and Christmas decorations in the world could not hide the sadness.

On Park Avenue, in a fourth-floor apartment in a prewar building, a middle-aged Yale graduate despondent after losing his corporate position shot and killed his wife and two daughters. I still see the outline of their Barbie dolls lined up against the window.

We passed a walk-up where a mother killed her own daughter in apartment 5C, after torturing her for years in the belief she was possessed by the Devil. When we pass that building I can see and smell the cigarette burns on her skin.

The sidewalk in front of a Third Avenue high-rise is cracked near the fire hydrant where a teenage girl, who'd broken up with her boyfriend, leapt to her death in her prom gown, wearing rosary beads around her neck. Although the blood is long washed away, I know those gouges in the concrete are from the force of her bones falling from the twenty-fifth floor.

Dermot Geary lived on Seaman Avenue in the Inwood section in upper Manhattan. Baker Field, where Columbia University plays football, is at the end of Seaman Avenue. Dermot's building was an aging five-story walk-up, the brick the color of a Thanksgiving yam. Gregory parked across the street. We walked slowly to the top floor.

"You going to be at J.C.'s funeral?" Gregory said as he knocked on the door.

"No, you can represent me."

I looked out the landing window as Gregory knocked again. I knew this area well because it was just past the northern end of my father's bus route, up Broadway. My mother and I would sometimes meet him on Dyckman Street when his relief driver took over. We'd wait in a greasy spoon on the corner, where I'd spin around on a wobbly counter stool. Burgers sizzled on the grill, the air redolent with hot grease.

"I think we drove up here for our health," Gregory said.

In a way I was glad. I wasn't yet completely sure how to ap-
proach Dermot. What if he didn't fall apart? We needed some
leverage, a carrot or a stick. Gregory and I walked down to the
basement and found the super, who told us he hadn't seen Dermot in a couple of days.

"What now, pally?" he said.

"Back downtown," I said. "We'll talk strategy in Brady's."

"You're buying," he said.

33

Next morning we were back on the road, driving uptown on First Avenue on the way to McTiernan's Neutral Corner. Woodsie McTiernan, the former fighter, owned the hansom cab that employed Dermot Geary. Before we left the office I asked Albie Meyers to check with the feds to see if Dermot or any of our group had left the country.

An army of rookie cops from the Police Academy was in the street, working the holiday traffic. Almost every intersection had a fresh young face. Traffic moved better than it did all year, despite the glut of cars and shoppers. It made me proud to be part of this city, one that was actually becoming safer. You could sense it, hear it in people's voices. But Christmas was always the best in the city. Manhattan blossomed in winter. The yule season took the sting out of the shorter days of December although from the red eyes of my partner it had been a very long night for him.

"What time did you get home?" I said. "Or did you?"

"I left a little after ten, eleven, maybe. Somewheres in there. I think it's allergies."

"Yeah, I can smell those allergies," I said.

"Everybody's a comic," he said.

Ninety-sixth Street is the classic dividing line on the East Side of Manhattan. Although gentrification has stretched and blurred the DMZ on the West Side, Ninety-sixth is still the line of demarcation on the East Side. McTiernan's Neutral Corner was on First Avenue, a few blocks north of the high-rent district. A line of Christmas trees enveloped the corner: blue spruce, Fraser firs, and Scotch pines. The smell of the trees enriched the morning air.

"I always hated this guy," Gregory said. "Gets a few drinks in him, starts looking for the cop on post."

I didn't know Woodsie McTiernan personally, but I remembered another boxer whom booze turned into a cop fighter—a battler named Hurricane Jackson. At a bar on Claremont Parkway and Third Avenue in the Bronx I saw a sixty-year-old uniformed street cop take Hurricane down with one swift vicious blow: a nightstick across his shins.

We found Woodsie on a stool near the cash register. The ex-pug was dressed in a gray double-breasted sharkskin suit. He wore half-glasses and was going through a stack of bar tickets. I introduced myself and Joe.

"What can I do you for?" Woodsie said.

"How are you making out with the hansom cab business?" I said.

"Weather could be better," he said. "Otherwise, I can't complain. Is that what this is all about?"

"This is about information," I said.

"I can do information," he said. "Up to a point."

He wore a strong cologne, something that would have the name of a toreador. Around his eyes were jagged doughy lumps of scar tissue, and his right ear seemed permanently puffy.

"The problem is," Gregory said, "that whatever we say here

can never leave this room. If this gets back to the people involved, we'll know it came from you. And we won't forget it."

Woodsie stubbed out a cigarette in an ashtray. He looked over
his half-glasses. "Is that a threat?" he said.

"What do you think?" Gregory said.

The Neutral Corner smelled like a locker room, stale sweat
and alcohol. The lighting was recessed and dim. The bar was
horseshoe shaped, the walls covered with fight posters, mostly
classic old fights: Kid Gavilan, Willie Pep, Sugar Ray Robinson,
Jerry Quarry, La Motta, Graziano, and a few Woodsie McTiernan.

"Let me tell you something," Woodsie said. "About six months
ago this yom comes in here, stands right where you are. It's three
A.M. and he sticks a forty-five in my mouth. He tells me to
empty the cash register, including the box under the bar, or he'll
blow my motherfucking head off. My point is: I was scared then,
but tell me, Officer, what the fuck can you do to me?"

"Impressive story," I said. "But look at us, Woodsie. Take a
good look. You really think that we can't figure out a way to hurt
you?"

"I seriously doubt that will happen," he said. "But I'm a reasonable man; I can listen. Maybe we're getting all worked up
over nothing."

"Big problem with society today," Gregory said. "Everybody
getting all worked up over nothing."

I said, "How much do you know about an Irishman who
works for you? Guy named Dermot Geary and a friend of his,
Mickey O'Brien."

"Geary I know, but are you talking about the little redhead
that's always with him? Little cocky guy, always putting stuff on
his lips."

"That's them," I said.

Woodsie laughed. "I was *definitely* getting all worked up over
nothing. Anything you want to know about those two assholes
just ask. If they're jammed up, it'll make my fucking day."

"Do they have IRA connections?"

"You got to be fucking kidding me. First of all, the little guy's name is not O'Brien, it's Lawton, Mickey Lawton. He worked for me, too, and he ain't even Irish. He's a Westie. Grew up on Tenth Avenue. He's hooked in with that psycho crew used to hang in the Green Beret on Ninth. Maybe somewhere back in his lineage he was Irish, but he's a New York product all the way. The other guy, Dermot, is a donkey, but he's a fucking zero. Just a fat shlump does whatever Lawton tells him to. The IRA wouldn't go near these guys with a ten-foot pole."

The bartender on the other side was watching ESPN, a preview of the NFL playoffs. The logo on the cocktail napkins stacked on the bar was crossed boxing gloves.

"I take it they're not your favorite employees."

"What employees? They quit. Both of them, the cocksuckers. Gave me shit for notice. Left me in a bad way. I still don't have the second carriage back on the street."

"When did this happen?"

"Four or five days ago. I had a call from the guy in Central Park Carriages. Says they never showed up for their shifts. But I never heard word one from Geary, or that little redheaded fuck."

"Do you have Mickey's address?"

"Everything I got is yours, pal. How about I buy you and your partner a drink?"

"Too early for me, Woodsie," I said.

"Hey, come on," he said. "I've been on the wagon for forty-six months. Haven't punched out a cop in ten years."

Gregory's beeper went off, and he looked around for a phone. Woodsie handed him the private line beneath the bar. Then he took a box from the same shelf, a little metal box with index cards.

"If I see these guys," he said, "anything I should say, or would you rather I just call you?"

"You expect to see them?"

"I owe them money," he said. "Not that they're getting dime one from me."

Outside, we squeezed through the tight corridor of evergreens. A tree salesman in a grungy Fordham sweatshirt and a three-day growth of beard was softening up a young couple with the classic Christmas tree lie: that the branches would fall and the tree fill out when they got it home in the warmth of their apartment.

"That was Albie Meyers on the horn," Gregory said as I took a last deep breath of pine. "I think they found Dermot. They got a floater up in the Three Four, sounds like our guy."

At the single most extreme northwest corner of Manhattan, in Inwood Hill Park, is a small hidden area under a railroad swing bridge used by Amtrak. The spot is secluded by rocks and thick bushes and overlooks the waters of Spuyten Duyvil. Spuyten Duyvil is a tidal strait that connects the Harlem River to the Hudson River. It's about half a mile long and also separates Manhattan from the Bronx. In the days before bridges those who tried to swim it courted death. In Dutch, Spuyten Duyvil means "spite the devil."

As you stand there, looking over the rushing water, the Hudson is to your left; south is a fantastic side view of the entire span of the George Washington Bridge. The only noise is a low steady roar of traffic on the Henry Hudson Parkway high above.

The body was covered with a soaked gray woolen blanket that read "Property of the City of New York." The ground around it was littered with beer cans and condoms. Gregory pulled the blanket back. The face was bloated and gray, but it was Dermot Geary. The right side of the head crushed and pulpy. His fly was open, his formal tailcoat was pulled up, and his pockets had been turned inside out.

"How did you identify him?" I said.

"Wallet and everything was intact," a young detective said.

"He had about two hundred dollars in his pocket, and this still stuck in his hand."

He handed Gregory a black-and-gold can of Guinness Stout.

"He lives over here on Seaman," I said. "We'd like to look at the apartment with you."

"You have a case going on this guy?" he said.

"He's on the periphery of a case," I said.

"What the hell does that mean, periphery?" he said. "Either he's in or he's not. I mean, you made the trip up here for some fucking reason. At least throw a couple of names my way. A lead, hopefully."

I knew I should help this guy out, it was the right thing to do. But I didn't want him charging through my case like a mad bull, just to keep his clearance rate respectable. And I definitely didn't want him talking to Fiona or Mickey.

"Give us a couple of days," I said. "I'll get back to you."

"My friend," the detective said. "Up here in the trenches we don't have the luxury of a couple of days. How about next of kin? Has he got relatives you know about? I need a notification. At least give me that."

"Call the Irish consulate," I said.

"You can't help me, maybe I'll just call it an accident, or a suicide," he said. "He was drunk, fell, hit his head on the rocks. Anybody drinking that thick bitter shit couldn't be in a right frame of mind."

"Call it anything you want. I said I'd get back to you, and I will."

"Don't leave me hanging here," he said. "I got a full plate back at the house. Give me something to go on, anything."

Joe Gregory sniffed the can of Guinness in his hand. "From the smell of this," he said, "I'd say he's dead two days."

When I got home that night Leigh was in the kitchen, watching Vito lip-synch Johnnie Ray singing "Cry." The old man writhed around the kitchen floor, tugging at the buttons of his shirt.

"Vito's coming to our Christmas dinner," Leigh said. "I asked him to bring Cookie."

Over Vito's homemade pasta fagioli I told him it was a pleasant surprise to find him still with us. I thought he'd be home with Cookie. I said I wouldn't blame him.

"Amigo," he said, "I went home this morning. My house is like an Irish wake. My kitchen counter lined with five-dollar whiskey. All J.C.'s people are staying there. Cookie has plenty of company with that crowd. Besides, I'd rather stay here and laugh with your lovely wife."

"You are making her laugh, Vito," I said. "And I really appreciate it. I appreciate everything you've done."

"Say no more, my friend," he said.

In bed that night Leigh tried to remember some of the stories that Vito had told her. Leigh whispered in bed whenever anyone was staying in our house. It was hilarious listening to her whisper her way through Vito's accent.

Then she was quiet, and I knew it wasn't because she was going to sleep. I knew from all the years, the little movements that signaled her time to sleep. I knew she was thinking.

"Did Joe and Cookie ever have a thing going on?" she said.

"What kind of thing?"

"You know, a romantic thing."

"I think so. Way back, before she married J.C., Cookie and Joe went out together."

"How serious?"

"I don't know. Not that serious. Why?"

"I just wondered," she said.

"What, what? Tell me, my *cara mia.*"

"Well," she said, lowering her voice even more. I had to move my ear close to her mouth to hear. "The other day, when Vito was showing me his family pictures, I had never seen a picture of any of them before. But when he showed me a picture of Johnny Boy I almost fainted. I thought it was a young Joe Gregory. He looked exactly like Joe."

34

On Monday, the morning of J.C. Counihan's Brooklyn funeral, I scoured Manhattan's West Side for Mickey Lawton, but I
couldn't get Joe Gregory off my mind. I kept replaying our recent conversations. After what Leigh had said about Johnny Boy
looking like Joe, I wondered if that was why he'd asked me if I
still avoided looking at pictures of the victims' faces. Maybe he'd
looked especially close at this one.

Over the weekend I'd called Joe twice. The second time I
asked him if there was anything he wanted to talk about. He told
me to get a life. I thought about showing up at J.C.'s funeral but
decided against it.

Mickey Lawton lived in a building on Eleventh Avenue across
from De Witt Clinton Park, far west enough to smell the Hudson. Apartment 5B was on the top floor. The door to the apartment looked to be solid steel, like the kind you see on numbers
joints in Harlem. It hurt my knuckles to knock. But the pain was
for naught. No Mickey.

I stopped in every bakery, bar, and bodega within five blocks, until I finally found him in the OTB on Ninth and Fifty-fifth. He was wearing an expensive-looking black leather jacket and smoking a fat cigar.

"What's up, Doc?" he said.

"Bad news, Mick. It's Dermot. He's dead."

"Oh, Jesus," he said, buckling at the knees. "Oh, Jesus Christ. I warned him about that place. Jesus Christ."

Ordinarily I'd ask why he assumed it happened at a particular place, but it wasn't in my game plan to come off as suspicious. This visit was a lullaby, an attempt to sing him to sleep.

I said, "I noticed Dermot's name on the daily incident reports. The detective who's handling it is having trouble finding a next of kin. I figured you might know."

"Yeah, Aunt Marge. Lives up in White Plains. I think she works for the phone company. Jesus, I still can't get over this."

"Marge's last name Geary?" I said.

"I think so," he said. "How the fuck did you find me, anyway?"

"Dermot had a piece of paper in his wallet with your address. I went there first, then walked around the neighborhood asking for Mickey O'Brien. But nobody owned up to knowing you."

"I'm not exactly a social butterfly."

"And people in this neighborhood wouldn't tell a cop whether they knew you or not."

"Yeah," he said, thinking about that. "You call Fiona yet?"

"She was my next stop if I struck out with you. I was hoping you'd tell her for me. It's not my favorite assignment."

"Don't worry about it," he said. "I'll take care of it for you. What happened to the poor bastard, anyway?"

"Drowned. Drinking beer near the water, up in Inwood Hill Park. Apparently he fell, hit his head on the rocks."

"I knew it. I warned him about that fucking park. Fulla junkies, that park. Jesus Christ. The fucking guy didn't like to drink in bars where it was safe and warm. You ever know an Irishman didn't like to drink in bars?"

"Never."

"Fucking A," he said.

The morning was dry and cold; steam rose from the manholes on Ninth Avenue. Two guys in Santa suits came out of OTB arguing about the daily double.

"When was the last time you saw him?" I asked.

"Oh shit, what's today, Monday? I saw him last Wednesday. We had a couple of beers up there by the *Maine* Memorial. Then he grabbed the train uptown, said he was going home."

"What time?"

"About six, seven," he said. "Where'd they find him, in the Hudson?"

"No, right in Spuyten Duyvil. Somebody spotted him from the Circle Line."

Across the street, the line for the TV talk program *The Gordon Elliot Show* stretched almost to the corner. I didn't know whether they were called punks or slackers or Generation Xers, but I could see that purple hair could come in a multitude of shades.

"Ever see shit like that before?" I said, pointing across the street.

"Scumbags," he said. "That's all you see over there. Every day it's something weirder. Fat broads with midgets, shit like that."

"I don't know what this world is coming to."

They all wore pants many sizes too large, dragging the ground and maintaining minimal contact with the ass. Chains were popular, chains that went from their wallets to their belt loops. The kind bikers and truckers wore, only longer.

"How you making out on the JFK thing?" Mickey said.

"Closed case. We found solid evidence pointing to these two brothers from Queens, the Lutz brothers. Unfortunately, they both were killed, so we'll never really know."

"I bet I know who whacked 'em," he said, and with his index

finger he pushed his snub nose to one side, meaning the bent noses, the Mafia.

"At least they saved the taxpayer the expense."

"Gotta be crazy to fuck with those guys," he said.

I gave Mickey Lawton my card and told him if he ever needed anything, to call me. I wished him a Merry Christmas and left him at the newsstand smoking his cigar and reading the sports page.

On the way downtown I stopped at the Federal Express office and picked up a couple of envelopes. I had to push my way through a crowd listening to a guy in a *Cat in the Hat* stocking cap playing steel drums near the subway entrance. The soft island bonging still rang in my ears when I got to the office.

"Your partner called this morning," Albie said. "Said to remind you he was going to the funeral."

Albie told me that he'd heard Gregory was in Brady's very late the previous night, claiming you can hear the ocean if you hold a can of Guinness to your ear.

"Did he sound in bad shape?" I said quietly.

"He sounded like the entire Russian army was marching through his mouth."

A handwritten note on my desk said that as per a telephone message dated that morning Gregory and I were transferred from Major Case back to the Chief of Detectives Special Homicide Team, effective immediately. O'Prey might have gotten wind of Gregory's holiday cheeriness and been anxious to wash his hands of us.

I picked up the phone and called Fiona's number, heard her voice, and hung up. Then I asked Albie if I could borrow his word processor for about an hour, I had something I wanted to write.

I began constructing a letter of my own. At first I struggled to find the voice of the letter, until finally deciding on the rhythm and speech patterns of our esteemed temporary boss, Declan

O'Prey. The letter was to Fiona Quinn, the writer was Johnny Boy's fictitious uncle Mike in Ireland.

My Dearest Fiona:
During my recent business trip to the States I had the opportunity to visit the son of my cousin John P. Counihan. Young Johnny Boy was a sweet lad, and I was happy to see him so much in love with an Irish gal. He even confided in me of your impending marriage, and I must tell you that I was thrilled. I was also warmed to see him so devoted to the cause. So many young people today are interested only in themselves. But, when Johnny Boy told me to expect a certain generous gift, imminently coming my way, I thought he was merely trying to please. Now I hear of how the poor boy died, so bravely, and I understand that he was serious after all. I will be in your fine city over Christmas and intend to ring you. As I always told Johnny Boy, our business is ours. It is for ourselves alone.

Yours in Christ,
Michael C. Counihan

I put my Uncle Mike letter in a plain white envelope and slid it into a FedEx envelope addressed to Fiona Quinn at her Central Park West address. I wanted the letter to be mailed from Ireland, and I needed my partner for that. Joe's stepmother, Ellen Gregory, stayed in their Emerald Isle home after Liam died. She lived in Dublin and ran a shelter for battered wives. I needed her address. I needed to find my partner.

The only message under Gregory's bulldog's paws was J.C. Counihan's obituary, but the funeral was long over. In all the years I'd worked with Joe Gregory he'd always accused me of being too analytical. He claims that sometimes the answers can't be figured; they come as a flash, a vision from the heavens. I tried to picture him in my mind. After all, I knew him better than anyone. I knew exactly what he'd be wearing: his good black overcoat, charcoal suit, and black wingtip Bostonians. After twenty years of day and nights, of laughter and murder, I even knew what he was thinking. Then I saw him. Standing. Looking down, his hands behind his back, the burly body shadowing the ground below. I saw him clearly. I knew exactly where he was.

The highest point in Brooklyn is on Battle Hill in Greenwood Cemetery. I found Gregory near two freshly dug graves, side by side.

"You look like shit," I said.

"Glad to see you, too."

I could smell booze, but it was old and stale. He hadn't been drinking in a couple of hours. I could see him swallowing, with the postbinge dry throat, looking more exhausted than drunk.

"Nice place," I said. "First time I've ever been here."

"Vito told me his father bought a slew of family plots in 1905. Then they decided they wanted to be buried in Italy. Boss Tweed is buried over there, he says. Albert Anastasia, Crazy Joey Gallo."

"You'd fit right in here."

"They got legit people, too. Samuel B. Morse, Horace Greeley, both Currier and Ives, Leonard Bernstein, Frank Morgan, the guy who played the Wizard in the *Wizard of Oz*."

It was the Central Park of cemeteries, without the skaters and joggers. I could see ships in New York Harbor. Birds actually chirped.

"That's good company," I said. "And speaking of good company, I need yours." I showed him a photocopy of my letter to Fiona and waited while he read it. "I want to send this to Ellen. Tell her to mail it right back."

"What if I say no?"

"I'll find somebody else."

We were standing in a wooded area that could have been rural

Pennsylvania. Among the hills and dales were granite and slate memorials carved in death masks or winged cherubs, even one in the shape of the Coney Island boardwalk.

"You get in touch with Brian Millard on this?" he said.

Brian Millard was the former second whip of the Nineteenth Detective Squad. He was now director of security for Federal Express.

"I was hoping you'd call him," I said.

"He'll pin down the delivery time," Gregory said. "So we're not sitting on our asses all day, waiting."

I pointed to a mausoleum bigger than my house. "That must belong to Boss Tweed's bag man," I said.

"Steinway," he said, smiling. "The piano guy. Got room for two hundred in there."

"I'll remember that for your retirement racket."

"You're always thinking, pally. Always thinking."

The grounds were pristine. None of the little white fences, plastic Madonnas, or small American flags so popular in Canarsie Cemetery, where Joe's mother was buried. Gregory was standing over a flat stone. John Patrick Counihan Jr. "Our beloved Johnny Boy," the inscription read.

"What if Fiona just laughs at your letter and throws it in the trash?"

"Could happen," I said. "Listen, why don't we get out of here. I need Ellen's address, and I have to get this to FedEx before they close."

"I asked Cookie point-blank," Joe Gregory said. "I got tired of waiting for her to speak up."

I felt his eyes on me, but I looked off and concentrated on the sun glinting off New York Harbor, reflecting off the glass towers of lower Manhattan.

"It's weird," he said. "Me with a son."

"You don't have to explain anything to me."

"Years ago, when I first heard she was pregnant, it crossed my

215

mind. Nobody said nothing, so I figured . . . no problem. Didn't think anything. Then, last Monday, the day J.C. died, I go out there and Vito has all these pictures out. I knew right away."

Joe Gregory and I were cut from the same Kelly green cloth; I knew how difficult this was for him. Our pain, like our religion, was between our God and ourselves. Ourselves alone.

"Give her time," I said. "So much has happened."

"Time, yeah. I'm fifty-seven years old. I'm not going to have any late-life kids. I don't even have a girlfriend, for chrissakes. J.C. is dead now, who does it hurt?"

"Maybe it hurts her."

We walked down the hill toward a lake surrounded by immense trees. The setting sun reflected in the water. I could hear the water in the stream, gurgling over rocks.

"Anything else I should tell Ellen?" he said. "About this letter?"

"Tell her to wear gloves when she's handling it."

"Listen, pally," he said, "it's not that I was close with the kid, or anything like that. I don't feel the loss like Vito. Vito really feels the loss. I never knew the kid."

"Maybe that's what bothers Cookie. She knows she never gave you the chance."

"I just want her to say something," he said. "I just want to know."

"I think you do know."

35

Four nights later, the Friday before Christmas, Gregory and I were backed up into the Tavern on the Green parking lot with a great angle on Fiona's residence on Central Park West. We were waiting for the FedEx man, our Oldsmobile hidden behind bushes ringed with thousands of tiny white lights. It was exactly six P.M. when the Federal Express van arrived, on cue. We'd asked Brian Millard to delay delivery until six. At that late hour it would be easier for Fiona to get out of the house.

"I hear somebody spotted Emil Lutz," he said.

"A cop from Auto Crime saw him in a Chinese take-out joint in Massapequa. Said he looked like shit."

Gregory had bought one coffee, one tea, and two hot bagels from H & H Bagels on Broadway. He got sesame, I got poppy. He sat back, watching them steam up the windshield. After twenty years as partners we were comfortable with our routines and our quirks.

"The cop should've grabbed him," he said. "They pay us for twenty-four hours a day."

"The cop had his family in the car."

"Maybe we'll get lucky and Chin's people will find him first. They don't care whose family's in the car."

The Tavern on the Green's parking lot was higher than street level. We had a clear direct view of the entrance and the flexibility to drive either way, north or south, in case she hailed a cab. It was the perfect surveillance spot, next to a floodlit Frosty the Snowman, bright enough to read by. The only problem was stalled traffic; buses and trucks could block our view.

"Hear from Cookie?" I said without taking my eyes off the front of the building.

"Today. We talked a couple of minutes."

"How's she doing?"

"Fine."

"She tell you Leigh invited her and Vito to Christmas dinner at our house?"

"She mentioned it."

Wreaths and candles decorated most of the building's windows. Balconies twinkled red and green. The entrance was covered by a long green canopy, running to the curb. The doorman wore matching green with gold trim and epaulets. He worked with a manic gusto, running from limo to lobby, blowing his whistle, smiling, patting the kiddies, knowing full well it was that time of year to grip and tip.

"Is that going to be a problem?" I said. "You and Cookie in the same room?"

"Why should it be a problem?"

"Just thought I'd ask."

Gregory didn't say anything further about it, not great, not shit, not you freaking asshole, not anything. Across the street, a woman with a shiny black fur coat yawned while her poodle pissed on the hydrant. A young couple with ice skates slung over their shoulders looked at us curiously as they cut through the parking lot, walking toward Wollman rink.

The FedEx man came out of the building, unlocked the door to his van, climbed in, and drove away. A small boy marched stiffly, up and down under the green canopy, like a toy soldier in *The Nutcracker*. Gregory and I ate bagels.

We took turns going to the bathroom in Tavern on the Green, hustling down their zigzag hall of mirrors. I'd just gotten back in the car when Fiona appeared in the doorway. She turned right and walked downtown on Central Park West. Gregory slowly edged the Olds into the roadway. Fiona wore a long black coat, in a city of long black coats. I focused on her red tam as it bounced along the sidewalk, disappearing behind vans and four-wheel drives. Follow the bouncing ball.

Gregory hung a full block back, pulling into hydrants and bus stops when we got too close. But Fiona was moving fast. I almost lost her in the crowd at Columbus Circle. She'd crossed to Eighth Avenue and was heading downtown; Eighth Avenue was an uptown traffic street. I grabbed one of the portable radios and got out.

The air was cold and crisp, a light snow teasing the city. I wore a woolen tweed cap, which had belonged to my father, in order to cut down on the recognition factor. But the tail was going to be easy, crowds of people in the street. New York City takes on a dimension all its own this time of year. The city is Christmas personified. People in overcoats carry shopping bags, their cheeks pink and ruddy. Fire escapes are decked out with reindeer and elves with blinking red eyes. Couples lug Christmas trees and kids on their shoulders. It is an old-fashioned, outdoor Christmas, like those before the malling of America.

Fiona turned west on Fifty-seventh Street. I got to the corner in time to see her enter Kennedy's Bar. I stepped into the alcove of a closed bank and keyed the radio. Gregory had parked behind the yellow tarp of a Con Ed street job. He blinked the lights twice.

"I'm thinking we should just drop in for a quick pop," he said as I got into the car. "See who she's talking to. We know everyone in this place. Even if she sees us, she'll see we're known."

We did know Kennedy's well. It was a warm place with good food, and cops we knew hung out at the back bar.

"I don't think so," I said. "Maybe we should call, see if anyone we know is there. They can watch her for us."

"Yeah, maybe. But a cocktail would be nice about now. I'm always thirstier in December."

Less than three minutes later Kennedy's door opened and the little red tam of Fiona Quinn was bouncing east. We watched her pass the Hard Rock Cafe, heading toward the huge snowflake that hung over Fifth Avenue. At Carnegie Hall she turned right, down Seventh, and wound up in another bar, Rosie O'Grady's.

"She's looking for Lawton," I said. "And she's in a panic."

"He hangs out in the same joints we do," Gregory said. "And that's not a comforting thought." But as soon as he said it, Fiona was out again.

I tailed her on foot through Rockefeller Center. The streets were packed with foreign tourists tossing around the cheap dollar. My feet felt damp and cold from getting in and out of the car. A man pulling a live camel went into the back door of Radio City Music Hall. Kids peeked in behind, hoping to see a Rockette in full spangle. My heels were starting to hurt from the cold. I leaned against the skating rink fence when Fiona stopped to tie her shoe.

Down below came the bass scraping of skate blades as people moved in circles under the giant Christmas tree to Gene Autry's "Rudolph the Red-Nosed Reindeer." Nearby, a line of white angels played golden trumpets as real little girls ran in circles, catching snowflakes on their tongues.

I followed her past Saks, weaving through a group protesting Santas wearing real fur. Past the grandeur of St. Pat's, and bell ringers, and guys selling hot chestnuts; the smell of their cooking gas always made me queasy.

Fiona picked up the pace, and we crossed avenue after avenue, walking faster all the time. We passed groups of loud, well-dressed young people, coming from office parties, arm in arm, dancing in the street. Every bar was packed, standing room only. Asses were jammed flat against frosted windows. On Second Avenue Fiona stopped for a glance into Eamonn Doran's, then on to Runyon's Bar.

She stayed in Runyon's for over ten minutes. I edged up to the window, but a crowd had gathered around the piano player. Everyone was singing "Deck the Halls," having more fun than I was. I saw a cop I'd worked with in OCCB, then I saw Fiona's red tam. She was on the pay phone, her finger jammed in her other ear.

Gregory had parked on the hydrant, across the street.

"She's on the phone," I said. I got in and took off my shoes and began to rub my feet.

"Not anymore, pally," Gregory said. "There she goes. Going back to the West Side again. I think she's trying to kill you."

There's an old cop story about a rookie detective who tailed this Mafia don from Manhattan all the way to the Bronx. The cop's bosses knew the Mob guy's marathon walking route. They didn't tell the rookie, who made the mistake of wearing new shoes. Four hours into the tail the cop's feet were in agony. When they finally got back to where they'd started, the Mob guy hesitated, then turned around as if to begin again. The young cop limped up to him, shoved a token in his hand, and yelled, "Take the goddamn subway, will you." I was ready to get a token myself.

This time she wasn't walking a straight route; instead she weaved: one block west, one block south. Working her way downtown. But at Times Square she hailed a red-fringed hansom cab. I didn't recognize the driver. When she climbed into the front of the buggy I stepped back and called Gregory. And waited.

The neon in Times Square has no season, all blinking and blaring and fuzzy panorama. A huge Pepsi can spouted jagged fizz. The ice cubes surrounding the giant Coke bottle had grayed with soot and weather. Hot pinks, blues, and reds advertised Japanese cameras. A pigeon disappeared into the Canon billboard. I wondered what kind of bird adapts to living behind wires and incandescent bulbs, neon tubes. My nose was running. I searched my pockets for a tissue as Gregory pulled to the curb.

"What's the matter, pally?" Gregory said. "That old horse too fast for you?"

"Speaking of old horses," I said. "Next time it's your turn on foot."

The city is darker below Times Square. From our angle only the Empire State Building seemed festive, its red-lit spire on a green base. Gregory drove through two lights, and we were again behind the fringed buggy and Fiona Quinn. We slowed down; the traffic was sparse. They turned west, and we waited at the corner until we could no longer hear the slow clip-clop of hooves. Gregory crept around the corner. I saw the buggy—and a familiar sight, up ahead: the Javits Convention Center. Suddenly my feet didn't hurt.

"Where the hell they going?" Gregory said. "I never saw a buggy this far from the park."

We were on West Thirty-seventh Street, heading toward the Hudson. The skyscrapers were only two blocks behind us, but it was as if we'd left the city. The only other traffic was lost Jerseyites, looking for the Lincoln Tunnel. We rode through a ramshackle lineup of questionable auto body shops, sheet metal factories, burned-out warehouses. The outskirts of any industrial town. There were no sidewalks, no shop windows, only gates and barbed wire. I began to get an odd sense, beyond familiarity.

Gregory stopped, let the buggy get two full blocks ahead. I picked up the binoculars. They were getting close to Eleventh

Avenue and the River Diner. I wasn't sure how close; it's tough to judge depth with binoculars.

The hansom cab stopped. Fiona climbed down. The driver and buggy disappeared into the warehouse on the right. Fiona kept walking west. Into the River Diner.

We drove up to the place the buggy went into, a place called Central Park Carriages. A guy was shoveling horseshit into a Dumpster. The place was just a one-story building that could have housed anything. But it housed hansom cabs, a lot of them. I had no idea the horses came this far south, over twenty blocks from the park. I hadn't noticed it when I was parked here with Rocky Lutz. It looked like another faceless warehouse. I remembered focusing on the gleaming Javits Center across the street. The lunch crowd walking around us. I remembered a guy carrying a red woolen blanket.

Gregory cruised slowly to the corner. In the mirror behind the diner's counter I could see Fiona's red tam and Mickey Lawton's red head. They were talking excitedly in a booth.

"You think this is coincidence?" I said.

"No, pally. I think you nailed it."

36

On Saturday at two P.M. I parked my Volvo opposite Declan O'Prey's building on Washington near Bank Street, in the West Village. I'd spent the morning going through organized crime files of a gang called the Westies, then I called O'Prey and filled him in on our plans for Fiona Quinn. He told me to meet him at his place and gave me the address. I let the motor run as I waited for Gregory. All I could get on the radio were talk shows and Christmas music.

It is a fact of life that opinions regarding your lifestyle often hinge on where you choose to live, even in New York. Especially if your abode is in the quaint and quirky Greenwich Village. I'd never figured Declan O'Prey for a Village resident. O'Prey came off as one desperately climbing the career ladder to the top rungs of the NYPD. Most of those people lacked any hint of an interesting private life.

Across the street, a dozen in-line skaters noisily bumped and zipped around the recessed playground of a schoolyard. Almost all wore masks, and all wielded hockey sticks. An orange rubber puck skittered across the blacktop.

Gregory pulled up behind me. I got out and walked back to the Olds. On the seat was a small Macy's bag. He picked it up as I got in the car and tried to shove it under the seat, but the box wouldn't fit. It appeared to be the shape of Rubik's Cube, but double the size. He let it sit on the floor under his legs.

"What's that?" I said.

"None of your business, that's what."

"Is it none of my business that your receipt fell out of the bag?"

He leaned down and picked up the yellow receipt. I was sure he'd paid cash. Joe Gregory didn't have a credit card.

"So what do you make of this?" he said, pointing at the building.

"I figured him for an Upper East Sider. You know the type: wifey is a tax lawyer, little Declan junior plays pickup sticks at some twenty-grand-a-year nursery school."

"I'll tell you what, pally," he said. "Looking back now, I'm thinking he always seemed a little light on his feet."

"Just because he lives here doesn't mean he's gay."

"Yeah, right," he said. "Maybe he's an artiste."

We crossed the narrow street. O'Prey's building looked like a converted factory, the brick a dark rose color. The front windows on all floors were large enough to light several rows of industrial sewing machines. Four apartments were listed. Each appeared to have an entire floor. I pushed the button. Off in the distance a car alarm shrieked.

"You line up a hotel yet?" I said. Our plan was to bring Fiona into a wired hotel room, where she'd meet our imaginary Uncle Mike. Christmas was the toughest time of the year to book any hotel room in Manhattan.

"Harold Sampel says he's going to take care of it for us," he said.

"Harold Sampel? Don't know him."

"Yes, you do. The guy who's a good dancer. Always dancing with the broads at a retirement racket. Thinks he's Fred Astaire."

"Where did he work?"

"The Two Oh Squad, then the Bias Incident Unit. He was a second-grader, now he's chief of security at that hotel on West Fifty-seventh Street. Used to be a Holiday Inn, then a Days Inn, I don't know what it is now. He takes care of visiting lecturers for John Jay College."

O'Prey buzzed us in, and we rode a small elevator to the top. The elevator opened into a small enclosed alcove with a coat rack, an umbrella stand, a white metal garden bench, and a silk ficus tree. O'Prey stood in the only doorway. He was wearing a white linen shirt with a band collar and extra baggy khakis.

"When the elevator stops on this floor," I said, "you know it's for you."

"I lock the elevator at night," O'Prey said, "so it can't open on this floor."

"Can't be too safe," Gregory said. "In this neighborhood."

We stepped into one huge room with a stretch of hardwood flooring long enough to accommodate a bowling alley. The ceilings were ten feet, the inner walls taken back to the original brick. Everything else was white. The building had been a piano factory, O'Prey said. The lofts below him had immense wooden supporting beams crisscrossing the ceiling.

"I bought this for the roof garden." He gestured toward a set of sliding doors. "Too bad the weather isn't nicer, we could sit out there."

Instead we sat in facing sofas, covered with loose-fitting white slipcovers. Between us sat a glass-and-copper coffee table containing the biggest candle I'd ever seen: the size of a gallon paint can, with three wicks burning. I showed him the letter I wrote to Fiona, then laid out the events of the last few days: the murder of Dermot Geary; the tail of Fiona to the River Diner. I tied it in with hunches and assumptions. It sounded logical to me.

"Is the Lutz family involved at all?" O'Prey said.

"Rocky definitely is. Probably Vincent, I'm not sure. At least, he supplied the guns. I doubt that Emil Lutz knew what was going on."

"So now we're after a maid and a buggy driver."

"Mickey Lawton drove buggies only because the Westies dumped him," I said. "He was too crazy. Everybody I talk to says he has a reputation for unpredictable violence."

The Westies are a gang of Irish-American hoods from Manhattan's West Side, an area called Hell's Kitchen. By simple cold-blooded brutality they ruled the West Forties and Fifties from the waterfront to the theater district.

"Too crazy for the Westies is very crazy," O'Prey said.

Mickey Lawton had been questioned in the parking garage murder of two CBS technicians. He was also suspected of murdering a Ninth Avenue barmaid who'd ridiculed his lovemaking. Informants said he walked back into the bar one afternoon with her head in a bag and her breasts in a jar. But nobody would admit to firsthand knowledge, and a case couldn't be made. The girl was never found.

"Mickey started as a teenager," I said. "As a numbers runner in the old Coliseum. That's probably where he met Rocky Lutz. Rocky was a loan shark and strong-arm for Sally the Goat, at the Coliseum, before they moved downtown to the Javits Center."

"That had to be a couple of years ago," O'Prey said.

"We figure they hooked up again in the River Diner. Workers from Javits eat there, and last night we found out that Central Park Carriages is behind the diner. Mickey stored his hansom cab there."

"What about the other two?"

"Fiona and Dermot were pawns," I said. "Fiona talked Johnny Boy Counihan into going along with them. She laid it on thick, swearing her love, promising to marry him as soon as they did this one thing, for 'ourselves alone.'"

"Is the IRA involved?" he said.

"We've checked with Intel, the feds . . . nothing."

"I know some people I can call," O'Prey said.

O'Prey made some notes on a white legal pad. He flipped through a Rolodex, found a number, and wrote it down. The immense candle smelled of vanilla. I could feel the heat from it.

"Do we need a wiretap on either of their phones?" O'Prey said.

"We don't have enough for a wiretap. That's our problem, we don't have much of anything evidentiary. That's were we need your help. We need technical assistance and backup. Plus a quality undercover from an outside source."

"We have hotel rooms lined up," Gregory said. "Compliments of Harold Sampel, an ex-cop."

"Why use an outside undercover?" O'Prey said.

"We need someone with a decent Irish brogue to play Uncle Mike. The idea is for Uncle Mike to put the squeeze on Fiona."

He shrugged and held out his hands. "Look no further, my good lad."

Gregory went to the phone to call Harold Sampel and reserve the rooms. O'Prey and I followed him to a wet bar near a window that had a view of the Hudson.

"Anthony," he said, "I heard you were threatened by Emil Lutz. I wish you would have come to me."

"He didn't exactly threaten me."

"He went to your home; that's close enough."

"I've taken steps to protect my family."

"I know you have," he said. "We've been watching your house all week."

Gregory nodded his head. He knew it.

"I appreciate that," I said.

"This guy's a prince," Gregory said, putting his hand over the phone. "When do we want to do this?"

"How about the day after Christmas?" I said. I was thinking of Leigh's Christmas party. The case could wait.

"Your decision, gentlemen," O'Prey said. He seemed more relaxed in his own place than he ever did in One Police Plaza.

Harry Sampel arranged for three adjoining rooms. Plus, he said he'd make sure the rooms across the hall were vacant. He also arranged for maid's and maintenance uniforms and a cleaning cart. Harry was a prince, but a cautious one. Gregory held out his hand and said, "Give me your credit card."

"Why do you need my credit card?"

"Just for looks. Harry says he needs it to cover himself until the city pays."

Gregory reserved the rooms, starting Christmas Day, so that the tech team would have time to work. He reserved them in the name Michael Counihan. Then he read my credit card number into the phone.

O'Prey said he would have his people handle the eavesdropping and backup arrangements. Then he took three glasses down from the cabinet. Gregory's scuffed leather address book lay open on the bar, next to O'Prey's lucite Rolodex.

"What's our next step?" O'Prey said.

"Uncle Mike calls Fiona," I said. "We can do that Christmas Day from the hotel room."

"Give me the number," he said. "We'll do it now. I'm not going to have you people come in on Christmas Day."

Like most cops who have been around, O'Prey had his own tape recorder and a suction cup that attached to the phone. We tested it with the weather number.

"I think Uncle Mike is a party guy," O'Prey said. "Wouldn't you say so, Anthony?"

"Most definitely."

I started to believe that O'Prey might do all right. A good undercover should enjoy his role. O'Prey opened his liquor cabinet and brought out a bottle of Old Bushmills Irish whiskey. He told Gregory to do the honors while he looked through an immense pine armoire that served as his entertainment center. Gregory poured while O'Prey shuffled his CDs.

The music came on loud, echoing through the big open space. It sounded like a party. Gregory and I sipped at our three fingers of Irish whiskey, so much finer and more delicate than anyone expects.

"Any time you're ready, boss," Gregory said.

O'Prey dialed the phone.

"Yes," he said. "I'd like to speak to Miss Fiona Quinn." He had a smile on his face, and his brogue was thicker than the fog over Galway. "Tell her it's Uncle Mike," he said as the Gallowglass Ceili Band played "The Plough and the Stars." Gregory looked at me and raised his eyebrows, and I knew he meant that we'd greatly underestimated Inspector Declan O'Prey. The guy had come three thousand miles to be a cop, and a cop he was.

Ice cubes tinkled, harps and fiddles played, as O'Prey said, "Good afternoon, Miss Quinn, and I trust you're having a wonderful day."

37

"To *famiglia,*" Vito said, raising his glass. "And friends that are family."

We stretched across the table to touch glasses. It wasn't easy with both table leaves in. Only five of us, but we needed the space for all the food. Vito had brought a fresh turkey, which Leigh had cooked with her family's southern recipe. Vito had made gravy for the pasta; the mussels and calamari he'd picked up at the Fulton Fish Market. Gregory's tie began tinkling as he reached to touch glasses with Leigh. He'd worn a tie that played "Jingle Bells" every time he touched it.

"Stop the music," Vito said, his Jimmy Durante imitation, as he stood and tapped a fork against his glass.

"Enough with the speeches already," Cookie yelled. "Every year he does the same thing. You could starve with all the speeches."

"My grandfather told me this story," he said.

"Oh, no," Cookie said. "Not that one again."

"It's about America," Vito said. "I have to tell it."

"I want to hear it," Leigh said.

"And you shall, *cara mia,*" Vito said.

"Don't encourage him," Cookie said.

Vito held his glass high in the air as if he were toasting the Grand Ballroom at the Waldorf. "My grandfather used to say that when he was a boy in Sicily he heard the streets in America were paved with gold."

"Hurry it up," Cookie said. "The food is getting cold."

Vito said, "But when he got here he found out three things. Number one: The streets were *not* paved with gold . . ."

Cookie mimed the story, holding two fingers up, like her father. Gregory's tie went off again.

"Two," Vito said, "they weren't paved at all."

"Give him the hook," Cookie said.

"And finally," Vito said, "my grandfather discovered that *he* was supposed to pave them."

Cookie yawned theatrically, then said, "If you don't stop him, he'll go on all night."

The party took off quickly, the way they do when people want desperately to laugh. Maybe I'd started the cocktails too early. Everything seemed funny. I'd been worried because of the strained connections between both women and my partner. The day's only tears surprised me. They were in my wife's eyes when she hugged Joe Gregory.

Food was being passed and backing up at Vito. I sat next to Cookie, and Leigh sat next to Gregory, with Vito in between the two women.

"It is such a pleasure to be with friends," Vito said as he poured the last of the wine. Then he went right to the cabinet and found the corkscrew. He knew more about my kitchen than I did.

After dinner Leigh and Cookie insisted that the men go into the living room while they did the dishes. Gregory and I didn't need any encouragement.

"What about women's lib?" Vito said, his face red from wine and speeches.

"It's taking a day off," Leigh said, but I knew she wanted a chance to talk to Cookie alone.

We went into the living room, and Vito went to the liquor cabinet and pulled out a bottle of sambuca I never knew I had. Joe Gregory admired our tree, then wandered over to the table and began looking through our family pictures. He picked up a couple of the Santa Claus figures that Leigh had scattered around the room. Some were made of glass, some wood or tin, one papier-mâché, one tiny pieces of rags.

"How come there's a different number on all these, pally?"

"The numbers are dates. Every year I give Leigh one, and I mark the year on it. We've done it for a long time."

"I can see that."

Vito pulled three cigars from his suit jacket pocket. He did it with a magician's flourish, but the cigars deserved the fanfare. He beamed as he handed them to us.

"These are Trinidads," Gregory said. "How the hell did you get Trinidads?"

"Contacts," Vito said as Gregory lit the cigars with the Zippo he'd had since his navy days. "I keep telling you guys, I got contacts."

Trinidads were legend among cigar smokers. They're made in Havana especially for Fidel Castro. I'd never seen one before.

"Aren't these illegal?" I said.

"So lock me up already," Vito said.

I walked over to the desk drawer, took out a package of my own, and handed it to Vito.

"I didn't know we were exchanging Christmas gifts," Gregory said.

"We're not. I just got this for Vito for keeping an eye on Leigh for me."

Vito tore at the paper like a five-year-old. His enthusiasm

made me wish I'd gotten something better. It was only an NYPD baseball style–cap with a patch in front; I'd picked it up at Frielich Police Equipment on East Twenty-first Street. But Vito acted as if it was the greatest gift he'd ever received. He put it right on.

"I'll wear this tomorrow," he said. "When we pick up Emil Lutz."

"Not tomorrow," I said.

"Why not? I know where he is."

"Where?"

"He's living on a boat out on the North Shore. Eastwinds, something like that."

"We can't go tomorrow," I said.

"Why not? What's more important than Lutz?"

"We have to go to the indoor range," I said, knowing it was a lame story, but I didn't want Vito lurking around the hotel. "The bosses are all over us because we missed the last shooting cycle. It's our last chance in this one. How about we go after Lutz one day toward the end of the week?"

Vito sat back and blew smoke at the ceiling.

"How about Wednesday?" I said. "We'll grab him on Wednesday."

"You're on," Vito said. "Wednesday's good for me. It'll give me a chance to verify my information."

Gregory's tie played "Jingle Bells" as the smoke from contraband Cuban cigars clouded the air above us. We sat back and listened to the soothing murmur of women's voices.

After everyone left, the house seemed empty and too big for two people. Vito went home with Cookie, still wearing his NYPD cap. Gregory departed for a yule nightcap of his own in Brady's Bar. Leigh and I cleaned up, then went to bed.

"I'm going to miss Vito," I said.

"I am, too. He was fun, he did his job. He protected me from the Mafia, or whatever."

"Why do you say that?"

"Oh, come on, Anthony. The first couple of days, all he did was peek out the windows. He walked me to school every morning; every afternoon he was there, waiting."

"I just thought it might be nice for both of you."

"It was," she said. "At first I was little annoyed with you for not being honest. But then I saw he was loving it. I think I replaced Johnny Boy for him for a while. He had someone to take care of, someone to laugh at his jokes. He's going to miss that kid terribly."

"What did you and Cookie talk about in the kitchen?"

"Work, women things."

"Did you ask her about Gregory?"

She picked her head up off the pillow. "You don't think I asked her if Johnny Boy was Joe's child?"

"No, I don't."

"I hope not," she said. "We talked about family, houses, things like that. We did decide the wives of cops should go straight to heaven."

"Goes without saying. Did she mention anything about her plans, about going back to Florida?"

"She might not. She said she's enjoying running the poultry store for now."

Leigh moved closer to me, putting her leg over mine, her head in the crook of my shoulder. I could feel her warmth and the steadiness of her breathing.

"I didn't expect to have a good Christmas without the kids," she said. "But I really had fun."

"Is that Cinnabar you're wearing?" I asked.

"I don't believe it," she said. "You noticed."

38

On Tuesday morning, the day after Christmas, the city seemed sleepy, still in holiday mode. You could hear the click of the traffic lights changing. The sun was barely peeking through the high-rises when cops began trickling into the Park International Hotel. One by one they rode up in the elevator, trying hard to blend in with the guests. It wasn't easy. The hotel was packed with Europeans traveling in large groups. The lobby sounded like the visitor's room at the UN.

"You going to be okay with this?" I said to my partner. "You don't have to be here, you know."

"This is a caper, pally," he said. "I never miss a caper."

Gregory and I arrived a little before seven. We came up through the underground garage, thinking Mickey Lawton might decide to case the hotel for police presence. Though we had cops watching his apartment, no one could confirm his current whereabouts. And I didn't trust him. This was his turf, and guys like Mickey are predators in the heart of their own jungle.

They know every vacant basement, the door to every roof, the exit from every dark alley.

"I should have brought pastries," Gregory said.

"You're slipping," I said, but I knew he was preoccupied, his mind racing a million miles an hour. I can always tell by the way his eyes move, darting back and forth. The Great Gregory is thinking.

We had three adjoining rooms on the left, at the end of the hall. Gregory and I were assigned to room 846 with the recording equipment and orders to stay put. The sting would go down in the center room, 848, where Uncle Mike was allegedly staying. The arrest team would be at the end of the hall, room 850, poised to burst through the door at the hint of a problem. All three rooms faced front, overlooking Fifty-seventh Street, between Ninth and Tenth Avenues.

"Last chance," I said as I stood in front of the door. "You really ought to think about being here."

"Open the door before I break your freaking arm," he said.

Inspector O'Prey met us in 846, where everybody ate and smoked so as not to leave telltale odors in the sting room. O'Prey told us he'd obtained background information on Fiona Quinn from his sources in Ireland. We filled him in on Johnny Boy and the Counihan family, in case Fiona quizzed him.

"Make sure you bargain with these bastards," Gregory told O'Prey. "If they offer you fifty percent, say you want sixty. Criminals always assume they're dealing with cops when they don't argue about the price. Always argue about price."

The key in these operations is anticipation. Anticipate every possibility. We discussed the plan until eight-fifteen, then O'Prey and Detective Kelsey Lucas left to check the center room. We could watch them on the monitor on the dresser. Tech Services had put in three mikes and two cameras, one in a vent, the other in a hollow VCR sitting on the TV. O'Prey's voice sounded deeper than the others because he stood directly under a mike in the smoke alarm.

Our room had two queen-size beds, one covered with coats and equipment. I retrieved a coffee-stained copy of the morning edition of the *Daily News* from the trash and staked claim to half of the uncluttered bed.

Lieutenant Jesse Keegan sat at a round table, wearing two sets of headphones. With one set he monitored the tail teams out on the street; the other picked up the sting room. We used headsets so that Mickey and Fiona wouldn't hear the police radio or the echo of their own voices in another room.

The only sound in our room was *Good Day New York,* the TV at low volume, and the heavy footsteps of Joe Gregory pacing the floor in front of the beds. Occasionally he'd stop to stare at a bubble in the wallpaper.

"What's wrong with your partner?" Keegan said. "He think this is a maternity ward, or what?"

"He's training for the marathon," I said.

"Sit the fuck down, Gregory," Keegan said. "You're making me nervous."

A pencil-thin shaft of outside light dissected the wall. The drapes were closed, anticipating the eyes of someone in a window or on a roof across the street.

"Why do I always get stuck with the boring guys?" Gregory said. "I'm going down the hall with the arrest team. See if they want any help with the collar. You guys don't need a real cop in here."

"Not a good idea, Joe," I warned. It wasn't. The arrest team was responsible for crashing through the door that connected the rooms, weapons raised and ready. It's an emotional and explosive moment. Definitely not a good idea.

"Go on," Keegan said. "Get the hell out of here. Drive them nuts for a while."

After he left I tried to concentrate on the fuzzy gray picture on the monitor. I could make out O'Prey, alone, sitting on the bed in 848. The room looked natural. The bedcovers were thrown back. A towel was slung across a chair. A suitcase lay open on the other bed; the luggage tags were Aer Lingus. I wondered how Joe Gregory was doing down in room 850, whether he'd volunteered yet to be the first through the door.

"Show time," Keegan said. "Fiona is on the street."

"She's early," I said. "Way too early."

Everybody scurried around, but the panic was premature. Fiona wound up in the McDonald's on Eighth Avenue and Fifty-sixth Street, where Mickey Lawton waited inside. They huddled for forty-five minutes. Then Fiona left, walking west, toward us. Solo.

"Mickey's not coming," Keegan said.

"I can't believe that," I said. But Fiona continued west on Fifty-sixth Street, nearing Ninth without him. I relayed the message to O'Prey, but by the time I got back to the room, Mickey was out on the street, almost a full block behind Fiona.

"He's checking for a tail," Keegan said, and he immediately ordered the cop following Fiona from behind to abandon the tail, turn off into a bar, a whorehouse, anything. We still had a female officer tailing her from the front, the hard way.

Ten minutes later Fiona entered the hotel lobby. She waited for Mickey at the elevator. I grabbed an extra headset from Keegan.

"What's the 'go' word?" I whispered. The "go" word was the code word that O'Prey would utter when he'd had enough of an admission of criminality. The arrest team would then come through the door.

"Mollycoddle," Keegan said.

"That's different."

"That's O'Prey."

Fiona and Mickey knocked on 848, and O'Prey opened the door with a big smile and a smattering of Irish gibberish, but they were too far away from a mike to pick up a clear conversation. Wiretaps and bugs were lessons in how people actually converse. People don't listen, they talk over one another, not waiting for the other person to finish. Most people don't speak in words, it's all huhs and ahhs and umms, and the transcriber eventually just writes in "unintelligible." With the brogues, this was going to be a transcriber's nightmare, one of those tapes you have to run over and over to figure out half of what was said.

O'Prey walked them into the center of the room and offered Fiona a chair. Mickey Lawton's eyes scanned the room as Fiona introduced him as Mickey O'Brien. She pushed aside the towel and sat.

"I know all about Mr. O'Brien," O'Prey said. "He impressed my nephew as quite the bold fellow."

"Your nephew was a strange fucking guy," Mickey said.

"Johnny Boy was an underachiever," O'Prey said. "That's why I'm glad he had such smart and ambitious friends. He was quite proud of his part in your big doings."

"What he had," Mickey said, "was one hell of a wild imagination."

Fiona sat rigidly and almost visibly shut her mouth. Mickey was acting as his own mouthpiece. No one was going to screw up his big score.

"I never thought of Johnny Boy as imaginative at all," O'Prey said. "Quite the opposite, in fact. I don't believe he had the imagination to make up a lie. Certainly not one as grandiose as your airport scheme."

"If your nephew," Mickey said, "told you we had anything to do with that JFK robbery, he sure as shit made up a lie at least one time in his life."

The more I thought about Joe Gregory, the more it bothered me. This is how tragedies happen, because people like me don't act. I should have been more forceful and stopped him from going. A cop's duty to his partner is sacred. Protect him at all costs. Even from himself. I'd let my partner get in a position to avenge the death of the son he never knew.

"Is that your opinion also, Fiona?" O'Prey said. "My nephew was merely imagining all this?"

"Yes, it is, sir," she said, her hands folded tightly in her lap.

O'Prey lit a cigarette and inhaled slowly. Surely this was against his marathoning credo, but the cigarette was a good prop. It allowed him to take a beat, slow down. Never rush it.

"I admit it's lovely to hear your voice, Fiona," O'Prey said. "It's such a lovely sound in this cold city. But I'm not going to play this game. I have a flight to catch, and I want our money."

"We don't have nobody's money," Mickey said.

"Is this how it's going to be?" O'Prey said. "You playing me for the fool? I hope you are not going to continue to go along with your friend's foolishness, Fiona."

O'Prey had his back to Mickey, working on Fiona. I knew everyone in room 850 was focused on Mickey. I wondered if my partner held a shotgun in his hands. Declan O'Prey held Fiona with a withering stare. He'd missed his calling; he was an actor.

"Perhaps your friend Dermot Geary might think differently," O'Prey said. We'd decided earlier that Uncle Mike couldn't know of Dermot's death.

"Dermot is dead, sir," Fiona said, swallowing.

"Pity," O'Prey said. "I suppose our redheaded friend here is responsible for that."

"We don't have to take this shit," Mickey said. "Come on, Fiona. We tried to be nice."

"You stay right there," O'Prey said, pointing at Fiona, his voice shaking. "Don't you dismiss me with the back of your hand. I'm going to tell you this, Fiona. This will end badly if you pursue this course. Do not let this worthless little man compromise your heritage."

Don't go this way, I thought. Never give a violent asshole like

Mickey Lawton a chance to be stupid; he'll turn this into a bloodbath.

"This is a fucking scam, Fiona," Mickey said. "This guy ain't shit. He's out for himself."

The tape was rolling. My partner will be on tape blowing away a punk like Mickey Lawton. A tape the media will dissect and interpret until they destroy him. Unless the machine malfunctioned. The recorder turned, less than a step away from me.

"Your dear ma will be bitterly disappointed, Fiona," O'Prey said.

"My mother has nothing to do with you people."

"Why don't you ask her that yourself," O'Prey said, gesturing to the phone. "Ask Elizabeth how she's feeling. Her arthritis has been bothering her, but she is going to get the care she deserves. And your brother Eamonn, ask how his studies at Trinity are progressing."

"Don't you touch my family!" Fiona screamed. "You have no right."

"He's bluffing," Mickey said. "Can't you see that? Let's get the fuck out of here."

"Give him the money!" Fiona screamed. "Give him the bloody money!"

That's an admission, I thought. Not a great one, but good enough.

"I ain't giving him shit," Mickey said.

"Now it will cost you sixty percent," O'Prey said. "And with every minute we play this silly game the tariff jumps ten percent."

"Tell you what," Mickey said. "I'll give you a hundred thou on the spot, and we forget about all this. A hundred large for your troubles, and we all walk away happy."

There, that's it. That's a goddamn great admission.

"Seventy percent," O'Prey said.

"Hey, first of all, it wasn't as much as the papers were saying. They're jacking the figure up for the insurance."

Say the word, O'Prey. What the hell are you waiting for? We have enough, let's go.

"And what is the true figure?" O'Prey said.

"Not even half of what they said."

"How much did you get?" O'Prey said.

"Two million dead presidents," Mickey said. "But that don't mean shit to you. 'Cause you ain't seeing a fucking dime of it."

Mickey suddenly reached into his jacket, and both Keegan and I jumped up. The adjoining door split off the hinges, and I lost my partner in the jumble of suits and blue vests and guns and screaming cops. I also lost Mickey in the bodies, but I didn't hear a shot. What I could hear was choking. Joe Gregory held Mickey in the air by the throat, his arms waving helplessly. Clutched in Mickey's right hand, the hand he'd stuck into his jacket, was a tube of Chap Stick.

39

They brought Fiona into our room. It was easier to work with suspects when they were separated; the level of bravado diminishes rapidly. Fiona resumed her position, hands folded in her lap.

"Did I perform as badly as everyone expected?" O'Prey said.

"You were starting to chew the scenery toward the end," I told him.

The operation was in a let-down mode, everyone breathing easier. Like the end of a big concert, when the roadies began breaking down the set. Tech Services disconnected the TV and the bugs, and we were working smaller: just two tape recorders, pen and paper. Mickey Lawton was still in 848, playing tough guy. We were waiting to question Fiona until the tech man gathered up his gear. He tossed everything in the brown-and-orange bedspread in order to carry it down to the end room, where he could pack it properly.

"Be careful with that bedspread," I told him.

That reminded me. I picked up the room phone and called

security for Harry Sampel. Someone was going to have to pay for the broken door. I didn't want this to get screwed up and charged to my personal credit card account. The city wouldn't pay it back during my lifetime. Sampel wasn't in at the moment, probably taking lambada lessons somewhere. I didn't leave a message; the less said the better.

O'Prey assigned Kelsey Lucas to stay with Fiona. Kelsey sat at the table with Joe Gregory while he read Fiona her rights. Fiona began to sob.

"Money is the root of all evil, Fiona," O'Prey said, still speaking in character.

"I wish I never saw a dime of it," she said.

"We're talking about the money from the JFK Airport robbery," Joe Gregory said for the benefit of the tape recorder.

"It's been nothing but trouble," she said.

"I take it that's a yes?" Gregory said.

"Yes, it is, sir," she said.

O'Prey started to open the drapes, thinking he was doing us a favor. But I stopped him. It was better to conduct interrogations without the ray of hope that sunshine allowed. Dark and dank, end-of-the-world conditions worked best.

"I want to talk to someone," Fiona said.

"You mean like a priest?" Gregory said.

"Someone with the authority to give me immunity."

"Immunity?" Gregory said. "What's that, some Irish rock band?"

"You know very well what it is. I want immunity from these crimes."

"Why the hell would we do that?" Gregory said.

"Because I can tell you everything you want to know."

"And I'll just bet it's out of spiritual remorse," he said. "Don't tell me you're a lapsed Catholic, Fiona."

"It's because I don't want to go to prison, sir. I will accept deportation; I don't know why I came to this bloody country in the first place."

"You can't just walk away from this."

"I can tell you everything."

"I'm not sure 'everything' is worth complete immunity. Like what, for instance?"

"Every detail of the robbery. Every detail."

"Were you present?" Gregory said. "And did you physically observe the crime?"

"Yes, sir. I was there. I can also tell you who killed the two guards, who killed Mr. Rocky Lutz, John Counihan, and Dermot Geary."

"Were you present for those crimes, and did you physically observe them?"

Fiona hesitated and took a deep breath. "All but Dermot Geary," she said. "However, I was told a detailed account. Direct from the lips of the killer himself."

"What about the murder of Vincent Lutz?" Gregory said.

"I don't know a thing about that."

"What about the guns used in these crimes?"

"I could show you where they are. But they're in the Hudson River."

O'Prey told Gregory to ask her where the money was hidden, but Fiona heard him and looked directly at the inspector.

"I can lead you to the money, most definitely," she said.

O'Prey had heard enough. He turned off the recorder and left the room to call the Manhattan DA. The deal depended on Mickey Lawton. If he refused to talk, then Fiona would get her wish. Kelsey turned on *Regis & Kathie Lee*.

Gregory walked back with me to the window. I opened up the drapes and let some light into the room. It didn't matter now. I knew once the DA was involved he'd want us back in a secure building, and we'd wind up in the precinct. I put my foot up on the windowsill, and my tie fluttered in the blowing heat.

"Maybe you'd better take a few hours off," I said. "I can handle this from here on out."

"You worry too much," he said quietly. "If I was going to shoot that little prick, I would have done it when I had the chance."

"What if he had pulled a gun?"

"Then it would've been legal."

I looked down at the traffic on a street that sloped toward the Hudson. On the side of a crosstown bus Michael Jordan flew spread-eagle toward Ninth Avenue.

"What you're telling me," Gregory said, "is that you'd feel more comfortable with me out of the room."

"That's exactly what I'm telling you."

"Then say no more," he said. "I'm outta here."

"Why don't you go to the precinct and get a jump on the paperwork."

"I'll think about that," he said as he snatched his coat off the bed.

Eight floors below us, the city in miniature moved silently and orderly. A doorman blew his whistle in the street. Tourists boarded charter buses, as if this were another ordinary moment on the streets of New York.

Shortly after Gregory left, O'Prey told us to pack up our prisoner and prepare to respond to Mid-Town North. The DA would be waiting. I was glad to be getting out of the hotel and into a safe place. A place with no queen-size beds, but a secure holding cage, all the proper forms, and a hundred cops running around. I wanted to deliver these people over to someone else, wash my hands of it. Fiona would get her deal; I could live with that. Five murders plus a ton of money were great bargaining chips for a skinny Irish maid.

A few minutes later I heard the door opening and closing in

room 848, the rustle of coats and feet. They were in the hall-way with Mickey Lawton. Mickey was flanked by two cops from Major Case. His leather jacket was draped over his shoul-ders, held on by a single button.

From the doorway, I watched until they were gone. We didn't want Mickey to make eye contact with Fiona, although I thought she'd already decided to play the hand she'd been dealt. Kelsey and I stepped onto a crowded elevator with the handcuffed Fiona and forged a New York memory for a group of wide-eyed German tourists.

The Mid-Town North Precinct is on West Fifty-fourth Street, just a few blocks from the hotel. It's west of Eighth Av-enue across the street from the infamous Studio 54, whose no-toriety has waned since its drug- and celebrity-filled nights of the seventies. Kelsey and I sat in the backseat of a marked car, Fiona between us. We were about six cars behind the car con-taining O'Prey and Mickey when we made the left onto West Fifty-fourth.

"They grab Emil Lutz yet, Anthony?" Kelsey said.

"Not that I know of."

"I hear he looks like one of those guys clinging to the wire fence in a Holocaust film."

"Couldn't happen to a nicer guy," I said.

Fiona had looked at both of us when she heard the name "Lutz." I thought about asking her, then decided to wait until the lawyers did their thing. But she volunteered, "I never did hear of that one."

"What's holding up traffic?" Kelsey said.

Because of the precinct, traffic was always backed up on this street. Cops jam cars into a block, like clowns in a Volkswagen. Cars public, private, and stolen were backed up against the brick wall of the old bus garage. They were squeezed to within inches of each other and angled halfway out into the street, forcing moving vehicles into a single lane. In the grimy windows were the appropriate vouchers, permits, PBA cards, and American flag decals. Bumper stickers on the private cars leaned toward the right: "America, love it or leave it."

We moved forward slowly until O'Prey's car reached the station house. Unable to get to the curb because of a line of chain-handcuffed hookers filing out of the wagon, they stopped and again held up traffic. Mickey Lawton's red head appeared as the cops yanked him out of the backseat. His head was down, hands cuffed behind his back.

"Check out this guy, Ryan," Kelsey said. "He's going to bitch to O'Prey about holding up traffic. Is he a cop?"

Up ahead, a man in an NYPD cap, his shield dangling from his raincoat, got out of a big white car, leaving the driver's door open. His car was directly behind O'Prey's, four cars in front of us. I knew who it was. I jumped out and ran toward Vito Martucci, trying to squeeze between the idling traffic and the angled bumpers. But I couldn't get to him. Vito took three or four steps from the Lincoln. I saw the gun in his right hand, and I yelled his name so loud that the cops snapped their heads around as Vito shoved the gun into Mickey's stomach.

Mickey screamed and crumpled. Then the curtain fell; Vito disappeared into a bear hug. Joe Gregory carried him, like a sack of mushrooms, toward the alley behind the precinct.

In the second-floor squad room I used a vintage Remington to type the affidavit for a search warrant for Mickey's apartment. Behind me four hookers sat on a long wooden bench, appealing to and abusing the plainclothesmen who'd arrested them. The smell of cheap perfume mixed with cigar smoke and garlic from a half-eaten gyro in the trash can.

"Stop frowning, pally," Gregory said. "You're getting wrinkles around your eyes. Nothing else can go wrong now."

"Please don't say that."

Joe Gregory filled out the arrest cards on Vito. We had no choice. O'Prey wouldn't listen to any alternative approaches. The only luck we had was that Vito never got a chance to pull the trigger before Mickey fainted.

"I asked Vito how he found out where we were," Gregory said. "You know what he says to me?"

"I got contacts."

"Exactly. He's in there now, happy as a pig in shit, acting like he's freaking John Gotti."

Before we finished the paperwork, O'Prey ordered us both into the interview room. He said he wanted us to handle the questioning of Fiona. Gregory looked at me and shrugged, as if to say "Should I go?"

"Come on," I said. "But I'll talk to her."

In the interview room we all sat around an old conference table that took up half the room. A reel-to-reel tape recorder sat in the center of the table. I started making an outline on a legal pad. Organization is the key to good interrogation. Start with small incrimination and work your way up, considering even the smallest lie to be legal tender. Fiona sat with her back to the holding cage, the kind of cage where J.C. Counihan's crazy monkey once threatened reluctant criminals.

"Have you your tape recorder working, sir?" Fiona Quinn said. "I want to make certain I have immunity from these crimes. I do, isn't that right, sir?"

The wall behind the fingerprint pad was grossly stained black where detectives tried to squeeze excess ink from the roller. The only window in the room looked over a small alley; across the alley was a school for drama.

"As long as you cooperate, exactly as we agreed," the DA said. Then she repeated the terms of the agreement, emphasizing the information Fiona had to give. Five murders, the robbery, the location of the money. Plus, she had to testify in open court. Fiona said yes to all the terms. I felt a chill go down my back.

"First let me begin," Fiona Quinn said, "by stating that it was I who killed John Counihan."

"Son of a bitch," Joe Gregory said.

40

I saw my father walking toward me in the glass door of Jimmy Neary's Bar. A tired, frowning man, wearing a dark overcoat and pushing his hair back with open fingers. I stopped, stunned. But it wasn't my father. It was me—my own fatigued reflection in the glass. My father would be in Fort Lauderdale, hitting red-striped golf balls into the moist electric night.

It was tradition for Gregory and me to have dinner at the end of a case. We drove under the huge snowflake to the east side of Fifty-seventh Street. At Neary's we both ordered the lamb chops, the best in New York, and mashed potatoes, and we spoke softly in the warm civility surrounding us.

"In the old days," Gregory said, "we used to call the Irish domestics 'pots.' Like Fiona, you know. I don't know what the hell it means: 'pots.' Maybe because they washed the pots, I don't know. In those days rich people would arrange to get these young Irish girls sent over here to work in their houses. They had a contract; the girls owed the people so many years. They used to have Wednesdays off, and that night they'd all be in Danny

Boy's, going nuts. Wednesday night was pot's night out. Wild woman night. Like they had only one night to let loose. And boy, did they let loose. Drink like fish, then try to rip your clothes off."

"My partner, young Casanova."

"I did all right," he said.

Fiona had confirmed our theory that Rocky Lutz and Mickey Lawton concocted the scheme. Fiona's role was to seduce the complicity of Johnny Boy Counihan with promises of love, marriage, and IRA appreciation. Mickey talked him into wearing the uniform coat that night, so his death would look like an accident. After Fiona shot him in the head she pushed him out to where Mickey, Dermot, and Rocky waited. Fresh from butchering two guards.

"She's going to walk away from this," he said.

Fiona was our fault; we never thought she was a shooter. She was the fortunate recipient of our bias. O'Prey predicted she'd be deported and live her days in shame and disgrace. He'd see to it.

"We got the main guy," I said. "Mickey Lawton used her, like he used Dermot, and Johnny Boy, even Rocky. The only reason Mickey didn't look for his own deal is because he never thought Fiona would betray him."

"It still ain't right."

"Justice is a witches' brew," I said. Joe Gregory's father, Liam, the greatest cop I've ever know, was the first one I'd heard use that line.

O'Prey's team recovered the money from a crude safe hidden in an old dumbwaiter in Mickey's kitchen; they were stacking cash when we left. Divers would begin looking for the guns in the morning. Fiona said that Mickey killed Rocky Lutz immediately after he saw him talking to me at the River Diner. Mickey had been the guy carrying the red blanket. I'd have to live with that; I live with worse memories.

"I guess Johnny Boy was in it up to his eyeballs," Gregory said.

"His heart was in the right place, Joe. Even if his head wasn't. He thought it was about love and the sacred cause."

"That shit over there causes more grief."

We split a bottle of wine Gregory picked from the Jack London Vineyards, simply because he remembered *The Call of the Wild*. For dessert my partner had vanilla ice cream with butterscotch topping.

Fiona had related Mickey's version of how he killed Dermot: drank with him all the way up into Inwood Hill Park, then crushed his skull with a blackjack while he pissed into the Spuyten Duyvil. Fiona told us everything, then asked if a priest could be arranged, as she wanted to receive the sacrament of penance. The last time I looked at her she was writing her story in that strange, even script.

"I'm taking Cookie out to dinner Friday night," Gregory said. "Think she'll like this place?"

"Definitely," I said. "What brought this on?"

"I've been thinking about things. I've always been a little jealous of you and Leigh. Single life ain't all it's cracked up to be. Cookie's all alone now. We got some history together. Maybe I can help her out with Vito. Who knows?"

Vito Martucci was someone I refused to see as a tragic victim. Rather, I'd remember him in my kitchen, tearing at his tie and doing his imitation of Johnnie Ray. We left him in Central Booking bragging that Mickey Lawton would never forget his face. He said he didn't care about the consequences. With the loss of Johnny Boy his heart had already been sentenced.

"So are you going to tell me what it was you bought at Macy's?" I said.

"An angel," Gregory said. "A crystal angel."

After dinner we went to the bar. Gregory ordered two Irish

coffees made with Irish Mist. He said the liqueur took the whiskey bite out of it.

"To us," he said, raising his glass. "The greatest detectives in the world."

The NYPD was one hundred and fifty years old. The city of New York was safer than it had been in two decades. I touched glasses with my friend.

"You know one thing I love about this city," Gregory said. "No matter how much money you have, you can always be rich."

"As long as you can get past the bouncers."

"This is on me tonight, pally."

"What a guy. Someday they'll be writing songs about you."

Like my partner, I loved this city: the noise, the lights, the pulse, the excitement. I loved hearing the music of a dozen languages in a single block, the smell of exotic foods, the push and shove, the sight of beauty in every possible shade. Most of all I loved my ringside seat.

"When I was a kid," Gregory said, "my mother used to send me down to the corner bar to pick up my father. My old man would grab me and hold me up under the beer taps and tell the bartender, 'Here, put a head on this.' I always loved when he did that."

"You'd have made a great father, Joe," I said.

"Who the hell knows? Cops like me don't make the best fathers."

In the end we were all stuck with the kinds of sons we were and fathers we weren't. As I drank, I again saw my reflection in the bar mirror, the Ryan profile. I was looking more and more like the man who loved warm weather and perfecting his grip or backswing. But I was in blustery Manhattan, ending another case, having a drink with my partner, and knowing that this was exactly how I wanted to live the rest of my days.

The door opened and two guys we worked with years ago walked in. Gregory called them over and insisted on buying.

"No problem," he said. "I happen to know the five greatest words in the English language: 'Put it on my tab.'"